Read and Buried

Center Point
Large Print

Also by Erika Chase and available from
Center Point Large Print:

An Ashton Corners Book Club Mystery
  A Killer Read

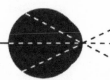

**This Large Print Book carries the
Seal of Approval of N.A.V.H.**

Read and Buried

An Ashton Corners
Book Club Mystery

ERIKA CHASE

CENTER POINT LARGE PRINT
THORNDIKE, MAINE

This Center Point Large Print edition is published
in the year 2013 by arrangement with
The Berkley Publishing Group,
a member of Penguin Group (USA) LLC,
a Penguin Random House Company.

The text of this Large Print edition is unabridged.
In other aspects, this book may vary
from the original edition.
Printed in the United States of America
on permanent paper.
Set in 16-point Times New Roman type.

ISBN: 978-1-61173-888-9

Library of Congress Cataloging-in-Publication Data

Chase, Erika.
Read and Buried : An Ashton Corners Book Club Mystery / Erika
Chase. — Center Point Large Print edition.
pages cm
ISBN 978-1-61173-888-9 (Library binding : alk. paper)
1. Mystery book clubs—Fiction. 2. Large type books. I. Title.
PR9199.3.C4748R43 2013
813'.54—dc23
                                        2013021339

Acknowledgments

I could very easily just reprint the acknowledgment page from *A Killer Read*. But a year has passed and so much has happened, I feel these same people need a new page to reinforce my indebtedness to them all.

I am truly blessed with a remarkable team at Berkley Prime Crime: Kate Seaver, editor; Katherine Pelz, editorial assistant; Kayleigh Clark, publicist; Marianne Grace, copyeditor; and the husband-wife team of Stanley Martucci and Cheryl Greisbach, who design the amazing covers for the series. Many thanks also go to my agent, Kim Lionetti of Bookends, Inc. Not only do these folks do such a great job . . . they're also really nice!

Mary Jane Maffini remains on my list as go-to person for everything! Her advice and humor have kept me on track throughout. Many, many thanks!

Lee McNeilly, my sister, will also be a permanent fixture on this list. Thanks for being such a great support and keen mystery reader!

My thanks also to Sylvia Braithwaite, colleague and friend. I very much appreciate your indulgence and thoughtful comments. Thanks also to mystery authors Avery Aames and Miranda James for taking the time to read and send along cover quotes. And speaking of which . . . it's such fun to belong to the Killer Characters gang. Blog on!

I also remain grateful for being a member of the Ladies' Killing Circle. Those deadly dames are also great friends! I should also thank my book club—the SPA Book Club (ask me what it stands for sometime), which is very different from the Ashton Corners Book Club, but a source of ideas and friendship.

And, as always, thanks to the readers who embraced the folks of Ashton Corners and continue on this journey with me.

Chapter One

◇◇◇

There is nothing you can do about the past except keep it there.
THE BRASS VERDICT—MICHAEL CONNELLY

Lizzie Turner, you'd like a signed copy of Derek Alton's award-winning book, wouldn't you?"

Lizzie looked over at the cash register where Jensey Pollard, owner of the Book Bin, stood waving a trade paperback with a moss green cover at her. The store was empty except for a tall, dark-haired man at the back. Jensey took Lizzie's delay in answering to be a yes and called out to the man.

Lizzie watched him as he walked toward her. She didn't recognize him but she was pretty sure she'd heard of the book, *Judgment*. If she remembered correctly, it had won a big award when it came out many years ago. She smiled, hoping to cover any look of bewilderment.

"I'm Derek Alton," he said, giving her the once-over as he held out his hand. He wasn't much taller than Lizzie, possibly around five-foot-eight. His eyes drew her attention—they were such an odd shade of green, Lizzie was certain he wore contacts. His nose looked slightly off-center but that gave him a bit of a bad-boy look, especially when paired with his short dark brown hair, graying at the temples. His smile looked practiced to her but she supposed that after years of book signings, he would be a bit jaded.

Jensey came around from behind her desk. "You know, Lizzie, *Judgment* is a mystery of sorts. And since it won the Onyx, I think it would be grand if he spoke to your book club. What do you say, Derek?" She had come up beside him and put her hand on his arm.

He looked at Jensey's hand and then at Lizzie. "I'd be delighted, although I'm only in town for another week."

Lizzie tried not to look cornered. She didn't know how the rest of the Ashton Corners Mystery Readers and Cheese Straws Society would feel about a guest. "I'm sure everyone would be delighted," she said carefully, fingers crossed. "We're actually having a meeting next Thursday, if that works for you."

Alton leaned back against the desk and appeared to be deep in thought. Lizzie had the distinct impression that he was giving her yet another once-over and maybe that's what he'd base his decision upon. It made her slightly uneasy.

"How about you tell me a bit about this book club and its members?" he asked.

"Well, besides me, there's Molly Mathews. She's involved in a lot of literacy projects in town and is an Agatha Christie fan. We meet in her

8

home." She paused to try to gauge just how much she should be saying about each member. "Then there's Sally-Jo Baker, a third grade teacher who's fairly new to town; Bob Miller, the former police chief now retired; Jacob Smith, a local attorney, also new to town; Stephanie Lowe, she's a bit younger, about to give birth at any minute so might not even be at the meeting, and also new here. There seems to be a theme here," she added with a chuckle. "And, last but not least, Andie Mason, who's in high school and just getting into reading in a big way."

"I'd be happy to do it," Alton finally said. "I'm staying at the Jefferson Hotel. If you'll give me your phone number, I'll call you for instructions." He pulled a pen and small notebook out of his jacket pocket and made some notations.

After signing the copy of *Judgment* that Jensey handed to him, Alton excused himself and left the shop.

Lizzie stared at Jensey, not quite sure what had just happened. She felt like she'd been railroaded not only into buying a book she'd not planned to purchase, but also into revising the book club schedule.

"I didn't realize you were having a signing here today, Jensey," Lizzie finally said.

Jensey giggled. "It wasn't really a signing. He just popped in and fortunately, I had a few copies of his books on hand so he signed them. Your walking in at that moment was opportune, don't you think?"

Jensey looked pleased with herself. Lizzie sighed then smiled, paid for the book and the two mysteries Jensey had put aside for her—the latest from Ellery Adams and Janet Bolin—and left.

The phone was ringing as Lizzie opened her front door. She picked it up just before it went to the message.

"Derek Alton here. Lizzie Turner, I hope?"

She nodded, taken off guard, but quickly realized an answer was needed. "Yes."

"I hope you won't think I'm too forward, but I'd like to take you out to dinner tonight. I'd like to know some more about your book club before I speak to them. It will give me a better idea of how to tailor my talk. Are you free tonight?"

Lizzie knew she had no plans but she hesitated. It wasn't really a date. But a part of her felt guilty, thinking of Mark Dreyfus, the heartthrob police chief she'd been dating for a few months. But Mark was working tonight. And it made sense that Derek would want to know about the book club, she reasoned, so she accepted.

He picked her up at seven P.M. and after a brief drive through town with Lizzie pointing out the main sights, drove back to his hotel, where he'd reserved a table at the restaurant. Lizzie was glad she'd worn her fairly recent purchase of a black pantsuit with a platinum satin shell. The Shasta

Room at the Jefferson Hotel was one of the classier spots in town. Ashton Corners, Alabama, had a good variety of dining spots, along with plenty of activities for all ages. But Lizzie didn't make it out to places like the Shasta Room very often.

Alton made a big show of examining the wine list after they were seated at a table for two. Although it was early evening and still light outside, the lighting was dim in their corner, three candles were lit, and a single red rose lay across her plate.

Uh-oh. Lizzie politely inhaled its fragrance and then set the rose alongside her cutlery. She adjusted the linen napkin the maître d' had placed on her lap and looked around the room.

The walls, ceiling, crown moldings and chair coverings were done in varying shades of neutral. The linens were pure white with a discreet "S" embroidered at each corner. The table and chair legs were dark oak. Shots of color came from the centerpieces of red poinsettia, towering paperwhites and sprigs of holly that anchored each table. String music wafted softly through the air.

Alton ordered a bottle of wine (without consulting her, Lizzie noted), then immediately began talking about himself. All she had to do was nod and make the occasional exclamation to show that she was suitably impressed.

"I'm still getting requests to read from

Judgment at many events and my publisher is thinking of doing yet another print run, so I thought it would be a good time to write a sequel. What do you think?" he asked.

Lizzie reined in her wandering mind and replayed his question before answering. "That sounds like a clever move." It was all she could think of to say.

Alton poured himself another glass of the California Baco Noir and beamed. "Just what I thought. Now, let's order before we get too wrapped up in talking."

Lizzie balked at his suggestion he order for both of them, instead choosing lemon chicken with braised roots while Alton ordered steak, done rare, and lobster tail.

"So, what do you do when you're not running the book club, Lizzie?" Alton asked after another long sip of his wine.

"I'm a reading specialist with the local school board," she replied. "And I do some tutoring and teach a literacy course at night school." She watched for a reaction.

Alton smiled pleasantly. "Interesting. I also taught, you know. Creative writing, of course. In fact, I still dabble at giving the odd workshop, but my novel writing is such a large part of my life, I hardly find time for other pursuits, even the more pleasurable ones." His smile slid into more of a leer and Lizzie cringed.

"Have you started your new book?" she quickly asked.

He stared at a point behind her right ear. "Early stages, my dear."

She wondered what that meant but he had already launched into describing the award ceremony where he received the Onyx for Best Fiction from the prestigious Hawthorne Society, even though it was close to eighteen years ago. Lizzie couldn't help but feel a bit sorry for him, that he was still consumed with that win after all these years. She wondered if he was a lonely man.

Their food arrived, saving her from further comment as Alton ate with gusto, stopping only long enough to refill his glass. Lizzie was still working on her first glass of wine by the end of the meal. She declined dessert, choosing a peppermint tea to keep her occupied while he ate a piece of pumpkin pecan cake. She tried to introduce the topic of the book club a couple of times, but Alton had slid into a silence punctuated by smiles and winks at her.

"Oh, look at the time. I should be getting home," she finally said, glancing over at the flashy watch on his left wrist. She couldn't read the dial but thought he'd never notice. "It was a wonderful meal. Thank you so much," she said as she gathered her clutch purse and jacket.

Alton stood abruptly and swayed for a moment, then grabbed her elbow and walked with her to the entrance. He stopped to sign the check at the desk then maneuvered her behind a tall ficus plant next to the coatroom.

"I'll see you home," he said, his hot breath brushing her left ear.

She moved away from him. "No, that's quite all right. I can take a cab. I really think you should just head up to your room."

He leered and grabbed her arm once again. "Good idea. Join me, won't you?" He leaned toward her to kiss her.

She turned away and removed his hand from her arm. "Thank you again for the dinner. Good night."

She rushed out the door and down the steps, asking the bell captain to get her a cab. He blew his whistle and one pulled into the driveway from the main street. Lizzie gave the cabbie her address then sank back and breathed a sigh of relief.

What a nightmare evening. What a letch. And they hadn't even talked about the book club. What an idiot she had been. Well, she'd just have to get the book club members on board for his visit and then act as if nothing had happened between them. Because of course, it hadn't.

Chapter Two

◇◇◇

God gives every bird his worm, but He does not throw it into the nest.

DEVICES AND DESIRES—P. D. JAMES

The phone rang on Tuesday afternoon as Lizzie struggled to hang the mistletoe above the doorway into the living room. She loved decorating for the holidays, even though the mistletoe was proving to be a challenge. This new tape she was using promised not to strip the paint when being removed. Unfortunately, it wasn't strong enough to hold the mistletoe in place. She'd give it one more try after taking the call.

Lizzie was smiling as she answered the phone but the smile disappeared at the sound of Derek Alton's voice.

"Lizzie, sweet lady, please do accept my apologies," he began.

Lizzie didn't answer, waiting for him to continue.

"I behaved abominably the other evening. And believe me, I paid for it the next day. I must admit I soothed my ruffled ego with several more drinks after you left. But you're not to blame."

Lizzie made a face. *What an egotist.* She still didn't say anything. He waited another beat before continuing.

"I was way out of line and I truly do apologize. Now, let's get back on track. Could we have lunch together tomorrow and discuss the book club meeting?"

Lizzie wasn't quite sure how to picture his face as he said this. With a leer? Eyebrows raised in anticipation? Or a sincere smile? It didn't really matter. "I'm afraid not, Derek. I have to work tomorrow and won't have time for a lunch break." She crossed her fingers. Just a little white lie.

He sighed deeply. "All right. I deserve that. So tell me, what do I need to know about Thursday night?"

Lizzie quickly filled him in on the format for the evening. "And we've got a couple of other readers who'd like to come. They got in touch with me after seeing mention of the meeting on the Book Bin's Facebook site."

"Okay, the more the merrier. Now, what time is it and what's the address? I know I have that all written down somewhere but you'd better give it to me again."

The doorbell rang and Lizzie glanced at the front door. *Saved by the bell.* Just the excuse she needed to cut the conversation short. "Sorry, Derek, there's someone at the door. We'll talk later."

She hung up and opened the door. Derek Alton stood facing her, cell phone in hand, a big grin on his face.

"Hi. I've found my pen and paper. Now what was the address?"

Lizzie tried to control her irritation. She took a deep breath, "Are you certain you need the address again?"

"Actually, I do not," he said, sweeping into the hallway. He looked the role of the confident author. Dark blue jeans, white shirt with the top two buttons open, dark brown plaid sports jacket. All that was missing was a pipe. "I really would like to know a bit more about the participants, though." *That smile does look sincere,* Lizzie thought.

He walked into the living room and surveyed the mixture of Rubbermaid containers on the floor, all marked as Christmas decorations. He glanced at the ladder and the mistletoe Lizzie had left perched on the top of it.

"Please, don't let me keep you from what you were doing. I'm very good at lending an eye to make sure things are on the level, so to speak." He chuckled at his wit.

Lizzie suppressed a groan. She was damned if she'd let his intrusion ruin her plans for the day. "This won't take me but a minute. Why don't you go sit down over by the window and I'll be right with you." She grabbed a hammer and a small nail, tired of trying to save the wall, and climbed the ladder.

"And what else have you been reading?" he

asked. She couldn't see him but it sounded like he was walking around the room.

"Mainly mysteries—we are the Ashton Corners Mystery Readers and Cheese Straws Society, after all. But we're pleased to expand the parameters with your book."

Alton laughed, obviously pleased with her comment. "How flattering. Now, tell me about the people I'll be speaking to. You mentioned a teacher."

"Right. Sally-Jo Baker teaches third grade at Ashton Corners Elementary School, which is also where I work. And—"

Alton interrupted her before she could continue. "You said she was new to town, if I recall. From where?"

"Fort Myers, Florida. Why do you ask?" She twisted around to look at him.

"Curiosity, my dear Lizzie. It's what keeps us writers going." His laugh sounded mirthless.

"Of course, we do have others in the book club who are new to town."

"So you mentioned. Quite a variety of people and tastes, it sounds like." Alton continued exploring the bookshelves across from where Lizzie stood.

"Yes. And speaking of tastes, we include refreshments in a big way. So eat a light meal that night."

"It's a good thing you mentioned that." Alton turned back and started over toward her. "You see

18

I have certain food allergies. I usually have only some tea or alcohol if it's available, and peppermint chocolate chip cookies that I bring so I won't be a problem to the hostess."

Unsure how to respond, Lizzie turned back to her project and was about to give the nail a final tap when a gunshot smashed her front window.

For a nanosecond she froze, then screamed and scrambled down the ladder, rushing over to the fallen Alton, while attempting to stay out of the line of sight of the window.

"Derek, oh my God, Derek . . . how badly are you hurt?" She felt for a pulse at his throat, trying to ignore the massive red splotch just below his left shoulder. "Oh God, Derek, just lie still, I'll get help. Don't try to move."

Her eyes flew around the room while her mind tried to ignore the obvious. No pulse. She needed help. *Get going.*

The front doorbell rang and someone pounded on the door. Nathaniel Creely called her name.

"Nathaniel," she shrieked. "Help, please." She struggled to her feet and somehow made it to the door and unlocked it.

Nathaniel, her eighty-year-old landlord and neighbor, shoved the door and grabbed her by the shoulders. "What's wrong? I heard a noise? It sounded like a gunshot. You're shaking. What happened?" Nathaniel's face looked as white as his hair, his blue eyes full of anxiety.

"In the living room." She pointed and sat with a thud on the stairs. "It's Derek Alton. He's been shot."

Nathaniel went into the room, knelt down beside Alton and checked his pulse, then reappeared at her side. He was already punching 911 into his cell phone. "Are you hurt?" He patted her shoulder as she shook her head. "Hurry. Someone's been shot," he told the operator, and then gave the address. "I don't know if there's a shooter on the premises." He looked at Lizzie, who shrugged and cast her eyes wildly around. "I don't know. Just hurry." He closed his phone, ignoring instructions to stay on the line, and took Lizzie by the hand.

"You're coming to my place until the police arrive. You'll be safe there." He took a good look in all directions after opening the door, then steered her across the front lawn, over to his door. As her landlord, he lived in the main house and rented out the two-bedroom side addition to Lizzie. The sound of sirens grew louder. "In here. Now, just sit and try to relax." He left the room but returned quickly with a beige wool cardigan, too large for Lizzie but cozy and warm.

"Who is he, Lizzie? A friend?" Nathaniel asked.

Lizzie shook her head. "Not really. He's a visiting author and he's supposed to be at our next book club meeting."

She sat hugging her knees and didn't even look

out the window when the siren ended in a whine as the police cruiser screeched into her driveway, followed instantly by second and third sirens.

"I'll attend to them. You just sit here," Nathaniel told her, and he left.

It didn't take long for police chief Mark Dreyfus to come rushing into the room. He hesitated, then sat beside Lizzie and wrapped his arms around her. She felt like she'd never stop shivering. He rubbed her left arm gently.

"I almost had a frigging heart attack when I got the call," he whispered in her ear. "Creely said you're not hurt. Are you sure you're okay?"

She nodded and felt some of the tension leaving her body. She longed for Mark to stay like that, sitting there with her in his arms for the rest of the night. But that wouldn't happen. Maybe later. She still marveled that after all these years, she and Mark Dreyfus were an item. After all those months of mooning about him in high school, she the book nerd and he the captain of the football team, totally unaware of her existence; then, meeting again, unfortunately at the scene of a murder a few months earlier, and being swept up in the excitement of a new romance. And now, yet another murder.

"What happened, Lizzie? Who is he?" Mark finally asked.

Lizzie took a deep breath to steady her voice. "His name is Derek Alton and he's an author who's in town visiting. He was going to speak to the book club on Thursday."

"Did you see who shot him?"

"No, I had my back to him when it happened. I didn't see or hear anything other than the window shattering."

"Chief?" A female voice called at the door, followed by a loud knock.

Mark kissed Lizzie's forehead. "I'll be back as soon as I can. I'm afraid I'll have to question you some more, but until then, you stay here and let Mr. Creely take care of you." He left. Bareheaded. *He must have forgotten his hat in the car.* What a crazy thing to notice, she thought. *I must be in shock.*

Chapter Three

◇◇◇

The tension in Iris' chest built up unbearably.
By rights, the hooks on her bra ought to snap.
DOG EAT DOG—MARY COLLINS

Lizzie sat for a few minutes longer and fidgeted. "Oh my God, the cats. I totally forgot. I have to go check on them. I'm worried they might have gotten out, with the police in and out like that."

"We'll go over after."

"No, Nathaniel, I have to do it now. I'm fine,

really I am. I'll just put them in my bedroom and make sure the door is shut." She hurried out before he could object any further.

Lizzie heard Mark talking to Officer Amber Craig as she entered the front door of Lizzie's side of the house. She stopped abruptly for a few seconds after she entered the living room, waiting until the room stopped swaying. Even though she avoided looking at the spot, she could see Derek Alton's body out of the corner of her eye. She took a deep breath, pulled the sweater even tighter around her and faced the two police officers.

"Lizzie, you should have stayed next door," Mark said, but he stayed where he stood.

"Don't come in any farther. This is a crime scene. We don't want you contaminating it." Officer Craig barked out the order.

Lizzie glanced at Mark. She'd already contaminated it. It was her house, after all. She shrugged and backed up a few paces.

"That's Derek Alton, the writer, isn't it?" Craig asked. "What's he doing here?"

Lizzie felt Mark's eyes on her as she answered. "He's visiting in town."

"No, I mean here, in your house." Officer Craig glanced at the chief and then back at Lizzie. "Was he a good friend of yours?"

"No. I met him just a few days ago. He was going to be our guest at the Ashton Corners

Mystery Readers and Cheese Straws Society this Thursday. He stopped by to find out a bit more about each of the members. He said he wanted to make sure to tailor his talk to each of them." She took a deep breath, hoping she wouldn't burst into tears. *It has to be shock.*

"I see."

Lizzie didn't like the sound of that.

"And you were where, when the shot was fired?" Craig continued.

Lizzie glanced at Mark. He was watching her closely, his face unreadable. "Uh, he dropped by unexpectedly. I've been putting up Christmas decorations." Her hand did a sweep of the room, exposing the fact that she'd been a bit slow at getting around to it this year. Mark's eyes stayed on the mistletoe. Lizzie swallowed hard. "I was on the ladder, hanging the, uh, mistletoe. My back was to the window. I heard the shot and Derek yelled out as he fell." A sob escaped her and she looked at the body. "He's really dead, isn't he?"

"Yes."

She looked at Mark. She thought she detected a slight sheen of perspiration on his head. His dark chocolate eyes were unreadable. She took a deep breath.

"I came to get my cats. I have to make sure they're safe." She turned and started toward the stairs.

Officer Craig was right behind her. "You can't go up there alone."

"Why? No one's hiding there. It's safe."

"It's not your safety I'm concerned about."

Lizzie stopped partway up and turned to look at her. "What? You think I'm part of this? Maybe going to destroy some evidence or something? Get serious."

"I'm very serious. You're not going up there alone."

Lizzie looked at Mark, who had come up behind Officer Craig. "I don't want my cats getting out with all the doors opening and closing. Please, Mark."

His face softened. "Can you take them next door? I'm afraid we'll have to go through your house."

"What? Why? What are you looking for?"

"I don't know at this stage of the investigation. But we have to be thorough. We don't usually get second chances with crime scenes."

"But he was shot in the living room, not upstairs."

"Is there something you don't want us to see?" Officer Craig queried.

"Yes. My private life." She looked directly at Mark. "Derek Alton was never upstairs in my house; therefore, there's nothing for you to investigate up there. It just feels like such an invasion of privacy."

Mark took a few moments before replying. "Go and find your cats, Lizzie. Officer Craig will help you carry them next door."

Lizzie straightened her shoulders and continued up the stairs. She heard Craig behind her, grumbling under her breath. That brought a small smile to Lizzie's face.

"Brie . . . Edam . . . come on kitties. Where are you?"

She checked in her bedroom. No cats on the bed. They weren't obvious in the guest room or in her office, either. She went back to her bedroom, with Officer Craig trailing behind her, and kneeled beside the bed. Both cats stared back at her from their hiding place under it. She spoke softly to them and slid partway under, snagging Brie and handing her to Officer Craig. Then she moved around to the other side of the bed and went through the same process to catch Edam.

"Hang on tightly," she told Officer Craig, who grunted in return.

They walked slowly down the stairs, out the front door and over to Nathaniel's. He relieved Craig of her charge and she left immediately, brushing cat fur from her uniform jacket, and muttering.

"You don't mind the cats being here, do you?" Lizzie asked.

"Not in the slightest, my dear. In fact, I've put out a dish of water for them in the kitchen and made sure all the doors and windows are shut."

"Thank you, Nathaniel. I'll go over again in a while and see if I can get their food and cat cages. Oh boy, what a day. And poor Derek. Who would want to kill him?" Now that the initial horror had passed, she still couldn't quite get her head around what had happened. She didn't know the guy well but she did feel sad his life had ended so brutally.

"Who indeed?" Molly Mathews announced as she stepped into the living room. "Oh, Lizzie honey . . . what a terrible, terrible thing for you to go through. You're sure you're okay? You weren't injured in any way?"

Lizzie looked quickly at Nathaniel.

"I took the liberty of giving Molly a call," he explained.

Molly walked over to Lizzie and wrapped her arms around her. Molly's white woven cape fell from her shoulders, revealing bold yellow and black silk Chinese lounging pajamas.

"I'm just fine, Molly," Lizzie said, torn between giving in to the urge to cry now that she was being coddled and keeping her eyes glued to Molly. "I just can't believe it, though." She wasn't sure if she meant the murder or Molly's outfit.

"Nathaniel, how about making us all some sweet tea?" Molly suggested as she guided Lizzie over to the couch. "Now, do you feel up to telling me what happened?"

Lizzie nodded as she sank back against the

overstuffed cushions. She couldn't tear her eyes from Molly. This wasn't the elegant, stylish Molly Mathews who had been a rock in Lizzie's somewhat turbulent growing-up years. True, she hadn't seen her friend in several weeks and that had been cause for concern. Molly seemed to have turned in on herself over the past few weeks, retreating from the world and her friends as she sorted through the aftermath of revelations about her deceased husband.

The Molly who had emerged was a transformation. Her shoulder-length gray hair had been swept up in a haphazard bun on the top her of head. A number of black chopsticks held it precariously in place.

"Are you okay?" Lizzie ventured, dying to know what had been going on in Molly's life all these weeks.

"Of course I am, honey. Can't you see? I've had a reawakening, is what it is. Now stop gawking and tell me what happened over at your house."

Lizzie gulped. "It was just awful, Molly. I was hanging Christmas decorations and had my back to Derek Alton, and then I heard a gunshot and glass breaking. I turned as Derek yelled out but he was already collapsed on the floor bleeding."

Molly patted her hand. "Just what was he doing at your place anyway?"

"He dropped in out of the blue. He said we could

talk while I continued decorating. I was hanging the mistletoe."

Lizzie's eyes narrowed. "That's what Mark is thinking, isn't it? Not who killed Derek, but what was going on in my house? I don't believe it."

Molly sighed. "Mark's a man, honey, and I'm certain he has strong feelings for you, so of course, he's likely to be a tad jealous. Especially since you've been out on a date with Derek."

Lizzie jumped up and started pacing. "It wasn't a real date. Derek wanted to talk about the book club, so sure, I had dinner with him."

"It's not me you have to convince."

"And how did you know about it anyway?"

Molly sighed. "Lizzie, you should realize by now that nothing goes unnoticed in Ashton Corners and also, that since I'm friends with the manager of the Shasta Room, I hear all."

Nathaniel appeared, carrying a tray of tall glasses and a plate of sugar cookies. "This should help," he said, setting it down on the coffee table. "I did detect a decided chill in the air when you were being questioned, Lizzie. I think Molly is right. As are you, my dear. Chief Dreyfus needs to focus on the murder, not the setting."

"Oh boy," Lizzie whispered as she sank back against the pillows on the couch.

"Indeed," Nathaniel said, and he passed the cookies.

Chapter Four

◇◇◇

Fasten your seat belts. It's going to be a bumpy night.
ALL ABOUT EVE—JOSEPH LEO MANKIEWICZ

How long have you had a relationship with Derek Alton?" Officer Craig asked Lizzie.

Lizzie looked over at Mark, sitting in Nathaniel's navy leather recliner beside the dark oak fireplace. Because of the usual moderate temperatures in central Alabama, the fireplace was seldom used. A tray of candles decorated the hearth, although they were never lit, either.

She addressed her answer to Mark. "I did not have a relationship with Derek Alton." She directed her gaze to Officer Craig in time to see a small smile disappear. "I met him at the Book Bin on Saturday and Jensey Pollard told Derek about our mystery book club and one thing led to another . . ." She paused to stare down Craig's smirk. "I mean, she suggested he should be our guest at the next book club meeting. He agreed. I bought his book, which he signed. Then he left."

"And next thing, he's in your living room being shot?" Officer Craig asked, her left eyebrow arched. Lizzie found it as annoying as her smirk.

"That's it exactly. He came to my house to talk about the book club."

"And you just happened to be hanging mistletoe?"

Lizzie sat upright. "Yes. He came in and said to go ahead with what I was doing, he'd just ask me some questions. He wanted to know more about the people who'd be at the meeting. He said it would help him tailor his talk. I had been hanging the mistletoe so I continued. I didn't stop to think, should I really be hanging mistletoe when this man is in my house, if that's what you're getting at. I had been struggling with it, so I hung the damned mistletoe."

"We've got that, Lizzie," Mark said unexpectedly.

She looked over at him but couldn't read his expression. Those dark eyes, usually so expressive, could be quite unreadable at times. Like now. She wondered if he could read the anxiety in her face. She must look a mess. She'd been wearing a Jaguars team sweatshirt that had seen many washings, jeans and thick socks when Alton arrived. She'd added pale blue Keds sneakers when she left the house. Her face lacked makeup and her long, dark brown hair had been pulled back in a casual ponytail. *Real enticing. You can see why Derek would try to seduce me right then and there.*

Officer Craig cleared her throat and spoke. "And you hadn't met him before that day in the bookstore?"

"No. Now wouldn't it be more productive to ask if I saw anything or anyone outside my house?"

Craig looked annoyed but asked, "And did you?"

"No."

Craig's look of annoyance deepened. "Just what are you trying to say, Ms. Turner?"

"That I know nothing about this man and why anyone would want to kill him. Nor am I a good witness because I didn't see anything. I had my back to him when he was shot." Lizzie could hear murmurs of Nathaniel and Molly talking softly in the next room. She wished she were in there with them.

Officer Craig looked over at the chief, then flipped her notebook shut and stood up, straightening her trouser legs as she did so. "That's all for now. But we'll want you to stop by the police station tomorrow and bring down your statement. You know the drill."

Mark stood and said, "I'm afraid you won't be able to stay at your place tonight. You can come back now and get what you'll need. We'll still be looking around for a few more hours and we'll board up the front window when we're finished. My office will let you know when you can get back in." He turned to go.

Lizzie asked, "And don't leave town?" That had been Mark's line the last time a murder had brought them together. He'd been quick to smile after saying it.

This time he gave her that unreadable look . . . and left.

The last time. That had been only a few months ago. And now a second murder in quiet, sleepy Ashton Corners. *It's like a bad dream.* Lizzie shook her head and tried to pick up on the conversational thread taking place around her. She looked around Nathaniel's living room, grateful to have her book club friends with her.

"This is unbelievable," Sally-Jo Baker said, dropping onto the couch beside Lizzie and patting her back. "What a terrible shock for you. You're so lucky not to have been hurt."

Lizzie nodded and took another sip of her wine. Maybe she should lay off it. Her mind felt wrapped in gauze and she didn't feel quite as upset as the other members of the Ashton Corners Mystery Readers and Cheese Straws Society. *Must be shock.*

The others had readily accepted Nathaniel's invitation to gather in his house that evening. They all wanted to hear the details of the demise of their anticipated guest. So, Sally-Jo Baker, Bob Miller, Jacob Smith and Andrea Mason had arrived in short order. Only Stephanie Lowe was missing.

"I do hope Stephanie is keeping her cell phone handy," Molly commented.

Stephanie had been in town for a short while but

hadn't divulged much about her background to anyone, even though it was increasingly obvious the unmarried nineteen-year-old would soon be giving birth. She'd eventually told them about the abusive boyfriend and his threatening phone calls, and her grandfolks who'd thrown her out. That was just over a year ago and she'd moved to Ashton Corners. The book club members had enveloped her into their protective fold and were eagerly awaiting the arrival of the baby.

Andie nodded enthusiastically. "I'm so excited. She should be having her baby any day now. Or maybe that's any week now. And now another murder. This is way too awesome."

Lizzie sighed. That didn't quite describe her own feelings about the crime.

"Are we sure this Alton fellow was the intended target?" Bob Miller asked.

Lizzie gasped. "Of course he was. It couldn't have been me."

"Of course it couldn't," Molly stated calmly, passing around the required plate of cheese straws, this time shaped as candy canes in honor of the season. "No one would want to harm Lizzie. She has no enemies."

Lizzie smiled gratefully at Molly. It was good to have a champion, because she didn't want to dwell on that possibility.

"I can't quite get my head around it all," Lizzie said. "But you know, it's a real shame he didn't get a chance to talk to the book club, because I think he would have been an interesting guest. I've just started reading his book *Judgment*, and it's set in a small town in Alabama. Of course, it's terrible he was murdered," she added quickly, feeling abashed that she hadn't mentioned that first.

"Maybe it's set in Ashton Corners," Andie quipped while staring at Molly. She hadn't taken her eyes off the new version of Molly Mathews since she'd arrived.

"I'm sure Ashton Corners wasn't even on his radar when he wrote this, Andie," Lizzie said.

"Well, I picked myself up a copy of the book on your say-so, Lizzie. Not sure if I'll even bother reading it now," Bob said. "Especially since it says on the cover it's a 'literary mystery.' I take it that means it's not a police procedural."

Molly tsk-tsked. "Here we go again. It'll do you right good to read a literary mystery, Bob Miller. Especially for its setting. I had meant to stop by the Book Bin and pick up a copy tomorrow. I wanted to be sure to have Derek Alton sign it." She sighed. "Such a waste. He must have been quite talented to win the Onyx all those years back. I should have read it when it first came out, I guess. Sally-Jo, have you read it?"

Sally-Jo glanced up from her tea. Her short auburn hair had been brushed back and tucked behind her ears. She wore little makeup, as usual, and even with glasses her hazel eyes looked enormous. "No, not yet. I didn't think I could make it to the meeting so I actually hadn't planned to buy it." She bit her bottom lip and brushed a crumb off the forest green sweater set she wore.

Lizzie glanced at her quickly. Sally-Jo sounded upset.

"You know, it's okay, Sally-Jo. I wasn't in any real danger," she said.

Sally-Jo looked puzzled then smiled. "I know but it's still a frightening thing to have happen." She turned to Molly. "Molly, I'm truly dazzled by your outfit tonight."

"Why thank you, honey," Molly replied. "You know, life goes on, even with death all around."

Lizzie couldn't think of anything to reply to that. "I didn't realize you'd been planning to skip the book club meeting, Sally-Jo? What's up?"

"My family," she answered with a sigh. "I just got word yesterday that they're coming to my place for Christmas."

"How many?"

"Fourteen. Only Megan and her family won't be here. They're going to visit Michael's folks in Dallas."

"That'll be a full house," Jacob said. He sounded out of sorts.

Sally-Jo grimaced. "Tell me about it. I warned you I had four sisters, three of whom are married with kids."

"And what about your renovation plans?" Lizzie asked.

Sally-Jo shrugged. "Have to wait, I guess. Christmas was a bad time to be starting on them, anyway."

Lizzie glanced at Jacob. "What about you? Had you been planning on coming to the meeting?"

He nodded. "Sure, I was looking forward to it. I did some research on the guy, and the review for his last book said it came nowhere close to being as well written as *Judgment*. Of course, that was the only mystery of the total of six books. I wonder what this new one he was working on was about?"

"A sequel to the first, I'd heard," Bob said.

Everyone looked at him in surprise.

He shrugged. "Well, I did a little reading up on him, too, since Lizzie had talked us into having him as a guest. Wanted to know what I was letting myself in for, expanding my horizons and all." He smirked at Molly. It took away about fifty years from his aging face, making him look devilishly handsome, Lizzie thought. Even wearing his trademark blue flannel shirt and worn jeans. His thick gray hair framed his craggy face, curling in the oddest places.

Lizzie thought that over. She knew Alton had won the Onyx for Best Fiction, given out by the Hawthorne Society, and that his second book had fallen far short of what was expected. Many had wondered if he was a one-book wonder. But she thought he'd managed to garner good reviews for the next four, although none of the others had won awards.

"Well, I plan to finish reading *Judgment*, and if you agree, we'll make it the book for my month. Which gives you until March, we're doing Molly's choice this month."

"And, I hope y'all are well into reading *Hercule Poirot's Christmas*," Molly threw in.

Bob groaned. "Pass the cookies, please. And Molly, I have to ask, what on earth is that you're wearing, woman?"

"Do you like it? I'm branching out a bit, trying new looks and along with them, a new attitude. Now, what are we going to do about this here murder?" Molly asked.

"Not a goddamn thing," Bob said quickly. "I'd think you'd have had enough of sticking your nose into murder and mayhem, Molly Mathews. You were just lucky you all didn't end up in jail as the number one suspect when Frank Telford was killed right outside your house."

"I wasn't guilty, so that wouldn't have happened," she threw right back, but she shifted uncomfortably in her seat, almost jarring one of the chopsticks out of her hair.

It had been close, Lizzie thought. Especially since the murder weapon had been an antique gun that belonged to her long-deceased husband. She shivered. Another death, so soon. She just couldn't get her head around it. Better not to think about it too much right now.

Nathaniel, who'd been invited to sit with the group but had been quiet most of the evening, spoke up. "I can see whereas you'd like to find this here killer, since it did happen at Lizzie's." He paused to accept a molasses cookie from the plate Sally-Jo passed around. Lizzie waited to hear the litany of reasons they shouldn't get involved.

"But the point is," Nathaniel continued, "it did happen at Lizzie's and who knows what the killer has in mind. He may think Lizzie knows something or spotted him. Her life could be in danger. And the way the police are thinking right now, that's not at the top of their priority list."

Lizzie looked at him in awe. Not what she'd expected to hear. Not what she wanted to hear. She'd not thought about any continued danger. That didn't seem too likely. Or did it?

"That's freaking scary," Andie shrieked. "We've got to figure out how to protect you. You can't go back to your house and you've got to borrow a car. The killer knows yours and could end up firebombing it or something."

Way too much Janet Evanovich in that girl's life. While Lizzie was pleased that Andie had suddenly taken to reading—she'd devoured most of the Evanovich books in the last couple of months— Lizzie wasn't sure about this sudden channeling of Stephanie Plum, Evanovich's sleuth. It was happening with increasing regularity.

"Just a minute . . . let's not get carried away," Lizzie interjected. "The killer must have had a view of my living room in order to shoot Derek Alton, after all, and he, or she, must realize I couldn't see a thing with my back to the window."

"Just how well did you know him?" Jacob asked.

"Now you sound just like the police."

"Sorry, that's the attorney in me," he answered with a small grin, which turned into an inquiring glance.

"I've met him exactly three times. That's it."

"Three times?" Bob picked up on her statement. "That would be first in the bookstore, right . . . and last in your living room. What about the second time?"

Lizzie shifted uncomfortably.

"As y'all know, I met him on Saturday morning at the bookstore and he called me later in the day, inviting me out to dinner. To discuss the book club. He wanted to know more about us and just what we might be looking for him to say. So, I accepted." She paused and chose her words with care. "We went to dinner but it didn't go quite as planned. He had too much to drink, talked mainly about himself and I left as soon as we'd finished eating. When he stopped by today, he apologized and said that he really did want to know more about each of us so he could tailor his talk." She looked around at them all, waiting for comments.

"Thorough man," Bob said. The tone of his voice let on that he thought exactly the opposite.

"Did he leave it at that?" Sally-Jo asked.

"What do you mean?"

"I mean, did he . . ."—she hesitated a moment—"make a pass or anything?"

Lizzie took a deep breath. "Well, he tried. But I let him know I wasn't interested."

"I bet he thought he'd give it another try," Bob said under his breath.

Lizzie glanced sharply at him. "He hadn't been at my place long, and he'd given no indication of anything like that before he was shot. The only problem . . ."

"What is it, Lizzie?" Jacob demanded. It sounded like his courtroom voice to Lizzie, although she'd never seen him in action.

"Well, you see, he just dropped in unannounced and I was decorating for Christmas and he said to continue while we talked. And so I did. I hung the mistletoe and that's when the shot rang out."

"Mistletoe?" Sally-Jo said in disbelief. "You hung mistletoe with that letch in the room?"

Lizzie looked at her in surprise. "I wouldn't say he was a letch. Okay, maybe he was. And, had I known he would be shot and the police would make such a big deal about the mistletoe . . . I would have waited until he left." She let out a big sigh. "I can't believe he's dead."

Molly moved over beside Lizzie and put an arm around her shoulders. "It's a big shock, honey. Especially since you were right there. And don't worry about Mark. He'll realize he's being silly after he's had time to think it over. I think you continued doing what you were doing and that's all there was to it. There's nothing of significance in it."

Bob snorted. "That's a very female reaction, Molly."

Lizzie sat up straighter. "Well, we're not here to discuss my actions. I'm wondering what Derek was doing in Ashton Corners to start with and if that's why he was killed. And I'm going to the Book Bin tomorrow to ask Jensey Pollard if she knows."

"Action . . . that's a good remedy for everything," Molly agreed. "What can I do?"

Lizzie looked a bit bleak. "I'm not sure at this point."

Andie jumped into the fray. "Well, I'm going online tonight when I get home to find out everything I can about Derek Alton. If he has any dark secrets that might have gotten him killed, I'll find them."

Lizzie smiled her thanks.

"And I think I'll just wander over next door right now and see if I can pick up any details. I see they've got Ronny Biggs working the crime scene. He owes me, that boy does. I gave him a job when I was chief and taught him a thing or two about crime investigating when his own brother wouldn't hire him." Bob stood up. "Thank you kindly, Nathaniel, for your hospitality. I'll just head on home after that and give you a call tomorrow, Lizzie."

Lizzie nodded then said good-bye as the others decided to leave also, save Molly, who took her time.

"Is everything all right with you, Molly?" Lizzie needed some reassurance about the change in Molly.

"As right as rain. Are you sure you're all right, honey?" she asked. "I sure wish we'd just ambled on into the Christmas season without any dramatics. I'm right tired of murder and suspicions."

"And it's just started, Molly. Who knows where this will all lead?"

Chapter Five

◇◇◇

How the past can tyrannize, delimiting our scope of activity—the choices we make, the things that happen to us, what we choose to do.

MCGARR AND THE P.M. OF BELGRAVE SQUARE—BARTHOLOMEW GILL

W *rong bed.* Lizzie cautiously opened an eye. Wrong curtains. Where am I? She bolted upright in the bed, sending the cats leaping onto the floor. Nathaniel's house. Yesterday's murder. It all came back in overwhelming detail.

She shivered and crawled back down under the covers. Brie and Edam joined her again within seconds.

Derek Alton had died yesterday, in her house. She hated to think ill of the dead but she'd not been impressed with him. He'd come across as egotistical and much more interested in the adulation than in the writing process. She'd worried about that, just what the book club would make of him, and since it had been her suggestion he be their guest, she'd been troubled.

Not enough to kill him, though. Of course the police couldn't think she was the killer. She'd been in the same room and the shot had been fired from outside. The police. She couldn't even begin to know what went through Mark's mind yesterday. He looked none too pleased about Derek being in her house. Even less, that she'd been hanging mistletoe at the time. Was he jealous? Or just being professional, trying not to let his personal life interfere with the investigation of a murder?

No, he was not happy with her; that was certain. And if she were to reverse the roles, she knew deep down that she'd be jealous, too. What had she been thinking, going out to dinner with Derek? And Mark didn't even know about that as yet. So, she'd made her own bed, so to speak.

She hoped Mark would get over it and soon.

Now, the real question was, who would want to kill a visiting author? Surely no one in Ashton Corners. She'd been born and raised here. It was a wonderful town, large enough to provide all manner of arts, entertainment and outdoor activities but on the cozy side so you'd always meet someone you knew when out doing errands. The town itself had been part of the reason she'd returned after college and a year of working in Huntsville. The other part was the need to be close by to her mama.

Derek Alton was a visitor. So, someone had been targeting him. Someone had followed him to town. That had to be it.

She made herself get out of the warm, cozy bed,

once again disturbing the cats, got dressed quickly and went downstairs to find Nathaniel sitting at his kitchen table, cup of coffee in hand, reading the *Birmingham News*.

His thinning white hair was in need of a cut, unusual for Nathaniel, since he normally took such pride in his appearance. A true Southern gentleman was how Lizzie had once described him to a friend.

He glanced up at her and smiled. "Good morning, Lizzie. I hope you slept well after all that. And that the cats did as well. Please, help yourself to some coffee."

Lizzie poured herself a mug and sat down across from Nathaniel. The round birch table fit nicely into the large kitchen, about twice the size of her own. No surprise, since his beloved wife, now deceased, had been a terrific cook. Two of the walls were decorated with traditional country-style wallpaper in cream, yellow and brown, with the bottom halves a pale green wainscoting. The remaining walls were covered in appliances and dark mahogany cupboards. It still held the aroma of a woman's touch although Charlaine Creely had died long before Lizzie moved back to town.

"I had a good sleep in a comfortable bed, thank you. And the cats were pleased, also. In fact, they've snuggled back in."

"That's good. Now, I baked us some fresh

scones," he said as he got up and went to the oven to remove the baking.

"Smells delicious. Now I'll regret not having gotten up earlier for a run. But that's not going to stop me from eating one." She inhaled deeply as he placed a plate of scones on the table in front of her.

He chuckled. "I'm glad you didn't get up early. You needed a good rest after yesterday's turmoil. The police called earlier to say it's okay to go into your house, so I put in a call to Ford Guiger to come and replace the window. He should be here in a couple of hours. As will Noreen, my house-cleaner. She'll tidy it right up."

"Thank you, Nathaniel. Oh boy, I still can't believe what happened yesterday. Is there a story about it in the paper?"

"Yes, but not a very long one." Nathaniel opened the paper to page four. "Birmingham folks aren't too concerned about an author dying, it seems. But it will be big news when the *Ashton Corners Colonist* comes out on Thursday, I'll bet."

Lizzie read the story over quickly. "Just the facts. That's good. And no mention of it being my house nor the address. Also good. I'd hate to have gawkers passing by, or worse yet, reporters."

"What are your plans for today?"

"I have to go to school for a couple of meetings I've scheduled with some children and their parents. Do you mind if the cats stay here until I get back?"

"No, that's quite all right by me. I have an appointment early afternoon but I'll be here all morning so I'm happy to supervise the goings-on at your place, too."

"That would be great. I appreciate it. I'd better get going, though, or I'll be late for my first appointment." She snatched another scone to have as a snack.

Nothing stays a secret long in a town the size of Ashton Corners, Lizzie thought as she ventured from the school staff room to the vice principal's office. She'd already been inundated with questions from several teachers wanting details of the shooting and she'd been at school for only twenty minutes.

She gave them very little information, mainly because she didn't have any. She let her mind play with suggestions of what her next move should be while she set up for her first appointment of the day. As a reading specialist with the Ashton Corners School District, she was charged with assessing children who appeared to be reading below their expected level, referred either by their teacher or by parents. Part of her job also involved making recommendations to teachers as to programs and techniques, and designing staff training sessions.

A third-grade boy, who, from what she could see, would be happier out on the playground than sitting in a classroom, appeared for his second appointment in as many weeks, along with his mama. Lizzie went over the test results with Mrs. Cline, trying to emphasize her son Tory's strong points, even though reading wasn't one of them. Mrs. Cline had her own ideas about how well her son should be doing, and Lizzie had to remind herself that tact was the best way to deal with such single-mindedness. She wondered if Mr. Cline might be more inclined, so to speak—she smiled at the thought—to view his son with some sense and sensibility. She kept her smile in place as she saw them out the door and then went to the staff room.

Lizzie realized she kept glancing at her watch, about three times in the past fifteen minutes, and hoped it hadn't been obvious to the two fifth-grade teachers seated across from her. They'd been meeting through the lunch hour, going over Lizzie's suggestion for integrating a new reading program into their work plans at the start of the new term. Finally, the meeting ended as the school bell rang. Lunch over.

Lizzie tried to avoid the few stragglers still in the staff room, anxious not to have to answer any more questions about the murder. She made it out the door and beat a hasty retreat to her car in the school parking lot. She liked most of the teachers she worked with but, as in any small community, she sometimes felt as though they were living in one another's back pockets.

Her afternoon was clear until two thirty, when she had a meeting with the principal, Herbert Slocam, and she planned to head home in the meantime. She remembered to switch on her cell phone as she started her car. An instant buzzing alerted her there was a message from Officer Craig, who wanted to know when she planned to bring her statement into the station. Now was as good a time as any, she guessed.

As she pulled up to the station, she noticed that Mark's black Jeep wasn't in the parking lot and breathed a sigh of relief. She wanted to talk to him but not with all his colleagues around. Officer Craig looked up from her computer screen as the desk officer called over to her. She nodded to him, and Lizzie was told to go ahead.

"I thought you'd come by first thing in the morning," Craig said without even a hello.

Lizzie bristled, as she often did when in her presence. "I wasn't aware a time was stated, by either of us."

Craig glared at her and held out her hand. Lizzie pulled the handwritten statement out of her tote. She really had meant to drop it off on the way to school but had totally forgotten. No way she was about to let Officer Craig know that, though.

"Was there anything you wanted to add to it?

Something that might have come to you as you went about your business all day long?"

Lizzie bit back her instinctive retort. "No. There wasn't a whole lot to tell in the first place. So if that's all, I'll just go and let you get on with your work."

"If you do happen to think of anything more, be sure you call." It sounded like a warning of some sort.

Lizzie nodded and left, glad to have it over and done with. She headed home and again felt happiness and relief at being able to pull into her driveway. No police van or cruiser blocked it. Better yet, a brand-new window had been installed in her living room. All traces of yesterday's violence had been eliminated from the outside. She braced herself as she opened the front door, dreading the bloodstained carpet in the living room.

Thank God for Nathaniel. Lizzie smiled at the sight of a clean hardwood floor. The small area carpet, fortunately one she hadn't been overly fond of, had been removed and any traces cleaned away. His cleaning lady must have come in just after she left him this morning.

She glanced at the mistletoe hanging right where she'd stuck it when the bullet had been fired at Derek Alton. She sucked in her breath as her internal video of the scene went into replay. How could such violence have happened here, in her

51

house? Who had known Derek was stopping by? Lizzie hadn't. He'd taken her by surprise. But he must have told someone, or else he had been trailed. A stalker?

And why would anyone want to kill him? He was a stranger in town. So had he really been stalked all the way to Ashton Corners? She wanted some answers. Her house was the crime scene, after all. And the location had not sat well with Mark Dreyfus. She didn't believe for an instant that Mark would let this color the way he viewed the investigation. But, if she could maybe figure out who had killed Derek, it might put her back in his good graces all the more quickly.

She walked into the kitchen and picked up the phone to dial Molly.

"Oh, Lizzie . . . thank you so much for calling. I've been wondering all morning how you are. How are you?"

"As well as can be expected, I guess." She felt better already just hearing the melodic Southern lilt of Molly's voice.

"Well, that was quite a shock you had yesterday. Quite a shock. Why don't you just come on over here for supper before the literacy class tonight? I'll cook up some of the Bourbon and brown sugar tenderloin you like so much."

"Thanks, Molly. I'll take you up on that."

"Good. See you later then, honey. Come on over whenever you're ready."

Lizzie smiled as she replaced the receiver. That sounded like the old Molly she knew and loved. And had missed. She glanced at the clock. Just enough time to collect her cats from Nathaniel and get them settled back in before she had to return to school.

When Nathaniel didn't answer the bell or her knocks, she let herself in with the key he'd given her. She found some paper and a pen to leave him a note thanking him for everything, and telling him she'd taken the cats home. Then she set out to find them.

They'd settled right back on the sofa bed they'd all slept on the night before, curled around each other. They eyed her warily as she opened the cat cages. She scooped them in and carried them home.

Edam cautiously toured the main floor, checking it out thoroughly, creeping toward the spot in the living room and walking warily around it. Brie headed straight upstairs. Lizzie filled their bowls with dry treats and went to look for Brie. She found her curled up on her bed, obviously still exhausted from the change in routine.

She assured herself the house was secure, pausing as a sharp pang of panic shot through her when she entered the living room. She could almost see Derek's body on the floor, the large bloodied spot on his back getting larger, the same terror gripping her. She sat down on the arm of the settee and took a deep breath. It had happened. It was over. She had to move on. Figuring out who the killer was would certainly help.

But for now, she had to get back to school.

Chapter Six

◇◇◇

She turned to give me a commiserating smile. "Men. You can't live with 'em and you can't shoot 'em."

POLISHED OFF—LILA DARE

L izzie glanced at the clock on her bedside table. She didn't want to be late for tonight's literacy class but she wanted to find her new Iban stretch bracelet. She was certain she'd placed it on the dresser before going back to work. She glanced down at Edam and Brie, engaged in grooming each other on the floor. Had one of them chosen it as a toy? She got down on her hands and knees and searched under the bed. Nothing. She grabbed a flashlight and shone it under the dresser. Bingo. It had obviously been played with and had slid to the back wall. Grabbing the long ruler she kept on hand for fishing cat toys out from such a spot, she managed to retrieve the bracelet.

The ringing doorbell sent her scrambling to her feet and, with a final look at the cats, now up on the bed in their favorite spots, she ran downstairs.

Mark had his back to her, looking out at the street, when she opened the door. She had just enough time to close her open jaw before he turned around.

"I know you've got a class tonight but I have a few more questions for you," he said, stepping forward.

"Oh, sure. Come on in." Lizzie closed the door behind him and followed him into the living room, wincing as her memory clicked on an image of the body. "What is it you want to know?" *No "Hello, how are you?"* Okay, she'd play it cool, too.

Mark sat on the green-striped settee and waited until she'd sat on the taupe wicker chair in front of the window.

"I need to know, as close to verbatim as possible, what you and Derek Alton discussed over dinner." His face showed no sign of emotion, although Lizzie thought his voice cracked a bit at the mention of dinner.

Taken totally by surprise that he knew about the dinner, Lizzie tried to gather her thoughts before answering. "Well, we started off with the usual pleasantries—comments about how he was finding Ashton Corners, the weather . . . the usual."

She paused to study Mark. He held his pen and notebook but wasn't writing. She shifted uncomfortably. Time to make the intent of the dinner clear. "He'd asked me to dinner to discuss the book club evening. However, he ended up doing most of the talking and it was all about himself."

Mark was staring at her, although he didn't say a word. She felt disconcerted and tried to pick up the train of her thoughts.

"And how long was the dinner?" Mark asked.

"A couple of hours, I'd guess. I didn't really look at any clocks." And Mark should remember she disliked wearing a watch, she thought.

"And then?"

Do not squirm. "I took a cab home." *No way I'm telling any more details.*

"So, he picked you up? You didn't drive over to meet him?"

"He had a rental and he suggested we take a quick drive around town on the way to eat, so I could point out some of the sights."

"Humph," was all Mark said. Lizzie didn't like the sound of it.

"And that's the reason he stopped by yesterday," Lizzie continued quickly. "He realized he'd been a bit of a bore and apologized and asked about the book club. I filled him in some more about the members."

She thought a moment. "I'm not sure if this matters, but when I mentioned we have refreshments at our meetings, he said he always brings his own cookies with him because of an allergy." She took a deep breath. "And then he was shot."

Mark stood abruptly. "Thanks. I can see myself out since you've got to get ready. I'll probably have some more questions soon."

"Any clues? Any ideas who killed him?"

Mark shook his head.

"Any motives?"

"No."

Lizzie continued sitting long after he left. He'd been so abrupt and businesslike. How totally frustrating. And, he hadn't even asked about the ending to the evening. He probably imagined the worst. She leapt up and stalked upstairs. Men could be so infuriating.

Chapter Seven
◇◇◇

Waking is like rising from the dead. The slow climb out of sleep, shapes appearing out of blackness, the alarm clock ringing like the last trump.

THE CROSSING PLACES—ELLY GRIFFITHS

Wow, Miss," said Sonny Dolman. "You're like some kind of murder magnet."

Jolene Racine favored him with a dirty look and jumped in. "That's a really uncool thing to say, Sonny. I'm sure she doesn't go looking around for people who are about to be murdered."

Lizzie suppressed a smile. "You've nailed it,

Jolene. Thank you. Now, if we could just concentrate on the topic, which is three types of point of view. But first, we'll start with everyone reading out loud last week's assignment. Who'd like to go first?"

Jolene's hand shot up a fraction of a second before Sonny's. Lizzie nodded at Jolene, who opened her notebook to a page marked by a pink Post-it note and started reading. Lizzie was impressed. Jolene had worked hard all term at the evening literacy classes and her essay showed it. She had most of the grammar correct, it sounded like she used proper punctuation and she'd obviously done some research to include in the original short paragraph they'd been given to work from. She'd have no trouble with her GEDs, Lizzie thought with satisfaction.

"Well done, Jolene. You're up now, Sonny."

Sonny sat up straighter in his comfy club chair. Since the classes were held in Molly Mathews's library, there were none of the classroom basics like desks and upright, uncomfortable chairs. Lizzie thought back briefly to the first class she'd taught in this room, two years ago. She'd originally been worried that the magnificence and comfort of the room would be a distraction but she'd soon learned that most of her students, all in their late teens, were focused on passing their GEDs and a little thing like an awesome room wouldn't deter them.

Sonny cleared his throat, looked at the other two students, flashed his fifties' *Grease* facsimile smile and read.

Lizzie hadn't been quite sure what to expect. Sometimes Sonny turned in well-thought-out papers; at other times the homework contained meandering thoughts that were all over the map. Tonight, he was right on target. Lizzie smiled and thanked him; he beamed and did a small bow to the others, then sat and slid back down to his slouchy position.

She listened to Melanie's paper, which was consistent with the work she'd been doing since joining the group six weeks before. Passable. Lizzie missed Stephanie being in class but she was pleased that she'd wanted to keep up with the work at home. Lizzie would drop off the new assignment tomorrow and go over her latest paper at the same time.

Jolene interrupted her musings. "Isn't it time for the break? I can't wait to get another look at Miz Molly. It's been real weird, her not being around for the last few weeks. Just leaving the juice and cookies out for us. Very *X-Files*, ya know? And tonight . . . did y'all see the geisha outfit she's wearin'?"

"This is the first time I've ever seen her and you could have knocked me over," Melanie agreed. "She looks weird."

"Not weird," Jolene replied. "She's doing her own thing."

Lizzie glanced at the antique brass clock on the end table. "Of course. Take five, everyone." They dashed out of the room except for Jolene, who held back.

"Do you mind if I ask you about my book?" she asked, somewhat timidly for her.

Lizzie did a mental head slap. "Oh, Jolene. I'm so sorry. What with everything that's been going on, I haven't had time. I'll read it before you go on Christmas break, though. I promise."

Jolene grinned. "That's okay. I thought it was something like that. Think I'll get myself a cookie and tea."

Lizzie made a note in her agenda to read Jolene's partially finished sci-fi manuscript on the weekend. She'd been pleased when Jolene had asked for her comments. The least she could do is be timely about giving them. She looked up as Sally-Jo entered the room.

"Hey, Lizzie. I don't know about your class but mine is sure hyper tonight," Sally-Jo said as she sank into a chair. "Got a minute?"

"Sure, what's up?" asked Lizzie.

"I was just wondering how you're feeling? I saw your car in the school parking lot today and couldn't believe you were at work, but I didn't have a free moment to look for you."

"I had to go into work. Too many appointments to take a day off. And also, I'd just sit around and brood if I stayed home. It seems sort of surreal now. But a bit freaky when I walk into my living room."

Sally-Jo sank into one of the cushy chairs across from Lizzie. "I'll bet. You'd said Derek just turned up out of the blue. Was he asking anything specific about us?"

Lizzie nodded. "He said he wanted to find out more about the members and see if he could tailor his talk a bit better."

"Did he ask our names or for any specifics?"

"I'd already told him our names and a bit about everyone when I first met him. Yesterday he'd wanted some more details."

"Like what?"

"Sally-Jo, what's going on? Why are you asking me these things?"

She didn't have a chance to answer. Jolene came bouncing back into the library followed by Melanie and Sonny.

"Oops, sorry," Jolene said as she spied Sally-Jo.

"No problem. I'd better get back to my class." She gave Lizzie a small smile as she left the room. Lizzie wondered what all that had been about.

The rest of the evening passed quickly and the students left with a new assignment due the following Monday, which was the next time they would meet. The literacy group met twice a week, Mondays and Wednesdays. Lizzie went looking for Sally-Jo, only to find that she'd already left. Her classes were held in the sunroom, which was a 1980's addition to the grand old house. With the size of Molly's house, the entire adult literacy program could be hosted there, but the majority of students attended weekly classes at the Community Center on Main Street. These were the overflow students, with Lizzie and Sally-Jo volunteering to teach at the mansion. In fact, Molly Mathews had volunteered her house as a location for many good causes over the years and her generosity had earned her numerous awards in the community.

"Jacob came by a bit early and we had a nice visit in the kitchen," Molly explained. She straightened the obi wrapped around her waist. "He and Sally-Jo left as soon as her students cleared out."

Lizzie accepted the cup of hot tea and cinnamon pecan drop biscuit Molly offered her and slid along the built-in banquette in the corner of the kitchen. "That's a very colorful outfit, Molly." She wasn't sure how much to say about it.

"Yes, isn't it? The dark red cherry blossoms on the white background caught my eye the minute I entered the store." She did a slow twirl for Lizzie. "I'm quite happy with it."

"Umm. How did Sally-Jo seem to you tonight?"

Molly sat down across from Lizzie, her own tea in hand. The rather wide sleeves of the silk Japanese kimono draped on the table as she sipped. "I didn't really get a chance to talk to her. Why do you ask?"

"Maybe it's nothing. She just seemed sort of jittery and was asking me all sorts of questions about Derek. Like if he'd asked about anyone specifically."

"His death has shaken us all to some extent, even though we hadn't yet met the man. Anticipating meeting him brought us all a bit closer to the tragedy." Molly absently swept back a stray lock of her gray hair that had fallen across her forehead and dangled in front of her left eye.

Lizzie watched the graceful movement and thought back to the many times Molly had pulled Lizzie's own dark brown hair back and into a ponytail. When Lizzie's mama had been unable to look after her properly, it was Molly who had hovered, stopping by every day, making sure there were meals prepared, the laundry done and Lizzie not lacking for anything.

"And had he?" Molly asked.

"Excuse me?" Lizzie tried to connect back with the train of conversation.

Molly took a sip before answering. "Had Derek asked about any of the book club members in particular?"

"I'd told him a bit when I'd met him at the Book Bin, though we didn't get around to talking much about the book club the evening we went to dinner. The day he was killed, he had come over to apologize and to ask some more about the members but we got sidetracked into talking about cookies and then he was killed."

"Cookies?"

"Yes. He has—had—an allergy, so he said he'd bring his own."

Molly nodded absently. "So, when he stopped by yesterday, would you say he'd really been thinking about us and wanted more details? Or was that merely a ploy to get into your house?"

Lizzie gasped. "Don't even think that when anyone else is around, just in case they can read your mind."

Molly chuckled. "You did say he made a pass at you the other night, right?"

"Well, yes. But I left right away. It didn't get out of hand."

"You could have been seen as a challenge to him. Maybe he was having another go."

Lizzie stared at her before answering. "Do you really think that or are you just messing around with possible plots?"

Molly leaned across the table and put her hand on Lizzie's. "I wouldn't blame him at all for trying again, honey, but if that wasn't on his mind, I guess he wanted to give us a good show. Too bad we didn't get to see it."

Chapter Eight

◇◇◇

I wasn't sure who had told what lies to accomplish it.

THE PROFESSIONAL—ROBERT B. PARKER

Yesterday's news was old news. *Thank God.* Lizzie had been cornered only a couple of times at school during the lunch hour by curious teachers. But she'd been thankful to make an early escape after her final afternoon appointment.

Back at her house, she tried to finish the Christmas decorating but found it impossible to get enthusiastic when she actually stood in the living room. The cats, too, were having problems adjusting, skulking into the room and sniffing madly at the site where the body had been. Maybe it was a bit disrespectful, hanging festive décor so soon after the murder. She decided to put it off a week and then give it another try. She planned to put the tree itself up on December 17, something she'd done every year, following the pattern set when she was a child. The tree would remain in its full glory until the twelfth day of Christmas, January 6.

Usually she found this time of year and all the rituals exciting. Now, she found it hard to stir up any enthusiasm. *Give it some time.* She nodded to herself and sank onto the settee facing the window. She wondered what a white Christmas would feel like. They'd had the odd, light snowfall in late December before but nothing deep and lasting. Maybe some year she'd take a trip at Christmas, spend it up north. Maybe Lake Placid in New York, or even Canada, just outside Montreal in the Laurentians. She'd read about some nice ski lodges up there. Who was she kidding? She'd never go away at Christmas. She had Mama to visit, and Molly, too. And hopefully this year, she'd do something with Mark. If he were even speaking to her.

She'd have to address that. But was it better to wait until Mark brought up the topic? She didn't want him to think she was reading too much into their relationship. How did she really know how he felt? Maybe he hadn't been upset about Derek being at her place. Maybe he had been frustrated at having to deal with another murder, so soon. That cheered her somewhat.

The next evening, Lizzie finished carrying the trays of food into Molly's library and waited until all the book club members were seated. It really was the perfect place to hold the monthly meetings of the Ashton Corners Mystery Readers and Cheese Straws Society. The floor-to-ceiling dark oak bookcases covered three walls, framing the two internal doors, one going to the hall and the other to the powder room. The remaining wall was covered in plush beige brocade drapes, which, when drawn, revealed double French leaded-glass doors opening onto a stone patio. And beyond the patio, which wrapped around the back and two sides of the house, there was an acre of green grass, gardens and shrubbery.

Lizzie drew her attention back to those inside the room. She was pleased to see that Stephanie Lowe had made the effort to attend although she had great difficulty in settling her body, all nine-month-pregnant bulk of it, into a comfortable sitting position. Her gaze settled on Jacob Smith.

"Where's Sally-Jo?" she asked.

Jacob shook his head. "I'm not sure what's up. She phoned just as I was getting ready to leave and begged off. I think she's starting to feel the pressure. I don't think she's all too thrilled by the prospect of her family descending on her for Christmas."

Lizzie frowned. She knew Sally-Jo wasn't looking forward to the visit, mainly because it meant her parents, sisters and their families but well-organized Sally-Jo always had a plan of action. She'd have to call her later.

Andie Mason finished her walk around the perimeter of the room, looking behind the curtains and staring out the windows for a few moments. She finally sat down, close to Lizzie.

Lizzie just gave her head a slight shake. *What is*

that girl up to? She looked at Molly, seated on the edge of one of the club chairs. Not a very flattering style of dress she'd chosen for the evening. What was going on? "I guess we should get started. Anyone like to lead the way?" Lizzie asked.

Molly waited a suitable amount of time in case anyone was dying to jump in. None of them would dare. "Before I begin I wanted y'all to take a look at my outfit tonight." She stood and did a slow turn. Her eyes twinkled as she sat and explained.

"This dress was all the rage in England in the early nineteen twenties. I was so lucky to track it down and even luckier to be able to buy it. These Egyptian prints on the bodice were popular after the discovering of old King Tut's tomb in Egypt. The dress is entirely shapeless, more like a long box, but I thought it would add a little touch of the world of Agatha Christie, about the time she published her first novel, *The Mysterious Affair at Styles*, in nineteen twenty. And that was a full twenty years before *Hercule Poirot's Christmas*, my choice for this month, for obvious reasons. But I thought, as well, that it would give y'all who haven't yet read an Agatha Christie"—she paused for effect and gave Bob a steady stare—"a suitable introduction."

Bob stood and helped himself to a couple more cheese straws, sat back down and focused on Molly. He eyed her top to toe but didn't comment on her attire. "I tried, Molly. I really tried. But it was so painful. So slow moving, just like I was strapped to the back of that old tortoise, wandering in and out of sentences and paragraphs, and then finally, reaching the end. Hallelujah. That's my only comment."

Molly's face dropped about a mile. Andie's head swiveled back and forth between the two of them. Stephanie looked as shocked as Molly, while Jacob and Lizzie managed to hide their smiles.

Lizzie tried to salvage the meeting. "Well, I thought it was plotted in true Christie style and Poirot . . . well he's my favorite of her sleuths. But you know, with this book, I think she's gone more over to the dark side. There's more violence in it, or is that just my imagination?"

"Very good, Lizzie," Molly said with a big smile. "It's true. I'd read that her brother-in-law had said her books were lacking in luster or some such thing, utter hogwash if you ask me, but she deliberately added more blood and violence to this one. Of course, she kept that Christie magic in it, with the house party in the country."

"And the double whammy of a locked room mystery, too," Lizzie added.

Molly nodded.

Bob jumped back in. "Okay. I get it. You two really know your Christie and I'm mighty impressed. And that's quite the getup you're wearing, Molly Mathews. But next month is my turn and I'm suggesting we read *Sixkill* by Robert B. Parker. That's the last Spenser book he wrote before he died. You'll see what I'm comparing Christie to, Molly. And if you don't like the book or the style of writing, I promise to not take your opinion personally. And, well, you did say this here book club was supposed to broaden our reading horizons, didn't you? This will definitely broaden yours."

All eyes were on Molly, awaiting her answer. She took a few moments, sighed and then smiled. "You are so right, Bob. On all counts. Now, does anyone else have anything to add about this month's book?"

Stephanie held up her left hand tentatively; her right hand still held the knitting she'd pulled out of her bag as soon as she'd sat down. She had almost finished the baby blanket, this one in yellow and green. "Well, I . . . y'all know I'm trying to widen my reading, too. I like her style, like having all the characters right there so we meet them right close to the beginning and then you can try to figure it all out knowing the murderer is one of them. But I sort of agree with Bob—it's kind of slow moving. But I did like it," she added quickly. "And I've gotta say, you look amazing."

Molly nodded. "Why, thank you, Stephanie. Jacob?"

Jacob swallowed hard. He glanced from Bob to

Molly. "I was never into mysteries growing up and through school years but I've been enjoying them lately. So, I must admit I haven't read a lot of Agatha Christie. I like the settings. Those big British estates . . . there's a right gallant feel about them."

"That's it?"

He nodded. "I'll stop while I'm ahead." He grinned at Molly.

She shook her head but Lizzie could see a smile playing at the corners of her mouth as she asked, "Would anyone like a refill of tea?"

Andie leapt out of her chair. "Let me get that for you." She grabbed the pitcher and walked around refilling glasses.

Jacob took a big swallow and said, "Has anyone heard anything more about the murder inquiry?"

"They're probably still trying to get all the background info on Alton," Bob answered. "Since he's an out-of-towner, it'll take a bit of desk work. And then, there's his hotel room to search, which they've surely already done. And his movements around town to try and track down where he went when he was here."

"Did that officer you talked to over at my place tell you anything?" Lizzie asked.

"Well, he thought it looked like a hunting rifle had been used, seeing as the bullet didn't do any damage. Other than kill him, that is. Around here, that doesn't narrow down the search any, I'm afraid. Assuming this isn't a random killing, someone knew him and someone had it in for him. So we need to find out, who, besides you, Lizzie, did he know in town?"

Lizzie shrugged. "Well, Jensey Pollard at the Book Bin introduced us but I don't know how well she knew him. She is a bookseller after all. It was natural he'd stop at her store. And I hear she'd added to the store's Facebook page a note about his talking to the book club. I had emails from two people who wanted to join us tonight, had he but lived. I didn't get around to stopping by the store yesterday, but I will real soon and I'll ask her some more about him."

She added after a slight pause, "Derek didn't mention knowing anyone else in town, when I was talking to him."

"Andie, what did you find out about Derek Alton on the Internet?" Molly asked as she chose a slice of Bourbon pound cake.

Andie replaced the plate on the hand-carved oak side table and sat down across from Molly. "He's on Facebook and has a website that talks mainly about his award-winning book and lists the other books. You can click on each title and get reviews, covers, the whole bit. Plus links to buy them. And lots of pictures of him at signings."

"What about his personal life? A bio? Anything like that?" Lizzie asked.

"Well, in Wikipedia it says he's taught creative

writing at night school and at college, but that's about it. I didn't see a location listed or a status—like if he's married or has kids or any of that stuff. He hadn't even listed where he was born or went to school. I guess I didn't get too far into the articles. There were quite a few on the Net. I'll go back and look at those. Also, there were lots of Derek Altons listed who weren't our guy, so there's a lot of weeding out to do."

She took a bite of her pecan cookie. "Oh yeah, it said that he has some food allergies and always brings his own cookies to events."

"He told me that just before he was murdered," Lizzie said, pausing a minute before adding, "By the way, are you into exams yet?"

Andie focused her attention on the Judith Fields watercolor of a swamp lily hanging on the wall behind Molly. "Well, yeah, sort of."

"I could probably take a stab and say they'll be starting in about a week and run until school breaks for Christmas, right?"

"Uh-huh. That sort of sucks, you know."

Lizzie shook her head. "Right. Well, I think you should give the Alton research a pass for now and concentrate on your studies. I'll do it."

"I can do both, really I can."

"I'm sure you can, but what if, for some reason, there's a problem with one of your marks? Your mama's going to have my head."

"And I won't allow you to come to any more

book club meetings, if that happens," Molly threw in for good measure, although Lizzie knew that she would never follow through on that threat. "Besides, if Lizzie loses her head, we may have to abandon the club anyway."

Andie folded her arms across her chest and gave her own head a shake. Her black and blue hair, cut blunt to chin level, swung around and her nose ring danced. "All right. But just until I ace my tests. Then I'm back on the case."

Lizzie smiled to herself. Some case. But at least she wouldn't have Andie's exam marks on her conscience. "One thing does nag at me."

"What's that, Lizzie?" Jacob asked.

"Why now? What made this the right time to kill Derek Alton?"

Chapter Nine
◇◇◇

I took a deep breath unwilling, though ready, to face the world with another murder on our hands.

GRACE INTERRUPTED—JULIE HYZY

Fridays were usually good days. The end of the work week. Choir practice night. What's not to like?

The answer would be, this Friday, Lizzie thought to herself as she opened the front door to

Officer Amber Craig. How could an early morning visit from this woman be a good start to a day?

"Are you leaving for school soon?" Officer Craig asked, without so much as a good morning.

Lizzie's first appointment was at ten with the vice principal but she felt the sudden urge to get there early. "Yes."

"This won't take long." Craig didn't wait for an invitation but walked into the living room while Lizzie got settled.

Lizzie glanced nervously out the window, thinking she'd sit in her comfy bucket chair in front of it. *Nothing to worry about.* No one with a rifle in any case. Her eyes narrowed as she thought she saw a quick movement at the end of the driveway, but the police cruiser blocked her view. *Stop being paranoid.* She decided to sit on the settee instead, though.

"What can I do for you, Officer?"

"Tell me all about your relationship with Derek Alton."

Lizzie didn't miss a beat. "There was no 'relationship,' as you put it. He was a visiting author and would have spoken to our book club at last night's meeting, had he not been shot. But of course, you know that already. I've said it before."

"Do you go out for a romantic dinner with all visiting authors?"

Lizzie tried to appear unbothered by the

75

question. "It was a working dinner to discuss the book club and help him focus his talk. It was *not* a romantic dinner."

Craig pulled out her notebook. "According to Mr. Trent at the Shasta Room of the Jefferson Hotel, Alton called ahead and asked for a 'secluded table for two, with low lighting, candlelight and a single rose.' Now, that sounds to me like someone thought of it as a romantic dinner." She cocked an eyebrow and stared at Lizzie, with a slight smirk on her face.

Lizzie squared her shoulders. "You asked me about the dinner and I'm telling you, to my mind, it wasn't a romantic dinner. It was a working dinner."

"So you say."

"Yes."

"And, did he try to kiss you during the dinner?"

Lizzie groaned inwardly. She'd bet Mr. Trent had been lurking and had told all. "Well, yes, but I didn't reciprocate."

"Sounds like he planned the evening from start to finish, though. He picked you up?"

"He came early and we drove around a bit before going to dinner. I showed him some landmarks in town on the way to the hotel."

"Huh. Right. And after this unromantic dinner?"

"I took a cab home."

"Why?"

"Let's just say he'd had too much to drink."

"Sure. We'll say that. So tell me, Ms. Turner, why you lied to the police." Craig's voice was deceptively low.

"I didn't lie."

"You were asked about Derek Alton and you weren't entirely forthcoming."

"But I didn't lie." Lizzie shifted in her seat. "I just omitted telling you certain things."

Lizzie waited for Craig to say something, and when she didn't, added, "For obvious reasons."

Officer Craig still didn't comment. Lizzie kept her mouth shut. After a couple of minutes of silence, Craig closed her notebook and stood.

"I'll pass along the information to the chief. We'll be in touch."

Lizzie bristled. Craig seemed to be enjoying this. "I don't like your tone of voice, Officer Craig. You're implying much more happened than did. It was a dinner. Period. Nothing more. And besides, the chief already knows."

"So tell me, did Mr. Alton take the hint when you hung the mistletoe?"

Lizzie exploded. "No. There was no hint, no message, no kiss under it. I already told you, but in case you've forgotten, I was decorating the house when he stopped by. Unexpectedly."

"Right. That's what you said. That's all, for now." Craig put her hat on and left.

Lizzie didn't know whether to throw a pillow at the bookcase or a book out the door at Officer

Craig. She was so frustrated. She glanced out the window when she heard Craig yelling. In a few moments, Andrea Mason stood up on the other side of the police cruiser. Lizzie hurried to the door.

"And just what were you doing? Tampering with my car?" Craig shouted at Andie.

Andie sauntered past Officer Craig, toward Lizzie. "Nope. Nice seeing you again, Officer Craig."

Lizzie watched as Craig walked around her cruiser, checking it carefully. She got into the front seat, pulled out her notebook and made an entry before driving away.

"What were you doing, Andie?" Lizzie asked as Andie joined her on the porch.

"I was just walking past on my way to school and I saw her car and she came marching out the door so I ducked. Instinct, I guess."

"Uh-huh. Now what were you really doing here?'

Andie looked around, up and down the street, and then answered. "I was just checking out your car, actually."

"My car?"

"Yeah. You park it out there in the open. Anyone could tamper with it."

"What do you mean 'tamper'?"

"Well, you know. Let the air out of the tires. Break a window. Plant a bomb under it."

"A bomb! Where did you get that idea? Who would want to kill me? Oh no . . . not your theory about the killer thinking I got a look at him."

"Or her."

"Whatever. Your mind is working overtime here, Andie. It's not going to happen. I'm not in any danger."

"How do you know?"

Lizzie had to think about that. "Well, the killer used a rifle or shotgun, so he—or she—wasn't up close. So how could the killer think I'd see him or her? It's more likely the person would have been seen by a neighbor."

"But our killer might not be thinking straight."

"Our killer, as you call him—"

"Or her—"

"—is probably trying to keep a low profile right now. Hoping not to attract the attention of the police. Now, I think you should maybe put the Janet Evanovich books aside for a while, say, for the duration of this investigation, and concentrate on your studies instead."

Andie made a face. "Hmm, I gotta head to school. Just promise me you'll check under your car before getting in each day."

"Andie . . ."

"Promise me or I'll quit book club."

Lizzie sighed. "All right, I promise. Now, off to school and have a good day with no more thoughts of killers and explosives."

Andie grinned, stuck her earbuds into her ears and sauntered off.

Lizzie shook her head but glanced at her car before going back inside.

Her appointment with the vice principal, Vanda Striker, was a no-brainer. They went over a list of recommendations Lizzie had made for presentations she could include in future professional development days for teachers. She was given a schedule, which would allow her to share Striker's office on a more regular basis. That would make it much easier for her to slot in appointments with students and their parents. Lizzie mentally cringed as Vanda went over the plans for the upcoming Christmas pageant, for which Lizzie had been conscripted into the role of master of ceremonies. "It sounds like a lively program you've got planned, Vanda, but I would really prefer not to wear an elf outfit," Lizzie said, trying not to sigh too loudly.

"Nonsense, Lizzie. We'll all be in one costume or another. I just thought an elf would be the most likely to emcee the afternoon, being Santa's helper and all. One of the first-grade mamas has volunteered to sew it, so you don't even have to do that. Mrs. Farnshaw will meet with you when she picks up her son after school today and take your measurements. You are here all day, aren't you?" Vanda asked, suddenly concerned.

Lizzie sighed. There was no escaping it. "Yes, I'm here. But I have a short meeting with the principal at two thirty."

"Oh, that's no problem. He won't mind waiting. This is important. I'll just fix it with him, don't worry."

Lizzie shrugged. She'd long ago learned the easiest way to deal with Vanda Striker was to leave the worrying up to her.

Lizzie hung up her jacket in the entrance hall in the St. John's Episcopal Church basement and shivered. They were in the middle of a cold snap and the church hadn't yet adjusted its thermostat. Maybe she should keep the jacket with her. She left it where it hung, hoping she'd warm up after a short while of singing.

Lucille Miller waved at her as she made her way over to the chairs, forming a semicircle with the well-worn grand piano at the base of the seating plan. Lucille gave her a big hug, surprising Lizzie. Not Lucille's usual greeting.

"Don't mind me," Lucille said, squeezing Lizzie's arm. "I'm just getting so wound up about the concert. I can hardly wait. And to top it off, Bob actually has agreed to come. I can't imagine what's gotten into the old coot but I'm surely happy about it."

Lizzie wasn't about to tell Lucille that her brother was coming because Molly had bought tickets for them both. Her early Christmas present to him, so he couldn't very well refuse. Lizzie wasn't sure where Lucille stood when it came to Molly Mathews and her brother. Not that there was anything going on. Not yet, anyway. Both Lizzie and Sally-Jo were hopeful, though.

Lizzie was saved from further conversation when one of the tenors whisked Lucille away, asking for her help in setting up the coffee urn. Lizzie sat and pulled her music out, setting her water bottle on the floor beside her chair. She wanted a short quiet time to relax before singing. She'd hoped to have it at home but as soon as she'd pulled in the driveway after school, Nathaniel had appeared. He came bearing gifts in the form of butter tarts, a new recipe for him, and Lizzie had invited him in to share them along with a glass of wine.

Nathaniel had barely left when her phone rang and a frantic Sally-Jo had asked Lizzie to track down Jacob and tell him she was being taken to the police station for questioning, and to ask him to meet her there. Lizzie eventually got hold of him as he returned to his office from court. She relayed Sally-Jo's appeal and then debated going down to the station herself, but she was reluctant to face Mark, and she did have to get to choir.

So, here she was, trying to focus on Benjamin Britten and his wonderful *Ceremony of Carols*, while her mind raced through possible reasons for

Sally-Jo to be taken into the station, rather than being questioned at her own home. It could be nothing more than an overzealous Officer Craig—highly likely. She was sure to hear all about it when she got home from choir.

Stanton Giles called for quiet and then took them through the usual warm-up session. Ten minutes of scales and tongue twisters followed by work on the Britten, starting at the beginning movement, which was also the end one. As the evening progressed, Lizzie was swept away by the music, as always, and after a reminder of their extra rehearsal on Sunday night, she dashed home to check for messages from Sally-Jo.

Nothing. In fact, no messages at all. What was going on? She picked up the phone and punched in Sally-Jo's number. "Sally-Jo, it's Lizzie. What happened at the police station? I'm home from choir. Please call me soon." She hung up and chewed her bottom lip, wondering whether to worry or be annoyed. Sally-Jo should have realized how concerned Lizzie would be.

Maybe that was it—Jacob had rescued Sally-Jo and they went out for dinner or a drink. She could have taken the time to call and leave a message, though. That's what cell phones were for, after all.

Lizzie walked over to the cupboard above the kitchen counter and grabbed the jar of almond butter. She snagged a spoon from the drawer on her way into the living room. She avoided looking at the location of Derek's final living breath and sat down on the settee to think. What was happening with everyone?

First, Molly going into her couple of months of self-imposed solitude only to emerge as a reincarnated Auntie Mame. Then Sally-Jo and her odd behavior. She really hadn't been herself for the past few days. No nightly phone calls; no hanging around the staff room at lunch; nothing but the call asking Lizzie to find Jacob.

But Molly as Auntie Mame? Lizzie remembered how she'd loved that movie and persuaded Molly to take her three times to see it when it had a week's run at the Sunset Drive-In Theatre. Of course, Lizzie would sit through just about anything in order to go to the drive-in. Even all the older movies that were the specialty at the Sunset.

She had just plopped a second spoonful of almond butter into her mouth when the phone rang. *Damn.* Hard to talk with a mouthful of almond butter.

"Yes?" At least she hoped that's what it sounded like.

"Lizzie, is that you?" Jacob asked.

"Uh-huh. My mouth is full, sorry."

"Okay. I'll do the talking. I'm still here at the police station with Sally-Jo and she's not telling them, or me, anything. Maybe you could come down and talk to her. I know it's late but if she refuses to answer my questions, I can't do anything for her."

Lizzie had rushed over to the fridge and grabbed some water from her Brita, as Jacob talked. She took a gulp to clear her throat. "I'll be right there. Why are they being so tough on her? What do they think she knows?"

Jacob sighed. "I wish I knew. Maybe you can find out. I'll try to convince the chief to let you in to talk to her."

Lizzie hesitated. Mark was questioning her. That sounded serious, and as much as she wanted to help Sally-Jo, she was very aware of the fact that Mark had been avoiding her. Which made it difficult to just waltz in as if everything was okay between them. Which it should be because she hadn't done anything wrong. Sort of.

Chapter Ten
◇◇◇

"Great," I said to myself. "Just great."
GRACE INTERRUPTED—JULIE HYZY

Lizzie could see Jacob through the window at the police station, pacing in the small front lobby. When she entered the building, he stopped and rushed over to her.

"I'm glad you came, Lizzie. I don't know what's gotten into her. This is not at all like Sally-Jo."

"Won't they let you in there with her? You're her lawyer, aren't you?"

"She refused to have me there," he said, looking totally forlorn.

Lizzie opened her mouth to answer at the same time the door to Mark's office opened. Mark closed the door behind him, glanced at Lizzie and walked toward them.

"She sits there like a stone. This isn't good," he said to Jacob, then shifted his weight to his left leg as he turned to Lizzie. "I don't know what's going on with her but we need some answers and it's looking bad for her when she won't talk. This is highly unusual, but I'm going to let you talk to her, try to get her to cooperate. I don't have anything to hold her on but I'm tempted to lock her up until she starts explaining things."

"Lock her up? What's this about, Mark? What do you think she's done?" Lizzie asked, forgetting her own discomfort at seeing him.

"She's being questioned in the murder of Derek Alton."

"Yes, we all are. But why bring her in here? Why the heavy tactics?"

Mark's cheek twitched. "Believe me, Lizzie, these are not heavy tactics. I have reason to believe there was a connection between her and the deceased and until she gives me some answers, it's looking shaky for her."

"What connection? What makes you think that?"

Mark took his time in answering. "We found a notebook among Alton's possessions. He'd written the date, time and location of your book club meeting but nothing else about the book club itself. Except for Sally-Jo Baker's name followed by several exclamation marks."

Lizzie thought back quickly to their first meeting. She had mentioned everyone's name and Derek had written down her phone number. But why Sally-Jo's name?

"But she was teaching Tuesday afternoon," Jacob interjected.

"We checked on that. She took some personal time in the afternoon. The vice principal covered her class. Right about the time Alton was murdered."

Lizzie gasped. "Oh, but it's just a coincidence. That's all. Sally-Jo is not a murderer even if she did know Derek Alton. And who's saying she did?"

Mark sighed. "I'm not going to debate this with you, Lizzie. Will you talk to her or not?"

"Yes, of course I will. I'll do whatever I can to help."

"Good." He walked to his office and held open the door for her.

Sally-Jo looked up when Lizzie walked in. She'd been sitting in one of the two hard-backed chairs, pulled up to Mark's desk, leaning her head on her arms, folded on the desktop.

"Oh, Lizzie," she wailed. "What am I going to do?"

Lizzie rushed over to her. "Sally-Jo, what's this all about? Why aren't you telling Mark what he wants to know?" She put her arms around Sally-Jo and hugged her.

Sally-Jo seemed to relax, then stood up, almost knocking Lizzie over. "It's such a mess. I just wish it would all go away. I wish I'd never met Derek Alton."

"When did you meet him?"

Sally-Jo looked startled. "Mark hasn't told you?"

Lizzie shook her head. "I think the only thing Mark knows is that Derek had your name written in his notebook."

Sally-Jo's shoulders shuddered and she sat back down. "I'm so embarrassed. It's something I thought I'd put behind me and hoped never to think about again. I certainly didn't want you or Jacob to know. I was such an idiot."

"Sally-Jo. You stop that and tell me right now. We love you. Nothing's going to change that. But we all need to know what's going on so that we can clear your name. Please, tell me. I'll stand by you no matter what."

Tears rolled down Sally-Jo's cheeks. She looked at Lizzie and tried to smile. "Promise?"

"I promise." Lizzie pulled the other chair over so she could sit down facing Sally-Jo.

Sally-Jo took a deep breath and brushed away the tears. "I met Derek when I was a freshman in college. He was writer-in-residence and taught a creative writing course. I took it because I needed the credits and it looked like fun. I'd never really thought about writing but he told me I had talent when I handed in a short story. He wanted to 'help me grow as a writer.' " Sally-Jo held up her fingers to indicate quotation marks. Lizzie braced herself for what she thought was coming. *Old, sad story.*

She sighed. "We had an affair but I ended it after a few weeks. I came to my senses and realized as I watched him with the other girls in the class that I was probably one of many who were getting 'extra help.' I felt like such a fool. I dropped the course and picked up something else for the second term."

Lizzie waited and when Sally-Jo didn't appear to be adding more to the story, said, "You were young and impressionable. And I'd imagine he was quite irresistible. Did you see him after that?"

Sally-Jo shook her head. "When I heard that he'd be talking to the book club . . . that's why I asked you what he wanted to know about us and if you'd mentioned my name. I decided I would skip that night. Beg off at the last moment. I had no desire to see him again, especially if he knew I would be there. I would have been mortified."

"I think you'd be smart to tell Mark the entire

story. He won't go telling it around. But he also wants to know what you were doing the afternoon Derek was shot."

Sally-Jo gasped. "Oh God. I hadn't thought about that. I wasn't at school. I'd asked Vanda Striker to fill in for me for an hour. But I didn't kill him. I didn't even know he was at your house."

"What did you do?"

"Well, I couldn't get Derek Alton being at our meeting out of my mind. So, I guess I panicked. I knew I had to talk to him and made him promise not to say anything about us. And I thought Jensey Pollard would know where he was staying. I didn't want to see him but I was desperate. Can you understand that?" She looked sheepishly at Lizzie.

Lizzie smiled. "Did you go to the Book Bin?"

Sally-Jo nodded.

"Well, that's great. Then you've got an alibi. Jensey Pollard can vouch for you."

"No, she can't. The store was closed. She'd tacked up a sign about having gone to the bank."

"Yeah, that's annoying when she does that."

She leaned over and hugged Sally-Jo. "Just tell Mark, okay? I don't think that's a strong motive for killing him. It will be all right. I'm sure."

Sally-Jo nodded.

"And you need to tell Jacob, too."

Sally-Jo hesitated but after a few seconds answered. "I will," she said softly.

• • •

Lizzie had a hard time getting to sleep that night. Too many details clogging up her brain. It had been a real shock to hear about Sally-Jo's past relationship with Derek. She just hoped Jacob had been okay with the news. But why wouldn't he? He had hidden the fact of his marriage from Sally-Jo and all of them for some time. He was not the one to take the high road.

She knew for certain that Sally-Jo wasn't the killer. No way. So, if Derek had a hidden past— and that seemed certain—was there anyone else in Ashton Corners who also knew him? Otherwise, the only other possibility was the stalker theory, someone who followed him to town. That was certainly possible—he was a high-profile type of guy.

Maybe Jensey Pollard knew something about him or might have some ideas as to why he came to Ashton Corners. Why was he here? It was pure luck that Lizzie met him at the Book Bin. Natural for him to stop into the local bookstore and offer to sign stock. But he wouldn't come to town purely for that reason. It was unlikely Jensey had invited him, because she hadn't organized an event. So, back to the question . . . why was he in town? Maybe Jensey would have some ideas. Time to stop by the store and stock up on some holiday reading material.

And then there was Mark. Mr. Cool himself at

the station. She thought back to the first time she'd seen him, number twelve in the red and beige uniform of the Ashton Corners Gladiators. A football hero if ever there was one. But he was two years ahead of her and light-years removed in the fold of cute cheerleaders surrounding him. He made her toes tingle every time he glanced her way, even though she knew in her heart of hearts that he didn't know she existed. What a shock to find out he indeed had noticed her and, furthermore, wanted to date her. Of course, it took the previous murder in Ashton Corners to bring them together. That was three months ago. Oh boy, a lot had happened in such a short time.

Brie, fed up with Lizzie's tossing and turning, jumped down off the bed. A few seconds later, Edam curled up in the abandoned warm spot at her left side. She reached out and stroked the soft fur, concentrating on the movement, willing her brain to clear itself and finally let her rest. The next thing she knew, a horn fanfare roused her to consciousness. She opened an eye and reached over to shut off the radio.

Focus. It's Saturday. Day off. Shopping. House cleaning. Ugh. Both eyes popped open as she remembered her date with Mark. Last weekend he'd asked her over for dinner tonight. She wondered if it were still on. He did have the excuse of an active investigation, if he wanted to avoid her. *Don't be paranoid. He'll call.* Of course he would. But what if he didn't? Should she call him to confirm? She couldn't just assume and show up at his house. Or could she? Pretend nothing had happened. *Oh God . . . why is nothing simple?*

She willed herself to get out of bed, slid her feet into slippers, pulled a bathrobe around her and trudged downstairs to the kitchen. Definitely lacking energy here. She should go for a run. No, she'd given herself the day off. She opened the cupboard, ground some espresso beans and turned on the espresso maker, meanwhile grabbing a spoonful of almond butter. Espresso cup in hand, she made her way into the living room, then opened the front door to retrieve the newspaper. She almost dropped her cup. It was snowing.

It never snowed in Ashton Corners. All right, maybe it did, but she couldn't remember the last time it had happened. But this was definitely snow and there was already a light covering on the ground. Why couldn't it have waited until Christmas? Or maybe it would stick around till then. Not likely.

She realized she was shivering and closed the door. She positioned the bucket chair so it faced outside and curled up in it, taking a sip of espresso. For a moment, all felt right with the world, until thoughts of driving crept into her mind. She had all-season tires. Surely they would get her through any snowdrifts. *Like there's going to be that much snow.* She should shovel her front walkway, though, and Nathaniel's, also. She couldn't allow him to do that. But she didn't have a shovel. So, she'd borrow one. This would be an adventure, that's for sure.

A golden retriever that lived up the street came bounding over the lawn, stopping for a roll and leaping up when his owner caught up to him. She longed to be out on the lawn frolicking with the golden. Dogs greeted snow with such abandon. All joy. No dreary thoughts holding them back. No conscience saying, *Do housework.*

She finished drinking and left the newspaper on the coffee table. She'd read it later. She wanted to get outside. She felt like a little kid.

She decided to skip breakfast and stop for brunch downtown and hurriedly got dressed. She added an extra pair of socks, then pulled her rain boots on, added her heaviest jacket and gloves and went next door to knock on Nathaniel's door.

It took several minutes for him to answer, and when he did, he was still in his bathrobe. Lizzie tried not to let the surprise she felt show on her face. Nathaniel was always up and dressed with daylight. She hoped he wasn't ill. His coloring looked just fine. Slightly on the pink side. Oh well, he was taking the morning off, too.

"Sorry to bother you, Nathaniel. Look at this amazing weather. I just thought I'd borrow a shovel and clear our walks, in case it gets any deeper."

Nathaniel cleared his throat. "Oh my. Yes, it's highly unusual, especially this early in December. That's most kind but I can do the walkways later, when it stops, Lizzie."

"I'd really like to do it, Nathaniel. I want to be out in the snow. Besides, it's good exercise."

"Well, okay then. I have a wide-blade shovel in the back shed. It's probably behind the mower, though. If you don't mind, I'll let you go and find it yourself." He looked down at this bathrobe.

"No problem. I'll keep it in case I need to shovel again and then return it when it stops snowing."

"Sure. No rush. And, thank you, Lizzie." He closed the door and she made her way around to the shed. That was odd, she thought. No invitation to join him for something freshly baked. Not that she needed anything. Especially since she wasn't running this morning.

It didn't take her long to clear both sidewalks, but she realized it might be time to drag out her weights and give her arms a toning. Nothing like a little physical labor to point out what body parts are out of shape. She thought she'd leave the driveway until the snow stopped. She looked toward the house and noticed for the first time that footprints led up to her car. She followed them as they circled the car and stopped at the front end where the snow was messed up.

Andie, she'd bet. But it seemed early for her to be out on a Saturday. What if it wasn't Andie? What if she'd been right . . . someone trying to rig her car with explosives? No, that was just too unbelievable. Still, Lizzie hesitated for only a moment before getting down on her hands and knees and peering under the car. She couldn't see anything, but what did that mean? Probably the tracks belonged to Andie. Sure. That was it.

Chapter Eleven

◇◇◇

Not my problem, I thought. Doesn't have a thing to do with me.

STATE FAIR—EARLENE FOWLER

The tiny bells above the door at the Book Bin jangled as Lizzie walked into the store. She spotted Jensey with a customer so she browsed the front display of newly received titles. She had decided to stop by and pick something to read over brunch. And, to ask Jensey a few questions.

The customer demanded a lot of attention so Lizzie began wandering through the stacks. She loved the cozy feeling of the Book Bin. The tall, dark shelving covering the outer walls, the shoulder-high units placed at an angle taking up half of the floor space. There were comfy chairs in various locations. In the back corner, a small monitor and DVD player showcased a variety of TV mystery series. Customers with the time to stay could watch while seated on the floral-covered love seat, enjoying a cup of coffee from the drip machine located in the tiny alcove at the far left. The experience led to happy customers and, Lizzie guessed, a large number of DVD sales. If she owned a bookstore, it would look a lot like the Book Bin.

Lizzie had amassed a small pile of new paperbacks in her shopping basket and her stomach grumbled. She looked around for Jensey and found her alone at the front desk. Lizzie piled the books on the desk as she greeted her.

"This snow's a bit of a surprise," Lizzie said.

"I'll say. It's been a few years since I've looked outside and the ground's been white. I wish it had waited until closer to Christmas, though."

"Me, too. Maybe it will put everyone in the holiday spirit and they'll decide they need to do extra Christmas shopping."

Jensey laughed. "You know, that happens. In fact, that customer I was helping, she had a long list of people who were all getting books under the tree. Now, let's see what you've chosen." She started scanning the books Lizzie had piled on the counter.

"You must be shocked at what happened to Derek Alton," Lizzie said. "I find it hard to believe it was just last week I met him here in your store."

Jensey grimaced. "It's unbelievable, Lizzie. When I heard the news, I was speechless. I didn't know him well but it was no less a shock."

Lizzie nodded in sympathy. "I can imagine. That was the first time you'd met him?"

Jensey glanced at her sharply. "Why, yes. What makes you ask?"

"I'm just wondering why he came to town. Was he visiting someone? Did he tell you?"

Jensey shook her head. "No. I hadn't really thought about it. He'd only arrived in town the day before so I was pleased that he'd taken the time to stop in here. Fortunately, I had a few copies of *Judgment* on the shelves—the book sells quite regularly even after all these years—and a couple of his other titles, so I asked him to sign them. We talked a bit about the town but he didn't mention anyone. And then you arrived. Oh dear, of course, he was killed at your place, wasn't he? That must have been very disturbing for you. How are you?"

Lizzie shrugged, trying to feign a nonchalance she still didn't feel. "I'm getting over it. Like you, I was shocked."

"I'll bet. That's so terrible." Jensey reached across the desk and patted Lizzie's arm. "Did he talk to you about his new book at all?"

"No. He seemed more interested in hearing all about the book club."

The bells over the front door jangled again and three teenage girls entered the store. They giggled as they made their way to the fiction section. Jensey watched their progress and then finished putting Lizzie's order through. She bagged the books as Lizzie hunted for her credit card.

"Thanks, Lizzie. Excuse me, I should see if they need some help," Jensey said as she finished the transaction. She grimaced and escaped from behind the desk while Lizzie gathered up her purchases.

Lizzie wandered out to the sidewalk, selected from the bag a book by Mary Jane Maffini that she'd been meaning to get for some time now, *The Busy Woman's Guide to Murder*, and stashed the rest in her car before walking across the street to the Oasis Diner. The restaurant teemed with chatter and cutlery as Lizzie found a vacant table for two by the front window.

She took a quick look around the interior, almost expecting to see Stephanie Lowe waiting on tables. But that wouldn't happen. Stephanie had been ordered by the doctor to stop working a few weeks ago until after the baby's birth. She was lucky enough to have an employer who valued her work ethic and willingly gave her an extra two months' leave, which would lead into the six-month maternity leave that awaited her.

Lizzie smiled as another server glanced over, then she gave her full attention to the menu. She decided to treat herself and settled on smoked salmon eggs Benedict. A mug filled with steaming coffee was placed in front of her and her order was taken, all within seconds.

She glanced around the restaurant again, hoping not to see anyone she knew, which would require a stop at the table and a chat, then felt secure in pulling out the Maffini book. She was well into the third chapter and totally riveted when someone sat on the chair facing her.

"I can't believe you planned a Saturday morning brunch and didn't include me," Paige Raleigh whined. She turned around and snagged a menu off the now vacant table behind her.

Lizzie grinned. "And I can't believe you'd be able to sneak out on your hunky husband and two darling daughters. Besides, it was a last-minute decision. But, I am happy to see you. As always."

Paige lowered the menu and smiled. "Me, too. I have actually eaten, but when I saw you sitting here I thought, not too early for lunch. Brad has the girls out trying to build snowmen in the backyard, and I had to pick up some color swatches at the Paint Emporium. We're finally going to do the family room, you know. So here I am." She waved at a server, who came and took her order and returned immediately with a mug, filled it with coffee and topped up Lizzie's at the same time.

"So, what's new?" Paige asked, blowing at the

steam arising from her mug. "I wouldn't have been surprised if you'd been out making snowmen, too. This is interesting white stuff."

"I love it. I've already shoveled the sidewalk at home. I'm glad there's not enough of it to make driving tricky, though, I have to admit."

"That's the one and only beauty about driving that tank of an SUV. I feel I can take on any weather that's thrown our way." She took a tentative sip. "Ouch, hot. I haven't talked to you since the day after that author's death. Are you coping all right?"

Lizzie nodded. "It's still sort of surreal, except when I walk into the living room. I avoid looking at the spot where he died, and you know, the cats are still spooked in there, too. But other than that, life goes on."

Paige studied her face. "And Mark? Any changes there?"

"I still haven't really talked to him." Paige's eyebrows shot up and Lizzie hurried on to explain. "Sally-Jo was questioned and I went into the station, at Jacob's request, to try to get her to answer questions. She just sort of clammed up. Anyway, Mark had to talk to me then, but it was strictly business."

"What's this about Sally-Jo, or shouldn't I ask?"

Lizzie chewed her bottom lip. Paige was her best friend and she didn't often keep things from her, but she knew that Paige seldom kept things from Brad. The less said the better.

"Well, she had known him briefly in her college days. The police are looking for any ties he had with anyone in town. They want to know just why he came to Ashton Corners."

"Hmm. I'll bet Lucille Miller knows. She seems to find out everything. And I know for a fact she loves sharing her information."

"Lucille? How do you know her?"

"I don't. Not personally. But Kitsey Chantell, she runs the quilting club I belong to, she's Lucille's niece and we hear the darnedest things. From Lucille's lips to Kitsey and passed along to our eager, gossip-mongering ears."

Lizzie laughed. "And here I thought you gave yourself totally to quilting at those gatherings."

"Oh, we do . . . we're quite able to quilt and gossip at the same time." Paige nodded. "Now, all I ask is that you don't get yourself run off the road or find yourself at the wrong end of a gun this time."

Lizzie laughed but it lacked mirth. "Not on my agenda, Paige. Once was enough." She reached out and squeezed her friend's hand.

Mark phoned at the exact moment Lizzie unlocked her front door. She stumbled in, dropped the bag of books and a cloth bag filled with groceries she'd picked up at the Piggly Wiggly, kicked off her boots and dashed to the phone. She got it just before it went to the message.

"Hi Lizzie, I've only got a minute to talk. I'm calling to say I'm sorry, but I have to cancel out on tonight. There's just too much to do with the murder investigation. You know how it is."

Well, he didn't sound sorry at all. She took a moment to reach in her grab bag of emotions and pulled out the agreeable, controlled voice. Slightly aloof but not mad. Definitely not mad. Nor sad. "That's too bad but I understand, Mark. You have to keep at it this early on in the investigation. Any leads?"

"Sorry, got to go. We'll talk later." He hung up before she had a chance to continue.

And just what did that mean? "Talk" as in two people who date? Or as in cop to suspect?

Chapter Twelve

◇◇◇

"You never know," said Theodosia. "I wouldn't rule anything out at this point."
THE TEABERRY STRANGLER—LAURA CHILDS

Lizzie had to admit to herself that there had been no hint of intimacy in Mark's voice. It was as if he were canceling a business dinner. So, what did it mean? He was truly too busy to focus on anything other than the case? Or, he was too teed off at her for having gone out with Derek?

This was ridiculous. She was a grown woman who'd had dinner with a somewhat dashing man. Now dead. They'd met to talk about the book club over dinner, which hadn't happened. And she hadn't even liked the guy even though everyone seemed to think otherwise. Lizzie shook her head. There were more important things to dwell on than her shaky love life.

Like, who killed Derek? And how could she find out?

She shoved the groceries into their rightful spots then grabbed the jar of almond butter and a spoon, a notepad and a pen, and walked directly over to the wicker chair by the front window, avoiding looking at the floor. She wondered how long it would be until she could enter the room without seeing his body sprawled beside the coffee table. Imagine if he'd been a friend or a loved one! She sat, eating the almond butter, pen and paper on her lap. Not very inspiring.

Enough. She stalked upstairs, grabbing the bag of book purchases as she passed by it, and found some space on one of the bookcases for them in the spare room. This was also her home office, her multitasking room, and she clicked on the computer. She was damned well going to find out more about Derek's life. She used Google to search for his name and waited. The wait time seemed to be getting longer each time she used her computer. Maybe it needed an overhaul or something. She had no idea when it came to computers. Programs were fine; she could Excel with the best of them. But when it came to gigabytes and RAM, she preferred to rely on the techies at her favorite computer shop.

The screen finally filled with fifteen hundred hits. Most of the first page was stories about his untimely demise. She found a biography link and clicked on it. She read it over quickly, but as Andie had said, tons about Derek the author but nothing personal. The only thing even slightly interesting was the cookie factor. He was also listed on his publisher's website with links to various interviews over the years. There were several Facebook sites and a Twitter account with that name, but none were his. This was getting complicated, trying to sort through to find which hits were Derek Alton, author. Maybe she should let Andie have another go at it.

She read until the fading light in the room alerted her to the fact that it was time to eat. She'd spent an hour in front of the screen, and besides knowing all about his books and his writing courses, she still knew nothing about the man. Totally frustrating.

She debated briefly about calling George Havers, owner and editor of the *Colonist*, Ashton Corners's weekly newspaper, to see if he knew Derek or knew of any connection he had to the town. Mark would have already done that, she was sure, and Saturday mealtime wasn't the best time to intrude. She'd try him next week.

Supper was a thrown-together concoction of leftover veggie stir-fry and baked chicken strips, which turned out to be surprisingly tasty. She poured a glass of Shiraz and settled in with her meal and her copy of *Judgment*. She wanted to start where he had. Maybe some autobiographical bits had found their way into the writing. But how would she know? She just hoped there'd be something that would click. By midnight she was almost finished with the novel, but so far, no "aha" moment. Maybe tomorrow.

She glanced out the window and noticed most of the snow had disappeared. So much for her hopes it would stick around and present them with a white Christmas. Oh well, she'd simply have to watch the movie again this year.

She'd just crawled into bed when a thought hit her—she'd had two people contact her by email asking if they could attend the book club to hear Derek speak. She'd never met Xenia Henshaw, but she'd seen her face around town on numerous Realtor signs. Now, why had she wanted to meet Derek? The second, Calvin Knox, was from nearby River's End, a writer himself, he'd explained in his email. Was either of these the person Derek had come to town to meet? But if so, why would they be arranging to come to the book club?

She hadn't even thought to get back to them after Derek's death, and neither of them had shown up at the meeting. Obviously, they'd heard about the murder in the media. But she thought it rather odd they hadn't contacted her to cancel. That would have been the polite thing to do. But since when did politeness become a factor in a murder? Although, who said they were involved?

She had to get out and run. Funny what a couple of days playing hooky could do to one's psyche. When Lizzie was in run mode, desperation drove her out each morning. Her body craved the hour-long circuit and her mind then clicked in for the day ahead. Since the murder, she'd been sluggish, dragging herself through the morning routines, reluctant to leave the coziness of her house. Today would be different. She'd need to be bright and cheery for her afternoon visit with her mama.

She fed the cats, did her stretches, and set out taking the longer route, twisting back and forth through the neighborhood streets until she reached the town square, then across the small park with the red and white azaleas and camellias strategically planted throughout, and benches placed at intervals along the intertwining paths. At the far end, two blocks of asphalt brought her to Glendale Park, home to every fair and event the town council could devise to welcome in the various seasons and tourists.

Lizzie felt perfectly safe running by herself. Ashton Corners was known for its law-abiding citizens, despite the fact that two murders had taken place within the town limits in the past four months. No wonder Mark was feeling the pressure.

She adjusted her musing. Most of the townsfolk were law-abiding and anxious to keep their small town safe. She'd even been invited to sit on the Crime Prevention Council but had to beg off when it conflicted with the literacy classes. Lucille Miller was on it, as was George Havers. It was that kind of town. You were bound to know someone connected to something you were interested in, but it was still big enough that the majority of faces were nameless, which afforded that extra space for privacy.

Lizzie had missed that familiarity when she'd been away at college in Auburn for five years. It took her another year to earn her Reading Specialist Certificate from the University of Alabama in Huntsville and then she'd stayed on for another year to work. She'd been offered a permanent job with that school board but she felt the tug of Ashton Corners, although the three-hour drive each weekend to visit her mama would not have been a hardship. But she felt more comfortable being close by, in case she was needed in the middle of the night. A morbid thought, but there it was.

By the time Lizzie had circled around back onto her street, she felt she'd gotten the kinks out of her brain as well as her body. Time for breakfast, the weekly crossword puzzle in the *Birmingham News* and then a visit with her mama.

She looked down at her soggy feet. First she'd have to wring herself out. Slush will do that to a girl.

Chapter Thirteen

◇◇◇

It had seemed like the right thing to do, but it wouldn't be the first time her impulsiveness had led her into trouble.
SKETCH ME IF YOU CAN—SHARON PAPE

Lizzie pulled into the parking lot at Magnolia Manor and sat a minute, trying to clear her brain of any thoughts of the shooting, before going inside to see her mama. Although she often didn't know if they were communicating, Lizzie thought that Evelyn Turner could sense her moods. If Lizzie were uptight about anything, her mama would often become more agitated as the visit progressed.

She'd been visiting her mama almost every Saturday or Sunday for the past twelve years. And during that time, there were no major improvements in her condition. Evelyn had slowly retired into a world of silence after her husband died in a car accident when Lizzie was ten years old. The diagnosis was both psychological and medical, and at one point, the care and safety provided at Magnolia Manor, an assisted-living facility, seemed the only wise solution. Molly Mathews had been instrumental in finding the ideal spot for her old friend and in easing Lizzie through the difficult decision.

Lizzie was grateful to be able to spend time with her mama and she refused to dwell on the negatives. She took a deep breath, grabbed the small Christmas gift bag she'd brought and locked the car behind her.

She found Evelyn in the sunroom at the far end of the hall. That was a good sign. After hugging her, Lizzie put the gift bag on her lap, talking all the while about the approaching holiday season. She then pulled the tissue paper out and unwrapped a handblown glass cockatoo.

"This will look lovely on your tree, Mama. It reminds me of an ornament we had on the Christmas tree when I was little. Do you remember it? I think it was white and silver and red." Lizzie held the ornament up to the window so that the sunlight seemed to dance through it. After a moment, Evelyn reached for it, much to Lizzie's delight.

Lizzie sat on the wicker love seat next to her mama and talked about the events of the week, omitting those involving gunshots, while her mama continued to examine the cockatoo. Evelyn eventually returned it to the gift bag and looked directly at Lizzie. There was a moment when Lizzie was certain they connected, even though no words were spoken. It warmed her heart. She went on with her recital of the events, adding plans for the holiday season. She didn't mention wanting Evelyn to spend Christmas Eve and Day at her house, not until she had the approval of the medical staff at the Manor.

They moved to Evelyn's room when other residents started filtering into the sunroom to entertain their visitors. Lizzie read a few chapters from Jane Austen's *Sense and Sensibility* before leaving when the dinner bell sounded.

She realized, as she glanced at the clock on her dashboard, that she had just enough time to feed the cats before heading to Molly's for supper and then on to the final special rehearsal Musica Nobilis was holding before next Saturday's concert.

The cats took their time in joining her in the kitchen, finally being roused by the sound of dry cat food pouring into their bowls. Edam finished eating first and started rubbing his head against Lizzie's leg. The food had fueled Brie's energy level and she play-attacked Edam, eliciting an elongated hiss before they both ran off up the stairs. Lizzie stood and turned the overhead light on in the kitchen. The timer in the living room had already added light to that room. She tried phoning Molly but it went to voice mail after one ring. She must be on the phone. Lizzie left a message saying she was on her way. She grabbed her jacket and purse, locked the door behind her and dashed to the car.

Molly answered the door on the second buzz, phone still at her ear. She pulled Lizzie inside, glanced upward in annoyance and motioned Lizzie to take her jacket off and go into the kitchen. Lizzie couldn't even hazard a guess as to who was on the other end of the line, but Molly didn't seem able to get a word in edgewise. She'd been reduced to one-word responses.

The long, flowing, full sleeves of her gauzy V-necked overblouse floated through the air to punctuate her exasperation. The powder blue palazzo pants and white beaded sandals reminded Lizzie of an Art Deco painting she'd seen recently.

Lizzie poured them both a glass of Pinot Grigio, following Molly's pantomime actions, and then sat at the table watching the variety of expressions passing over her friend's face.

Finally, after about ten minutes, Molly was able to end the conversation and hang up. "Oh Lord, that woman talks like no other," she said taking a long sip of her wine.

"Dare I ask who?"

"Lucille Miller, that's who. It seems Bob went

and told her we went out to dinner last night and you'd think we'd gone and moved in together. She was a bossy young girl and she's gotten even worse in her old age. And don't you dare go telling her I called her old. That would get me another hour-long phone call, I'm certain."

Lizzie nodded and smiled. She could just visualize it.

"Now, dinner will be ready in"—Molly squinted at the oven clock—"ten minutes. I know you've got to be out the door by seven for choir. So tell me, how was Evelyn today?"

"She seemed in a good mood. I'd brought her a Christmas ornament and she appeared to be really pleased by it."

"Hmm. She always did like Christmas, even as a girl. And you were a hard one to keep from getting too excited before the big night. Which brings me to this Christmas. I never like to assume, as you know, so I'm just confirming you'll be here for Christmas dinner? I thought we might invite Stephanie to join us if she's still waiting to deliver her baby."

"Thanks, Molly."

"What? You don't sound that enthusiastic. Are you still thinking about bringing Evelyn over to your place?"

Lizzie nodded.

"What does the manager at Magnolia Manor think of your plan?"

"I haven't mentioned it to her yet." Lizzie sighed.

"Hmm." Molly paused. "Well, if you do, there's no reason why she can't come over here for Christmas dinner, unless they think it would be too many changes in one weekend. Anyway, we'll deal with it."

Lizzie smiled, feeling content. She'd missed sitting in Molly's kitchen. She'd missed talking to her for the past several weeks. She'd just plain missed Molly.

The oven timer went off and Molly set about pulling the meal out and serving it. "I thought it was a good night for roast chicken and all the trimmings."

"Oh yum. May I help?"

"You certainly may. Just put the plates in the oven for a minute or so to warm up then bring them over here and I'll just serve straight onto them. Save on the dish washing. Now, have you had any theories about who would want to kill Derek?"

"Not a one. I stopped in at the bookstore yesterday morning to see if Jensey Pollard knew anything about him but she said he just stopped by and announced himself. If he was in town to visit someone, she doesn't know whom."

Molly dished out the food then sat across from Lizzie. "Well, I'd say it's obvious he came to see someone. Why else would anyone come to Ashton

Corners? And I don't mean that in a derogatory way at all."

Lizzie took her time savoring the moist mouthful of chicken she'd bit into before answering. "Point taken. So the question still is, who? He arrived in town on Friday, according to Jensey, so he had plenty of time to make contact. Did they meet? Quarrel? And then did that person shoot him?"

"That phantom person would have to have been following Derek in order to know he'd be at your place, I'd think."

"Unless Derek told the person."

"What happened with Sally-Jo? I heard she was brought into the police station for questioning."

Lizzie hesitated. "She admits to knowing him but says she hasn't talked to him since her college days. No, there's got to be someone else here in town."

Molly put her fork down. "Now, if Agatha Christie were writing this, there would be an entire cast of people who had once known the deceased, and perhaps even conspired to all kill him. That's an interesting thought. Ashton Corners harboring several killers all united in killing one man, Derek Alton. Shades of *Murder on the Orient Express*."

Lizzie smiled. "How about if we were writing it? What would our next step be?"

"Well, I think the next step is trying to find the

identity of this mystery person. But how to do that?"

"I tried searching Derek on Google last night and Andie was right. There's a lot of information about Derek Alton the writer, but nothing personal. And no stories about him prior to his book winning the prize. I thought I'd give George Havers a call tomorrow and see if he knows if Derek had been in town for any events after his book came out. That might have been when Derek and this mystery person first met. Although I'm sure Mark has already asked George that same question."

Molly finished the last of her chicken and served herself some more. She passed the plate to Lizzie, who also took another piece. "Speaking of that young man," Molly said, "didn't you two have a date last night? How did it go?"

" 'Had' is the operative word. He called to cancel saying he was too busy with the case. I'm sure that's true but he didn't sound too sorry about it."

Molly leaned over and patted Lizzie's arm. "You listen here, honey. Our dear police chief is a man, and as such, his manly feathers have been ruffled. Some other male has been sniffing around his territory, pardon the expression. But like any smart man, and Mark certainly is that, in time he'll come around to realizing just how foolish he's acting. And then you can think, but not say, 'I told you so.' "

Chapter Fourteen

◇◇◇

But were their overt reactions because of their dalliances, or were they inspired by guilty consciences?

DEAD MEN DON'T LYE—TIM MYERS

L izzie went straight from Molly's to the choir practice at St. John's Episcopal Church, arriving just as the warm-up was starting. She eased into her seat and tried to quickly get into the mood for the practice. With the concert less than a week away, there seemed to be so many loose ends, small bits that hadn't been perfected, missed cues, words not memorized. But then again, she felt like this every time and she was sure most of her fellow choristers would agree. *Just think how the director must feel.*

At the break, Lucille Miller cornered her in the women's restroom. "Molly Mathews is acting a bit strangely these days, wouldn't you agree?" she asked without preamble.

Lizzie looked at Lucille in surprise. "No, I wouldn't. What makes you think that?"

"Well, we had a long phone talk and she wasn't very forthcoming. Short, clipped answers. She was almost bordering on rude. Now that's not the Molly Mathews I've known all these years."

"She did say something to me about you asking a lot of questions about Bob and her, like you might think they were having a relationship or something."

"Now, why would she say that? That's downright silly." She paused and peered over the rim of her glasses, which had slid down the ridge of her nose. "Or is it? Are they involved in some hanky-panky? Is she trying to cover it up?"

Lizzie tried not to smile. "That's not a question for me to answer, Lucille. You should ask Molly if you're so concerned."

"Of course I'm concerned. He's my only brother. And he had such heartbreak with that hussy he was married to. I don't want it to happen again."

"Molly's hardly a hussy."

"Aha . . . so there *is* something going on!"

Lizzie drew in her breath sharply. What a frustrating woman. "No. That's not what I'm saying and I think we shouldn't pursue this any longer. You'll just keep reading things into my words. Molly, via the Ashton Corners Mystery Readers and Cheese Straws Society, is trying to broaden Bob's reading habits and he's resisting. That's all I know." She thrust around desperately, trying to come up with a new topic.

Fortunately, Lucille was derailed by a couple of choristers entering the room. Lizzie ducked out and struck up a conversation with the accompanist, Tommy McCann, until Stanton Giles called everyone back to their seats to resume.

Lizzie loved the extra rehearsals involved in concerts. There was an added excitement in the air, a tension built on the fact that everyone was trying really hard to get it right, now that they were into the final phase. Only one more practice, and that was the dress rehearsal on Friday night, and then Saturday's concert. She must remember to check the condition of her long black skirt. She was pretty sure she'd tucked it in the spare closet in clean condition but she'd better make certain. The black long-sleeved jersey wrap top lay folded in her dresser. And her black pumps were used only for concerts, so they were fine.

"Lizzie, I read about the murder that took place in your living room. Pretty scary stuff. Are you coping all right?" Gaylene Pruitt, an alto and an assistant at the school board office, asked as she made her way to her seat.

Lizzie nodded, wishing she hadn't brought the topic into this joyous place. She tried to shake it away and focus on Stanton. Page five of the Britten, "There Is No Rose," one of her favorite parts, his right arm counting . . . two, and three, and four. Start singing.

The two hours passed quickly and Giles was pleased with how the concert was shaping up. He even let them leave on time. They kidded one another about how Friday's dress rehearsal better be bad in that case. Artistic superstitions abound.

Lizzie felt good about getting right to her run the next morning, although she felt entitled to take the short circuit. It was Monday, after all, and she did have to get to work. She waved at the neighbor three doors down, as he walked to his car, most likely on his way to the office. He'd left it parked on the street and did a walk-around before getting in, probably checking for any dents or scratches. Maybe she shouldn't feel foolish about following Andie's demands to check out her car before getting in. After all, who knew when vandals might strike. She shook her head at the thought. Not in Ashton Corners.

By the time she'd reached Nathaniel's place, she was ready for a shower and an espresso. She glanced at his door, wondering if he'd yell out an offer of freshly baked somethings, but no such luck. Odd, he hadn't made the early morning offerings in several days. Oh well, so much better for her waistline.

She went through her morning routine quickly but was startled when she spotted the time. It had flown when she hadn't been paying attention. She downed her protein shake breakfast, with a banana and almond butter chaser. The cats had abandoned her as soon as their food disappeared into their stomachs. So much for her appeal. She found them grooming on the bed and she quickly got dressed, choosing a long-sleeved black jersey T, blue cashmere vest and charcoal skinny cords along with black shoe booties. The drive into school was short, but it took her along winterberry-lined streets with colorful winter azaleas—bright red, pink, white and lavender—blooming in many yards. By the time she pulled into the parking lot, she felt in a good mood and walked to the staff room with a smile on her face.

That good feeling started drifting away at the sight of Vanda Striker hurrying down the hall toward her, waving a piece of paper in her hand.

"Lizzie, I'm glad you're here. We have to talk. Do you have a few minutes right now?"

Might as well get whatever it was over with. "Yes, but not too long."

"Good. Come to my office."

Lizzie followed her down the hall, Vanda out in front by a few paces. When they were both seated, Vanda shoved the paper across her desk at Lizzie. "This is the program for the Christmas pageant. I just don't have the time to proofread it and make sure it's all there. Can you take care of it?"

Lizzie sighed. *What next?* "Leave it with me, Vanda," she said as she made her way to the door and escaped down the hall.

She slid into the back of a second-grade teacher's class just as the children were pulling their readers out of their bags. Good timing. For the next half hour, Lizzie observed and made notes about the children's progress, as well as the teacher's progress, since the last time she'd done this. She felt heartened when she left the room at the end of the class, enough so to give the teacher a small nod and smile. That elicited a big smile in return.

Lizzie had an appointment scheduled with some parents for the next hour, in Vanda Striker's office. She made her way there slowly, hoping the office would be empty. It was. She set her computer and notes on the desk then invited the parents to come in and take a seat.

This meeting was one of the good things about her job. She delighted in giving them good news, that their child was responding to the suggestions, that his reading abilities had grown and that they would probably only get better. The parents left after thanking her profusely, much relieved that all their efforts had paid off.

By the time the final bell rang for the school day, Lizzie was looking forward to a couple of hours of quiet at home before heading to the literacy class after supper. However, she remembered her question for George Havers and decided to stop at the newspaper on her way home.

She parked a couple of spots over from the office on Main Street, on the opposite side from the police station, which unfortunately sat right next door to the *Ashton Corners Colonist* office.

She glanced at the station parking lot and saw Mark's black Jeep parked in his spot. None of the eight cruisers owned by the Ashton Corners Police Department were there, though. It must be a busy day on the streets.

George was standing at the counter in the waiting room when Lizzie opened the door to the newspaper office. A large smile spread over his face when he saw her, and he walked around the end to give her a big hug.

"How're things going, girl? It's sure nice to see you again." George had called to make sure she was okay after the shooting but they hadn't talked other than that in a few months.

"I'm good, George. And that's actually why I'm here."

He shook his head but the smile was still on his face. "I guess I shouldn't be surprised. Not after last time. Now, what information can I get for you?"

"That transparent, am I?" Lizzie smiled back. "I'm curious who Derek Alton might have known in Ashton Corners. Why did he come here? Was there an event in town after he won the Onyx award? Has Chief Dreyfus already asked you all this?"

"Whoa. Let's take this one question at a time. Would you like some coffee?"

She shook her head.

"Hmm. Smart. Let's go into my office." He led

123

the way in behind the counter and the several empty desks, all with computers on them, to the back room, which ran the width of the building. His office. He indicated the one straight-backed chair in the room that didn't have books or file folders cluttering it.

"Okay, starting at the end. The chief has asked me much the same thing so I just happen to have the answers at the ready. Derek Alton had never been in Ashton Corners as far as I can tell. There were no literary events, signings, or otherwise, so I know of no person he'd be here visiting. I'm sorry I can't give you more, but there's nothing in our files."

"How about a Google question then? I searched the Internet and couldn't find much about his personal life. It's like he just burst onto the scene with the winning of the award. Have you read *Judgment*, by the way?"

"No. I should, though. That's not so strange, you know. About the Internet. Considering all this cyber technology was in its infancy at the time Alton became famous."

"But I had searched for Molly's husband, Claydon, on Google in the fall when we were trying to find out if there was a connection between him and the murder of Frank Telford. I found lots about him and he's been dead a long time."

"Ahh. The fickleness of the Internet. It's only as good as the information that's available. Claydon

Mathews was an influential businessman, a town leader, a philanthropist and very wealthy. And that's generated a lot of press and other stories about him, most of which you can probably find on the Net."

"And Derek Alton, although the winner of one writing award, went on to publish several books that didn't get a lot of attention, hence, fewer stories and I guess if he were a private person, no interviews about his personal life. Right?" Lizzie ventured.

"That's about it."

"So any suggestions as to how to proceed?"

"Not if I want to stay on the good side of Chief Dreyfus."

Lizzie pretended to pout. "Could be a story in it for you."

George laughed, a deep, full sound from the bottom of his large belly. "Well done, Lizzie. If I come up with any ideas, I'll give you a call."

"Thanks." Lizzie stood and they shared another hug.

On the drive home she thought back to how much help George had been when she was trying to track down what had happened to her daddy. She'd wondered for a short while if his car accident had been premeditated, and George, once a journalism protégé of Monroe Turner, had been eager to help. She hoped that cooperation would continue.

She noticed a silver Prius parked in Nathaniel's driveway as she pulled into her own. As she let herself in through the front door, she realized she'd seen it several times recently and idly wondered who it belonged to. The cats were waiting at the bottom of the stairs. Obviously they'd finished all their dry food. At least they were back to acting normal.

She filled their bowls and then sorted through the small stack of mail she'd liberated from the mailbox on her way inside. A couple of Christmas cards. How wonderful. She'd mailed her own last week, early for a change. Good thing, too. She slit the envelope flaps, eager to know who the early birds were. Sally-Jo, not a surprise, and an old college friend with the yearly letter. After getting caught up, she went into the kitchen and started thinking about supper.

She glanced at the clock. She'd actually have time to prepare a real meal. She was rooting through the freezer in search of a chicken breast when the phone rang. A quick look at caller ID showed it was Sally-Jo.

"Hi, girl. How are you doing?" Lizzie asked as she answered.

Sally-Jo sighed loudly enough that Lizzie could just picture her sagging shoulders. "I'm not sure what to stress about more, the police and their questions or my family's upcoming visit. Can we just meet for a nice quiet supper somewhere before literacy class tonight? I really need to get out of here."

"Sure. I won't suggest you come here because I can't find one elusive piece of chicken, so I am unlikely to find two."

"You'd be busy cooking if we did that. I just want to sit and talk, okay?"

"Love to . . . How about Southside Jack's in half an hour?" Lizzie suggested.

"Perfect. Till then." She'd hung up before Lizzie could come out with a good-bye.

She hurried upstairs and freshened her lipstick and blush, then checked her tote to make sure she had everything tucked in there for class. She eyed the computer and wondered if she'd have time for another quick check of Derek Alton. Better not. She knew she'd probably get caught up in it and didn't want to keep Sally-Jo waiting.

Chapter Fifteen
◇◇◇

Mum's the word. Silence is golden.
  SKETCH ME IF YOU CAN—SHARON PAPE

S ally-Jo had snagged a corner booth on the far right side of Southside Jack's on Hooper Street. Lizzie glanced around as she made her way over. Nobody she knew in the small and almost full restaurant. It was a popular place with the older crowd, its menu of traditional Southern food and the muted beige and orange décor welcoming diners who like to have some conversation with their meal. It seemed surprisingly full for a Monday night.

She slid in across from Sally-Jo and paused long enough to take a good look at her friend. "How are you doing? You sounded harassed on the phone."

Sally-Jo grabbed a menu and scanned it as she spoke. "I feel like I'm hanging around, waiting for the proverbial other shoe to drop. Officer Frigging Craig laid it on real thick. She thinks Derek ditched me and I wanted revenge, so I killed him. Never mind it's twelve years later. She's trying to track down old college pals to get their version. I hate to have this all dragged up again."

"Is she likely to find someone who knew all about it and will verify your side of the story?"

"I didn't have any close friends. This was my freshman year, after all, and most of my friends from high school went to Miami State instead. I wasn't lonely. There was always someone to hang out with, but even my roommate had no idea what was going on. I made sure of that." She sighed.

"Well, I guess we'll just have to try to figure out who the murderer is, in that case," Lizzie said, reaching out to squeeze Sally-Jo's arm.

"Easier said, I'd think."

"Maybe, but we'll try. We need to find who in Ashton Corners Derek came to see."

They paused to give their orders to the server, spicy mango shrimp on coconut-lime rice for Lizzie and tuna cakes for Sally-Jo.

When he'd left, Sally-Jo asked, "Where do we start? You don't have any idea, do you?"

"I've already talked to Jensey Pollard and she didn't know. However, I've been thinking. I had emails from two people who said they'd heard Derek was coming to the book club and asked if they could come also."

"Really? How did they know about it?"

"Apparently Jensey Pollard posted it on the Book Bin Facebook page."

"So, who are these anonymous book lovers?"

"One is Xenia Henshaw. I've not met her, although I've seen her name on enough Realtor signs in the city. She works for Corners Realty, so is easy to track down. The other is someone named Calvin Knox. He said he's from River's End. He obviously heard about the murder, because he didn't show up. I'll email him and ask for his phone number so we can talk."

"If he's the killer, he won't want you to contact him."

"If he's the killer, I'd bet he also used a hard-to-track email address. I could just look in the phone book for a listing. But if he's the murderer, that's probably not even his real name."

Sally-Jo sighed again.

"But that's good, Sally-Jo. If he's trying to

remain anonymous, it's because he's hiding something. And that bumps him to the top of the suspect list, I'd say. We just have to figure out how to find him."

Their food arrived and they dug in, silent for some time. Sally-Jo finally spoke.

"You know Ellen Germain who teaches fifth grade? We went to the same college. She was a couple of years behind me and I didn't know her at the time. I came across her picture a few months ago in a program I'd kept from one of the drama club plays. She was just as surprised I'd been there when I told her, so I guess she wouldn't make a good witness for me. Forget I even brought it up."

"I wonder if she knew Derek Alton. Or better yet, his reputation?"

"I'm not about to ask her."

"But I can."

Lizzie watched the faces of her literacy students as they read over the essay homework she handed back to them. She was pleased to see that Stephanie felt well enough to join them for the final class of the session. Jolene scanned the pages, read the comments on the back and then grinned, looking around at the others.

Sonny took much longer but by the end of the comment page, he, too, was smiling, or what amounted to a smile for him. Stephanie had lost that tense, pinched look she'd entered the room with. She looked pleased with her comments, as well, while Melanie looked sullen but not surprised. Lizzie guessed she'd realized the GEDs were still out of her grasp and there was a lot more work to do. Would she be willing to carry on, was the question.

"This is the last class before Christmas," Lizzie said. "I think it's been a very productive session and I'm hoping you feel the same way, too. First class in the New Year will be on the first Monday." She'd given Jolene back her manuscript during the break. She just hoped her comments would be useful. She'd wanted to be encouraging as well. Hopefully Jolene would see it that way.

Jolene's hand shot up, surprising Lizzie. "We all"—she looked at the others one by one as they nodded, and she continued—"want to thank you and we have a Christmas present for you." She dug into her bag and pulled out a box, wrapped in bright red and green. She also produced a card in an envelope as she stood and walked over to Lizzie.

"Why, thank you. That's really very thoughtful," Lizzie said, accepting the gift and trying not to tear up. "May I open it now?"

"Oh yes . . . right now. We can't wait to see if you like it," Jolene said. She was almost as excited as if someone had given her the gift.

Lizzie grinned and pulled the wrapping paper off, then carefully opened the box. Inside was a set of bookends—two books carved in wood with a heavier metal base.

"This is wonderful," she said, knowing her eyes glistened. "Thank you. It means a lot to me." She cleared her throat.

"Sonny made them in woodworking class," Jolene announced, as proud as if she'd taught him.

"Wow, Sonny. They're amazing," Lizzie said.

Sonny sat back in his chair, shifting his weight to his left side, and slid his right leg forward feigning nonchalance. "Aw, it's nothing, Miss. I found that cherrywood at the dump."

Jolene gasped.

"No, really. I cleaned it up real good."

"Well, it looks great and I know just where I'll place them. Thank you. Now, class is over. Have a wonderful Christmas and see you in the New Year."

Jolene and Stephanie gave her a hug as they filed out of the room. Melanie waved in an off-handed way. Sonny hung back and stuck out his hand for a shake. "Uh, like, thanks," he said.

Lizzie nodded and watched him saunter toward the front door. A few minutes later she followed, after saying good night to Molly, who had donned a white linen caftan, white sandals and numerous strands of colorful beads for the evening. Sally-Jo had already left with Jacob, who was giving Stephanie a ride home, too.

Lizzie pulled the bookends out of the box when

she arrived home and set them up on one of the shelves of the bookcase. Then, too pumped to consider bed, she refilled the cat's dishes, walked upstairs, turned on the computer and went directly to her email.

She pulled up the original email from Xenia Henshaw and then checked in the phone directory for a number. Easy. Then she reread the one from Calvin Knox and, after some consideration, sent him an email asking for a phone number. She also called directory assistance, doubting they'd give her a number without an address, and she was right. She trolled the Internet for a while, trying different combinations of names and sites, but eventually gave up. After another check of her email, with no responses from either person, she turned her computer off and headed to bed.

There had to be another way.

Chapter Sixteen

◇◇◇

If all the things I don't know were laid out end to end . . .

THE THIN MAN—DASHIELL HAMMETT

Lizzie tried to shake the feeling of utter frustration that had gripped her since checking her email in the morning before heading to work. No replies from either Xenia Henshaw or Calvin

Knox. She tried to convince herself that neither of them had checked their email yet this morning and that she'd have answers tonight. But what she really thought was that both of them wanted to remain at arm's length. Who wouldn't, when someone had been murdered?

Now, seated at Vanda Striker's desk, she tried to clear her brain of anything murder-related and focus on the two upcoming meetings with parents. She'd booked the vice principal's office until noon but doubted they would take that long.

Her first appointment, with parents of a fifth-grade student, started with her outlining the testing that she'd done and the conclusion that he needed some serious remedial work. She braced herself for the usual response of denial ending with pleading and was pleasantly surprised when they were in total agreement with her assessment and suggested plan of action. The meeting wrapped up with Lizzie promising to send them her report, along with a suggested contact, before the Christmas break.

The second appointment proved to be a total contrast. Ten-year-old Michele's parents were adamant that their daughter did not have a reading comprehension problem and they rejected Lizzie's suggestion for extra help. Her only option was to leave the matter with them to mull over, then hold a follow-up meeting early in the new term and include the principal in the conversation.

She felt frustrated when she wandered into the staff room, her brown-bag lunch of tuna salad wrap in her hand. A group of eight teachers sat around the largest table and waved her over. They were in a jovial mood, the upcoming Christmas break on their minds, and she felt her tension easing as she settled in.

Ken Wicks, a sixth-grade teacher, plopped himself on the chair next to her as she unwrapped her meal. "How you doing, Lizzie? That was quite the scare you must have had last week." Concern was etched on his face, along with the many lines accumulated in his fifty-six years.

"I'm doing all right, Ken. Thanks."

"That was such a shocking thing to happen, especially in Ashton Corners. Not what you think about, that's for sure."

Lizzie nodded her agreement. "I just wish I knew why it happened and who he was visiting in town."

Ken looked at her questioningly. "Well, I thought he was here to speak to your book club. That's what Jensey Pollard said, anyway."

Lizzie didn't even try to hide her surprise. "She said that? It was Jensey who introduced us in her store and she suggested he speak at the next meeting. We weren't the reason he came to town."

"Well then, it could be almost anybody, couldn't it? That's important?"

"Probably. But only if he knew someone here."

"Well, why wouldn't he? He used to live here, after all."

Lizzie's mouth dropped open. "You're kidding. Are you sure? When was this?"

"Oh, I don't rightly recall. Maybe twenty-five years ago, or so. Could be less or even more. Huh, there's the bell. Well, you take care of yourself, you hear?"

Lizzie nodded absently. Derek Alton actually lived in Ashton Corners? Why had no one else mentioned it? She'd have to talk to Ken again and get more details. But for now, she had a presentation to make at the school board offices downtown.

She checked her email again as soon as she'd fed the cats. Her own supper could wait. Xenia Henshaw had responded and suggested Lizzie stop by her office the next day. Lizzie replied suggesting three thirty P.M. and received an almost immediate response confirming the time. Nothing from Calvin Knox. That was frustrating. How would she track him down?

She pondered her dilemma as she took a package of chicken strips out of the freezer and stuck it in the microwave to thaw. Next she scanned the vegetable selection and pulled out some sugar peas, red pepper and broccoli, thinking a stir-fry would taste great. Again.

She poured a glass of Shiraz when the food was

ready and sat down to try to enjoy the meal, without thinking about the predicament. No luck. Her mind kept wandering to the elusive Calvin Knox and who he was and where he was.

A knock on her kitchen door broke into her reveries. She opened it to Nathaniel holding two small measuring cups.

"I'm terribly sorry to bother you, Lizzie, but I'm in need of one teaspoon of turmeric and two of cumin seeds. You wouldn't happen to have any, would you? I'm trying to make a lentil curry." He glanced at the table. "I'm terribly sorry to disturb your meal."

"No problem. That's adventuresome of you. And I do have both." She measured out what he needed. "This is quite a change of menu for you, Nathaniel."

He grunted. "Thanks, Lizzie. I would have hated to have to run down to the store. I should have checked my supplies first." He paused with his hand on the doorknob. "Is everything all right with you?"

Lizzie nodded. "It is, although I'm totally frustrated trying to figure out who Derek Alton knew in town. And now one of the teachers said that Derek used to live here about twenty-five years ago. Does that bring anything to mind?"

Nathaniel thought it over a moment. "No. The name still doesn't ring a bell, and I can't offhand think of anything that might have happened that would make him stand out. Not in my mind, anyway. I'm sorry, my dear."

"Huh. I'll have to ask Ken for more details."

"Well, I'll let you get on with your evening. Thank you, again." Nathaniel pulled the door closed behind him and ambled past the window toward the front sidewalk.

Lizzie finished eating, thinking about how odd a dish that was for Nathaniel to be cooking. Then her thoughts wandered over to Mark, who hadn't made contact with her since canceling their date on Saturday. Was he still upset with her or just too involved in the investigation? She wanted to find out but hesitated phoning him. But if he didn't know about Derek having lived in Ashton Corners, he would want to.

With that rationalization, Lizzie picked up the phone and punched in Mark's home number. She hung up after four rings, just before it went to the message. Then she called the police station and asked for him, only to be told that the chief had left for the day. Totally frustrated, she declined to leave a message and pulled out the phone directory to search for Ken Wicks's number. Trouble was, there were three entries with that name and four K. Wicks listings. She decided to wait until the next day and talk to him at school.

By the time she had pulled into the staff parking lot, Lizzie had convinced herself that it would probably be better to talk to Ken again before telling Mark. He might be more grateful if she had more information to present as a sort of peace offering.

She'd gone in half an hour early, hoping Ken might have done the same. However, he wasn't in his room or the staff room. At lunch, she stopped in the main office to check her mail slot and glanced at the staff bulletin board. Ken Wicks was listed as having taken extra holidays and wouldn't be back until the school term began in January.

Lizzie waited until the secretary, Betsey, had finished her phone conversation, and then walked to her desk.

"Betsey, do you think I could get Ken's phone number? I didn't realize he was going to be off for so long and I need to speak to him."

"Sure thing. Yeah, poor guy, his mama's booked in for a gallbladder operation and he's going to stay with her while she recovers some. She's in her late eighties, you know. Spunky woman. I hope she'll be all right." She brought up a file on her computer and made a notation on a notepad, handing the paper to Lizzie. "Here's his number but I think you've missed him. His mama lives in Tucson and he was to have left this morning."

Lizzie sighed. There went that lead. But if Ken knew, others must also know. The question was, who? What did she know about Ken? Who were his friends? She headed down the hall to the staff room. Maybe someone in there could answer her questions. But the afternoon bell rang before she opened the door. She'd have to follow through later, but not after school because she had an appointment with Xenia Henshaw.

Still frustrated and not having anything scheduled for the remainder of the school day, she went to the library and worked on a purchase order for some new workbooks she wanted for the winter term. She'd already stretched her budget at the beginning of the school year but what with the mixture of problems she'd discovered in the fall, she really needed to expand the diversity of materials to use with the students. She went online and ordered, from her city budget for the literacy program, some more Rapid Reads from the Canadian distributor. She'd first come across them at an education conference last summer and found they'd been a big hit. The mysteries by some well-known writers were aimed at reluctant readers, and her students had given them the seal of approval.

She glanced at the old-fashioned school board clock hanging on the opposite wall. Still an hour until her appointment in town. She'd go now and stop in to see Mark to tell him about Ken's comment, and leave the rest of the tracking to him. She'd also neglected to fill him in about Xenia Henshaw and Calvin Knox. Now was as good a time as any, but he really didn't need to know about her appointment with Xenia.

She noticed Mark's black Jeep in the parking lot but no cruisers. So maybe he wasn't around. She didn't know if that would be good or bad. Of course it would be bad. She had information to give him, after all. *Stop being such a wuss.* She entered through the front door and spotted Officer Don Yost at the counter. She tried to peer around him to Mark's office but couldn't see inside it.

"I'd like to speak to Chief Dreyfus, if he has a moment, please."

Officer Yost glanced up from the official-looking documents he was reading. "Uh, actually, he's on a call, ma'am. Would you like to leave him a note?" He pushed a notepad and pen across the counter toward her.

She hemmed and hawed. No. "Thanks, but I'll try to call later."

"All right. You have a nice day now, you hear?" He went back to his papers.

"You also," she said, already at the door. *Now what?* She glanced at the dashboard clock. Still over forty-five minutes until her meeting with Xenia Henshaw. She sat in her car a few minutes trying to decide then headed to Mark's house. Just in case.

A cruiser sat parked in his driveway. She spotted Mark walking Patchett, his six-month-old bloodhound pup, along the sidewalk from the far end of the street. He appeared to hesitate when he noticed her, then Patchett starting pulling at the leash. Lizzie stayed put until they reached her. Patchett tried to jump up in greeting but Mark held him firmly in place.

"Hey, Lizzie."

She couldn't read anything into his greeting and with the sun shining in her eyes, couldn't really see his expression. She felt a deep sadness and realized she'd been hoping for a hug.

"Hey, Mark. I thought you should know, I had emails from two people who had heard about Alton being at the book club and they asked if they could attend that meeting. One was Xenia Henshaw and the other someone named Calvin Knox. I don't know either of them, though, and I never heard back from them."

"Was that unusual?"

"It's not like we advertise our meetings, but Jensey Pollard had posted it on her store's Facebook page."

"Why did you wait till now to tell me?"

Duh. "Well, I guess I wasn't thinking clearly after the murder. And it's not as if I've seen a lot of you since then."

Mark's mouth twitched. "Will you forward their email addresses to me, please?"

"Uh-huh. Also, I was talking to Ken Wicks, he's a sixth-grade teacher at the school, in the staff room yesterday and he said that Derek Alton used to live here about twenty-five years ago."

Mark looked suddenly interested. "He said that? He knew Derek at the time? I haven't found anyone else who admits that. Is Wicks at the school right now?"

"No, he's visiting his sick mama in Tucson and won't be back until the New Year. I thought I'd check with some of the other teachers who have known Ken for a long time. Maybe they knew of Derek also."

Mark eyed her a moment before speaking. "I'll take care of that, thanks. I'd like you to stay out of this investigation."

"Why? You've already asked me to help get Sally-Jo to talk. How different is that from me asking around the staff room?" She realized she was standing in an aggressive pose, arms crossed over her chest, feet apart.

A frown flickered across his face. "It's one thing to have you speak to your friend, quite another to have you poking around in the life of the murder victim."

Lizzie started chewing her lower lip as he spoke. "I think you're being unreasonable. In fact, I think you're being pigheaded about a lot of things to do with this case." With that, she stalked over to her car, got in without a backward glance at him and drove off.

Dumb, dumb, dumb. She wished she could take

it all back. She hadn't planned on a confrontation but she'd been upset about him for over a week now. She should have done some shopping while she waited to meet with Xenia Henshaw. Which was exactly what she'd do right now.

Chapter Seventeen

◇◇◇

Murder doesn't round out anybody's life except the murdered's and sometimes the murderer's.

THE THIN MAN—DASHIELL HAMMETT

T he bell over the door announced her arrival at the Book Bin. Jensey Pollard looked up from the catalogue she perused. Lizzie noticed the store was empty so she'd have all of Jensey's attention.

"Is this usually a slow time of day for you?" Lizzie asked. She was surprised, so close to Christmas.

Jensey covered a yawn with her hand. "You can never tell with the book business. There's really no such thing as a regular day, except for Saturdays. They're always busy, which is a damn good thing." She let out a long sigh. "And the Christmas daily rush usually starts around this weekend."

"It must be tougher these days what with e-readers and the like."

"You've got that right. It's tough being an

independent these days, what with online buying and the big-box stores, too. But I still have my regulars who check the Internet for new titles, then come in and buy them from me. And then, of course, there are lots of folks who are paper book junkies, like me. They need to be able to feel them, see them and often use them in decorating schemes." She laughed. "That's why I always have such a nice selection of hardback coffee table books on hand."

Lizzie made sympathetic noises, picked up the latest Krista Davis from the front display and casually said, as she pulled out her wallet, "Ken Wicks was telling me yesterday that Derek Alton had lived in Ashton Corners about twenty-five years ago."

Jensey fumbled with the page as she turned it. "Did he really? I wonder where he got that? I've never seen that in a bio anywhere."

"I know. I've checked but his bios are sadly lacking any real information and there's nothing previous to his winning the Onyx. But you've lived here a long time and you don't remember him." She left the statement hanging.

"No, I never heard his name until, like you, with the award. Now, can I put that through for you or can I tempt you with another title?"

Lizzie shook her head. "One per visit after last Saturday's splurge, I'm afraid." She handed over the cash. "Can you suggest anyone I should talk to in town who might know for sure, one way or another?"

"No. Why don't you just leave it to the police? I'm sure they've been real thorough. And you having so much on your plate and all."

Lizzie nodded. "You're probably right." But she wondered why Jensey was so concerned about her plate, which wasn't really that full.

Lizzie pulled into the empty parking spot in front of the Corners Realty at the stroke of three thirty. When she entered the office, the face she'd seen on so many Corners Realty "For Sale" signs smiled up at her from the reception desk. Lizzie walked over and introduced herself.

"Oh my, yes. And you're right on time, too. If you don't mind, we'll talk out here. I'm covering for our receptionist, who's just run out on an errand."

"That's fine," Lizzie said as she sat in the armchair facing the desk. "I won't take up much of your time. I just wanted to ask if you knew Derek Alton, since you'd inquired about attending the book club meeting last week."

"Oh my, Derek Alton. Now, that was such a shame, wasn't it? To think something like that could happen here in Ashton Corners. And he was shot dead in your very own house, wasn't he? That was just dreadful. How are you coping, dear?"

Lizzie inwardly cringed. She hated being called

"dear" by anyone, especially if that person might be only fifteen or so years older than she. "I'm doing all right, Ms. Henshaw. I guess you heard about it on the news?"

"Yes. Yes, I did." Her voice had taken on an edge. "I'm curious why you wanted to come to the meeting. We haven't had anyone ask to do that before and then we had two requests for the Derek Alton night, you and Calvin Knox. It seemed odd."

"Calvin?"

"Yes, do you know him?"

"The name sounds a bit familiar but he's not someone I socialize with. Does he live in town?"

"No, in River's End."

"Well, did he say why he wanted to attend the meeting?" Henshaw sounded like she was conducting an interrogation.

"Uh, no. Just that he was a fan. Like you."

"Well, yes. I loved *Judgment* and I was looking forward to hearing about the book he was working on. I'd heard it was to be a sequel. Did he tell you anything about it? I understand you'd had dinner with him." She leaned forward across the desk, a steely look in her eyes.

Lizzie guessed she'd better get used to having that dinner thrown in her face. Small towns and all that. "He didn't say anything about his book. He was saving that for Thursday." And that's all she planned to say about that.

"Uh-huh. A romantic dinner, then."

That woman would just not leave it alone. *I wonder if she's friends with Officer Craig?* "More a fact-finding dinner. About the book club. So, did you know him other than as an award-winning author?"

"No, not Derek Alton. I admired his talent and after reading *Judgment*, I wanted to meet him and talk to him. That's easy to understand, isn't it?" She was starting to sound hostile, so Lizzie thought it time to change the topic.

"I've seen your signs all over town. You must be one of the busiest Realtors."

"I've been very successful in this business but it's not easy for a woman, you know. The men in it are ruthless and I've had to work extra hard to reach the top."

"How long have you been a Realtor?"

"Over eighteen years now." She glanced at the sales award framed on the side wall.

"And are you an Ashton Corners native?"

The eyes narrowed again. "Why do you ask?"

"Just that it's probably especially difficult if you're new to the town and don't have any of the contacts that go along with growing up here."

Henshaw's shoulders relaxed. "You've got it."

"Where exactly are you from?"

"Oh, upstate but I consider Ashton Corners my home." She looked pointedly at her watch. "I really must get on with my work now. I have several clients to phone."

Lizzie stood. "I understand and I thank you for your time. Did you move here when you got your Realtor's license?"

Xenia shrugged her shoulders. "Around that time."

"By the way, are you sure you didn't know Derek when he lived here, if you've been around that long?"

She bristled. "Who told you he'd lived here?"

"I'm not sure . . . I've spoken to so many people about him."

Henshaw took a deep breath and slowly let it out. "As I already said, I didn't know Derek Alton. Now, you really must excuse me." She stood and walked around to the front of the desk.

"Thanks for your help," Lizzie said, and she left with a dozen questions floating around in her head. Primarily, had everything she'd been told been the truth?

Chapter Eighteen

◇◇◇

"At any rate, my friend," he said seriously, "I know now something I wanted to know. Let us leave it at that."

THE MURDER OF ROGER ACKROYD
—AGATHA CHRISTIE

Calvin Knox had been there all along. Lizzie couldn't believe she'd missed his name and number in the online 411 directory. Must have been a typo on her part. She copied down his phone number and address, picked up the phone to dial and then decided to pay him a visit instead. She glanced at the clock on her desk. Four thirty. It would take only half an hour to drive to River's End. She'd always wondered about that name, seeing as there was no river and therefore, no end. *Oh well.* She keyed the address into Google to search for directions on the computer, printed it out and hurried downstairs. She filled the cats' dishes, grabbed her keys and dashed out to the car.

The drive took her over to the 49 heading north past Gleeson. If she were out for a pleasant afternoon drive, she would have delighted in the passing scenery. Instead, she formulated questions as she drove along. And worried about whether he'd be home. She knew nothing about the man, where he worked, what hours, whether it would be safe to talk to him alone. Yet she felt certain if she alerted him to her visit, he'd make sure he wasn't there. He hadn't answered her email, after all.

She also wondered if Mark had already tracked him down and checked him out. That was likely but it didn't mean she couldn't do the same.

She easily found the address belonging to a two-story, four-apartment building. Calvin resided in the lower right-hand unit. Lizzie rang the doorbell and shifted from foot to foot while waiting for him to answer the door. It finally creaked open and a sleepy-looking man poked his head around the jamb. His thinning brownish hair hung in his eyes. He curled out his bottom lip and blew it away, then donned a pair of brown-rimmed glasses.

"Who are you?" he managed to get out before being overwhelmed by a coughing spell.

Lizzie waited until he'd finished before answering, backing away slightly. "My name is Lizzie Turner and I'm part of the Ashton Corners Mystery Readers and Cheese Straws Society. You contacted me about attending our meeting last week, the one that Derek Alton was supposed to attend."

His glasses had slid forward on his nose and he pushed them back up before answering. "Um, yes. Yes, I did."

"I didn't hear back from you."

"Thought there was no point since he'd died and all."

"Why were you planning on coming in the first place? Were you a big fan or did you know him?"

"I thought I did." He backed away from the door. "You had better come on in."

She walked hesitantly through the door and into the living area. A single couch, a worn-out wing chair and a battered coffee table took up much of the space. His small kitchen table was cluttered with a computer and papers, allowing only small portions of the yellow Formica top to peer through. The kitchen counter did little to hide the few but messy dishes piled there.

What appeared to be manuscript pages were laid out on the coffee table along with two coffee cups, still holding the dregs of whitened coffee, and a stained white ceramic ashtray semifilled with cigarette butts.

Lizzie was hesitant to sit on anything but had to once Knox had plunked down on the couch. She perched on the edge of the couch and tried to surreptitiously read the pages in front of her.

"So how did know Derek Alton?" she asked.

He stared at her a couple of moments before answering. "He stole my manuscript." He held up his hand to ward off any comments when he saw the look of incredulity on her face. "I know you won't believe me. Nobody has. I've told the publishers, the media, anyone who would listen, but I don't have any proof." He rested his head in his hands.

"I don't understand. Which book are we talking about?"

Knox reached for a cigarette and Lizzie cringed. He noticed the look on her face and put it back in the package. "You know how big a hotshot writer he became after his first book won that prize? Well, he just couldn't get it together for the second one. So he got a job teaching creative writing at night school. That was in 1995. I had a brilliant idea but couldn't quite get the hang of writing a novel so I took his course. He encouraged me, said I had real talent and offered to critique any of my work. So I gave him my manuscript. He took it and after several weeks, gave it back and said it didn't work and that rather than belabor it, I should just ditch it and start all over on something new. I was devastated but I believed him, especially when he told me I had talent. Just had to keep plugging away at it. So I did. And then, a couple of years later, he published his second novel, only it was my plot. My characters. He had changed it a whole lot but it was still my book. But I hadn't kept a copy of it so I couldn't prove it."

"Did you confront him about it?"

"I did but he said he didn't know what I was talking about. After I contacted his publisher, he got in touch with me and said he'd sue the pants off me if I didn't back off. And, he'd make sure I never got anything published in the future. I believed him, so I let him get away with it."

"So, why did you want to see him again? What did you hope to accomplish?"

Knox stood abruptly and walked over to the window. "I wanted to make him pay. I don't know how, but I wanted the famous author to pay."

"Did you shoot him?" Lizzie surprised herself by asking, then glanced at the front door in case she needed a fast escape route.

Knox turned and looked at her, a look of total surprise on his face. "Of course not. I don't believe in weapons of any kind. That was a long time ago and I'm still not published so his threats mean little to me now. I guess I wanted to embarrass him."

Lizzie pointed at the manuscript. "It looks like you're still writing."

"In my spare time. I have a job at Herren Farm Supplies, and I write at night. Every now and then I send it somewhere but it always comes back. I really don't believe anymore that I'll ever be published but I keep on sending it anyway."

Lizzie nodded. "Did you see him at all when he came to Ashton Corners?"

"No. He died in his full glory, not an embarrassment to his name. Lucky bastard."

Lizzie drove home quickly. She'd been creeped out by Calvin Knox's obvious hatred of Derek and his displeasure at not having had a chance to put his plan into action. But why had he told her about it? So she'd think him innocent? Basically admitting to having a motive but not to being a murderer?

He didn't sound like a murderer. Unless he'd built himself up to such a frenzy by the time Derek had arrived that he quickly abandoned his original idea and pulled the trigger instead.

That could be a possibility. She just wasn't sure how to prove or disprove it. She'd put it to the book club. In this instance, six heads would be better than one.

Chapter Nineteen

◇◇◇

Keep your eyes and ears sharp, won't you?
AMONG THE MAD—JACQUELINE WINSPEAR

A ndie stepped off the porch as Lizzie pulled into her driveway. She'd reached the car by the time Lizzie stepped out of it.

"Hi, Andie. It's nice to see you, but what are you doing here? Shouldn't you be at home studying?"

Andie shrugged. Her long white plastic skeleton earrings danced on her shoulders against the colorful backdrop of her black hair, streaked with blue. She was bundled in a cropped jean jacket, with a bright purple T-shirt riding lower onto her hips, just about meeting the top of her low-slung jeans. On her feet were her favorite New Rock Bishops. She shivered slightly, acknowledging the temperature, which had slid to the low teens as the sun went down.

"I needed a break and I hadn't checked on you in a few days. Thought I'd come over."

Lizzie hid a smile. Checked on her. Still playing PI. "Well, come on in. Have you eaten yet?"

"Naw. Nobody's home." She shrugged again.

"How about I thaw some homemade soup Molly gave me and we share it?"

Andie nodded. "Sure."

Lizzie stood waiting with the door open while Andie slowly circled the Mazda, flicking a small flashlight over the wheel wells. Lizzie sighed. Oh well, as long as it started and stopped with checking out her car. She'd had to replace her 2004 model after being driven off the road a few months earlier but she'd been pleased to find a newer version, same model and color at a great price.

Andie played with the cats while Lizzie tended to the soup and stuck a couple of cornmeal buns, courtesy of Nathaniel and her freezer, into the toaster oven. She filled their water glasses and called Andie over to the table.

"Is there something on your mind?" Lizzie asked.

Andie shrugged and took a tentative taste of the

sweet potato and red pepper soup. Lizzie knew when to wait her out. She tried her own soup and buttered the bun. They ate in silence.

When she'd finished almost half the soup in her mug, Andie said, real casual-like, "I don't think I'm gonna pass this term."

Lizzie put down her spoon. "Why do you say that?"

Andie slouched back in her chair. "I just am so thickheaded, ya know? I study and then take those practice tests and it's like I never saw the stuff before."

"What subject is giving you trouble?"

Andie glanced up at her through the cover of her long black bangs. "English."

Lizzie inwardly cringed. Had she not been doing her job as a tutor? Here she thought getting Andie interested in reading would be the first step and then she'd be more involved in the assigned material from her classroom. But maybe not.

"English Lit?"

"Naw. I think I can fudge what I don't understand in that." Lizzie cringed again. "It's like the grammar part, ya know?"

Lizzie let out a sigh of relief. Maybe she hadn't been using the wrong approach after all. And here was Andie, asking for her help, in a roundabout way. That, too, was a good sign.

"Listen, Andie. It can be done. Reading is the first step and you're into that now. You have to read the sentence and from that, be able to pull out the parts, identify them and then put them back together again. I can help you."

Andie sat up a bit straighter. "You can?"

"Sure. When's your exam?"

"Grammar is next Thursday morning."

Lizzie went and got her agenda from her purse and flipped through it. "Maybe we can combine some grammar with English Lit when we meet tomorrow. And could you come over here early Saturday afternoon? We'll look at next week's schedule at that point and decide how much more time is needed."

Andie tried to look nonchalant but a grin tugged at the corners of her mouth. "Awesome. Yeah."

"Good. I'll get some material ready but you've got to promise me two things."

"What?"

"You'll work hard at it and . . . you won't worry so much about it. Okay?"

Andie nodded and dug back into her soup. Lizzie wondered about the wisdom of her next statement but decided to say it anyway.

"I was hoping to get the book club together tomorrow night to go over some of the things that have come up about Derek Alton's murder."

"Yeah, way awesome." Andie had that eager sleuth look back in her eyes.

"The thing is, I don't want this interfering with your studying but I know you want to be a part of it. So, I'll make you another deal. If you'll call everyone tonight, starting with Molly to see if it's okay to use her place, then let me know who can make it, you can stay for the first hour of the meeting. Then you need to go home to study. The phoning helps me out a lot so that's your contribution."

"So we stay at Molly's right after the grammar thingy?"

Lizzie nodded. "Well, we'll take a break and slip out for a burger, maybe."

Andie mulled it over a few more seconds. "Fine."

They finished their meal then Andie made her excuses and left. Lizzie noticed the small beam of light from her flashlight as she circled the car one more time.

Lizzie checked the wall calendar the next morning as she waited for the last drops of espresso to land in her cup. She'd had a long run, more invigorating than usual given the continued low temperatures and high winds. Going was easy with the winds at her back. Coming home, it was twice the work but well worth it.

Christmas was closing in. The Musica Nobilis concert happened in three days; eight days until the school Christmas pageant; and then it would almost be holiday time. And once she no longer had work-related tasks, she could concentrate on shopping for gifts and finish decorating. She'd just have to bite the bullet—she cringed at her choice of words—and finish the job if she wanted all the trimmings in time for Christmas. But for today—school, Andie's tutorial session and then, book club. A full day. And evening.

Arriving at school, Lizzie skirted past Vanda Striker's office, hoping the vice principal wouldn't see her, and ducked into the library. She planned to use the morning to finish off term-end reports and get them out to the teachers by the end of the week. As a reading specialist, Lizzie's role started winding down earlier than the rest of the school staff. She had a few consultations booked for the next week, but aside from a meeting at the school board office, she would be available to help out in classrooms if needed.

She fired up the computer, focusing on her task. By lunch, she'd managed to finish about half the reports. Not bad, she thought, and grabbed her bag, making her way to the staff room. She retrieved the egg salad wrap she'd stashed in the fridge that morning and joined Sally-Jo, who had saved her a place at the table in the far end of the room.

"I wasn't sure if you were here today," Sally-Jo said as Lizzie sank onto her chair. "But I'm glad you are. I wanted a heads-up before tonight's meeting. Anything I should be aware of?"

Lizzie knew what she meant. She could hear the tension in her voice. She shook her head. "No. I've just been talking to those two people who wanted to come and hear Derek."

Sally-Jo lowered her voice. "My former college roommate emailed me. Officer Craig called her to check out my story."

That had been expected. "And, what did she say?"

"Like I thought. She'd no idea what had been going on, although she sure must know now. Or be hoping I'll fill her in on all the details. Not going to happen, though." Sally-Jo's fingers kept tapping out a random beat on the table.

Lizzie took a bite and chewed a few minutes. "Do you remember the names of any of the other girls from your class that he'd been playing around with?"

Sally-Jo looked surprised. "Not offhand. Why?"

"Well, if you did, they would hopefully verify that they'd had affairs with Derek around the same time. That would back up your reason for breaking it off with him."

Sally-Jo smiled. "You're right. That's a great idea, Lizzie. I'll look through my old yearbooks tonight and see if it sparks anything. By the way, have you had a chance to talk to Ellen Germain yet?"

"Nope. I haven't seen her at all but she's on yard duty with me today."

She glanced at the clock. "And I'd better get out there. See you later."

Sally-Jo managed a half smile, her mouth full of vegetable soup.

The weather forecaster had warned of unusually cold winds today, and Lizzie was happy she'd paid heed. Her lined Windbreaker, paired with a cozy fleece top complete with a hood, kept her from turning tail and running back inside. She slipped some black leather gloves on her hands and she was all set. She noticed Ellen huddled next to the back wall and wandered over.

"You must have missed the weather forecast this morning," Lizzie said.

Ellen looked startled. "Uh, oh yes, I guess I wasn't paying attention. Can't remember yard duty being this cold before," she said with a shiver for emphasis.

"You could borrow my gloves if you'd like," Lizzie offered. "They don't cover much but at least your hands will be warm."

Ellen shook her head. "Thanks, but no. I'll just keep my hands in my pockets and hope I don't have to take them out to pull apart any fights." She grinned. "By the way, Lizzie, I've been meaning to ask you something." She paused and took her time scanning the yard.

Ellen's gaze had locked onto something on the other side of the yard when she again spoke. "I heard about Derek Alton being shot at your house.

It must have been very terrible for you. But I was wondering, before . . . that . . . did he say anything about why he was in Ashton Corners? I mean, aside from speaking to your book club."

Kismet. "He didn't come to town to visit us. We managed to snag him, just on a chance meeting. I was going to ask you something, though. Sally-Jo Baker said you both went to the same college. Did you know that Derek Alton used to teach there?"

Ellen made a sound like a croak, which ended in a coughing fit. When she was able to talk again, she said, "That's right, Sally-Jo did tell me she'd seen my picture. Funny that we never ran into each other. It wasn't that huge a campus."

"Uh-huh. But did you know Derek Alton?"

Ellen shook her head. "Like I said, it wasn't too huge a campus but obviously you didn't meet everyone. I can't even remember half the profs I had. Anyway, his name didn't ring a bell when I read about the murder in the papers. He didn't say he knew me, did he?"

"Nope. He didn't mention any names."

Ellen started hugging herself and stamping her feet. "There you go, then. Look, I have to dash inside before I turn into an icicle. I'll just take a few minutes to warm up and then come back out, okay?"

Lizzie nodded. "It's quiet out here. Don't worry about coming back out. There's not much longer anyway."

Ellen gave her a small smile and hurried across the yard to the door. Lizzie was getting used to being asked a lot of questions about Derek, his death and his business in town. For someone who claimed not to have known Derek, Ellen seemed a bit on the defensive when talking about him. Of course, everyone seemed to be these days.

Chapter Twenty
◇◇◇

Tomorrow was looking much brighter.
FRIENDS IN HIGH PLACES
——MARNE DAVIS KELLOGG

Stephanie Lowe was the last to arrive at Molly's for the book club meeting. She waddled into the room and, with the help of Molly, eased into the straight-backed wing chair. Bob shoved a small needlepoint footstool over and she slowly hefted her feet onto it one at a time, and sighed.

"I'm sorry to be so much trouble to y'all."

"It's no trouble at all," Molly answered. "We're just so happy you're able to come and be with us." Tonight she wore off-white harem pants with a sheer, long-sleeved blouson top over a gold-colored shell, and almost by tacit agreement, everyone on arrival had told Molly how lovely she looked but had not made any further comments on her choice of clothing.

"Me, too, Molly. I can't tell y'all how much it means to me, your coming by and visiting and all. But it's nice to be out of the apartment. Thanks to you, Jacob, for picking me up tonight."

"My pleasure, Stephanie." He winked at Sally-Jo. She smiled back.

"Now before Lizzie gets to the talking, I think we need to start with the serious stuff," Bob stated. "Can I help you carry out the food, Molly?"

"Most of it's in here already." She pointed to the coffee table. "But there's still the tray of tea."

He looked over at the coffee table. "No cheese straws tonight?"

"Why, I swear that's the only reason you come over here, Bob Miller."

"Now Molly," he said with a sly grin, "y'all know that's not the main reason."

Molly flushed a pale pink. Lizzie and Sally-Jo shared a quick look. Andie helped herself to a sugar cookie and then passed the plate around.

When they were settled with cups of tea and plates of food, Lizzie explained why she'd asked them to meet.

"So, you think maybe this fellow Calvin Knox could've gotten tired of waiting and just decided to kill off Alton?" Bob asked, biting into the spicy cheddar cheese straws Molly had finally produced.

"I'm not sure. If he did, he's a very good actor.

He really sounded regretful that he didn't get the chance to embarrass Derek. But so far, they're the only two real suspects. He and Xenia Henshaw."

Jacob leaned forward in his chair. "You think Ms. Henshaw might have known him from a long time ago, if what Ken Wicks said is true?"

"She was adamant she hadn't known him, and anyway, it sounds like she wasn't living here at that time."

Bob said, "Well, I was chief back then and I never heard of the guy."

"What about Mr. Wicks?" Stephanie asked. "Could he have some long-standing grudge also?"

"Well, he admitted to knowing Derek had lived here before and I doubt he'd do that if he killed him. And, I don't think he said he knew him. I'd have to ask him again." She shook her head. "No, I really don't think he'd tell me about Derek if he were the killer. Why would he?"

"To throw you off?" Molly asked. "Just like Agatha Christie did in so many of her master-pieces—make the obvious less so by being obvious about it."

Lizzie shrugged. "Okay, well, I'll put him on the list, for now. That makes three of them. But I think Ken is a highly unlikely suspect."

"Didn't you say you were going to talk to Jensey Pollard at the Book Bin? What had she to say for herself?" Jacob asked.

"Basically what she'd said originally. She first

met him when he walked into her store and offered to sign any books she had in stock. That's when I wandered in . . . and you know the story from there. I did ask specifically if she'd known him from before and she said no."

Andie jumped into the discussion. "But she could be lying."

"Why do you say that?" Jacob asked.

Andie shrugged. "Like, doesn't everyone lie at some time or other? You must have lots of clients who lie, being a lawyer and all."

Jacob chuckled. "I'm not able to divulge that information. Client confidentiality and all that."

Andie grinned.

"Well, that's very true, young lady," Bob agreed. "Suspects lie all the time to the police. You can't just take a person's word for anything."

"That's very cynical," Molly said.

Bob shrugged. "That's life, I'm afraid."

"So, you're saying anyone who had contact with Derek, in any way, should be on the suspect list?" Lizzie asked, feeling a tad panicked.

"I think you're in the clear, Lizzie. But sure, I'd put Jensey Pollard on that list, along with the other three."

Lizzie did as she was told.

Bob cleared his throat. "I'm sorry to have to ask you this, Sally-Jo, and I surely hope you don't take any offense. But I was wondering why the police hauled you in for questioning?"

Jacob jumped to her defense. "Hauled isn't quite an accurate description, Bob. She was asked to assist in their inquiries."

Bob merely raised his eyebrows in response.

Sally-Jo sucked in her breath. She looked around the room then focused on Jacob, who gave a slight nod. "I guess y'all deserve to know but it's something I'm not too proud about." She took another deep breath. "Derek was my creative writing prof at college in my freshman year. We had a brief affair."

Molly smiled kindly at Sally-Jo. "That was a long time ago, honey. We all have done things when we were younger that we're not too proud about. But that's hardly a reason to suspect you of his murder."

"Thanks, Molly. I hope the chief agrees with you. I ended it and tried to forget it happened. I wasn't too thrilled when I heard he'd be our guest at book club. I'd planned to skip that night, by the way."

Jacob spoke up. "My money's on Calvin Knox at this point. But it might be hard to prove unless the police can get a warrant and search his house. They do know about him, don't they, Lizzie?"

"Yes, I told them about both Calvin Knox and Xenia Henshaw." But not about my subsequent conversations with them. Why should she tell Mark when she knew exactly where such a talk would lead? And she wasn't up to another confrontation just yet. Let the police do their own legwork. Or maybe she could try a little B and E some day when Calvin was at work. Get some solid facts. But of course, she wouldn't. Didn't have the nerve. And besides being illegal, she shuddered to think of Mark's reaction.

"You know," Bob said in between bites of a second cheese straw, "I'd like to run with this notion that Alton lived in Ashton Corners a long time ago. If it's true, then I'll bet it's someone from his past who's upset he's back in town and did him in, for whatever reason. I've still got my contacts at the county registry office. I'll have them dig back and see if there's a tax notice or anything for Alton. I'll also get Ronny Biggs to mention to the chief that it might be wise to have the phone company dig into past files, just in case Alton didn't own property. He was sure to have phone service. If we can find an old address, maybe we can narrow down the search."

"That would be great," Lizzie agreed.

"What if he did live here but he was a criminal so he had to change his name? He could have pulled a bank heist or robbed a gas station or just about anything. That's possible, isn't it?" Andie-with-the-vivid-imagination asked.

Bob answered. "Interesting thought, Andie. I'll get Biggs to check his fingerprints and see if he's got a record, if it hasn't been done already. Not too many people without something in their past to hide, that's for darn sure."

Sally-Jo squirmed on her chair and Molly stood abruptly and left the room. All eyes followed her out the door. Bob shook his head in wonder. "What?"

"You probably reminded her of her dead husband's secret past, I'll bet," Stephanie said.

Bob groaned. "I plumb wasn't thinking along those lines. She's got to stop being so sensitive about the whole thing." He stood to follow her.

"Maybe you should just give her a little time right now," Lizzie suggested. "I'll bet she'll be back shortly, carrying a plate of molasses cookies or something."

Bob shook his head. "Well she's not acting herself these days. First with her shutting herself away from us all these weeks. She wouldn't answer the door or the phone. And when she eventually did, she'd say she couldn't talk. And that meeting last month? It was downright spooky finding all the food and drinks ready for us along with a note to carry on without her. And then, all those crazy clothes she's been wearing." He paused to take a deep breath.

"But I sure hope you're right, Lizzie." He gave her a sideways glance and winked. "I'm still mighty hungry."

"Andie, isn't it time you were home studying some more?" Lizzie reminded her.

Andie glanced at her watch. "Yeah, sure. If y'all have anything for me to do, just let me know, okay?"

"Don't worry, we will," Sally-Jo assured her.

Stephanie shifted uncomfortably in her chair. "I'm sorry, Jacob. But I think I should be heading home, too. I hate to break up the evening, though."

Jacob stood quickly. "That's all right, Stephanie. I don't mind running you home. I can always come back if there's more to discuss tonight." He looked around the room, his eyes settling on Sally-Jo.

Bob answered for them all. "I think we've about covered enough for one night. I'll try to get some of that information, which is what we need before carrying on with anything. Lizzie, you did good tracking down those two. I'll give you a call as soon as I learn something." He stood then added, "Please say good night to Molly for me, Lizzie. And thank her for her hospitality."

"I'll give you a ride, too, Andie," Jacob said, and the three left behind Bob.

"Do you think Molly's really upset?" Sally-Jo asked as she helped Lizzie clear away the dirty dishes.

"I guess she must be. She usually takes everything in stride and she did seem to have bounced back lately. Until tonight. I'll see if she wants to have a talk before I leave," Lizzie said, thinking about the numerous times she'd been pounding on Molly's door, to no avail. And just when she'd be debating about whether to call the police, Molly would appear and tell her everything was just fine. She just needed some time to herself. And Lizzie, because Molly asked, just let it be. Although she'd continued to worry all those weeks.

"I'll leave, then. I've still got tons to do around the house," Sally-Jo said.

"I haven't asked how it's all going."

"Best not to ask at the moment. I'll have you over to do an inspection before I'm descended upon. I'm looking forward to your concert, by the way. Are you getting excited?"

"In a way. You know, this may sound crazy, but I always enjoy the rehearsals more than the concert. Guess I'm not much of a performer. I'm probably the only one in the choir who feels that way, too."

Sally-Jo laughed. "Well, you hide it real good when you're onstage. See you at school tomorrow. Just let me know if you think of anything you want me to do about all this. And you know, I feel much better now that it's all out in the open. Foolish, but better."

After Sally-Jo left, Lizzie started washing up the dishes. Molly came into the kitchen. "You don't have to do that, honey. That's what my dishwasher's for."

"I don't mind. And there isn't enough for a load. Look, I'm almost finished. I wasn't sure where to put the pitcher, though." Molly gestured with her head over toward the back counter. "By the way, everyone said good night and thank you."

Molly grunted and busied herself putting the leftover sweets into containers. Then she poured them each a glass of Pinot Grigio and sat at the table waiting for Lizzie to finish. "Just let them air-dry."

Lizzie drained the water out of the sink, gave it a quick wipe and joined Molly. She took a long sip of her wine and then sat, knowing Molly had something she wanted to say.

"I acted a bit foolish, didn't I?" Molly finally asked.

Lizzie leaned over and covered Molly's hand with her own. "Not foolish. Just surprising."

Molly sighed. "I'm doing quite well, you know. I don't dwell on what Claydon did that much anymore." She sighed. "That's part of this 'new me.' I decided that I'd been someone else's version of me all my life. First my parents brought me up to be the proper Southern miss. Then I was the proper Southern wife to Claydon. I realized, if I was going to get on with my life, to get beyond what Claydon did, I'd have to find out who I was and become that person. That's why I'm having fun with all these outfits. It's just a way of expressing myself. And, I'm also thinking I need to get away a bit and see some more of the world." She took a long swallow of her wine.

"Just because Claydon got involved in that get-rich scheme, and true, it did have some devastating results for some people, it doesn't change what you two had together. That was the real Claydon, the man you loved. And he loved you, too. Very much."

"But to cause so much havoc in other people's lives."

"He was remorseful, it seems. He tried to make amends over the years. He may just have been a young, cocky businessman who saw a good thing and didn't think beyond it. But later, he tried to do the right thing."

"The right thing would have been to tell me."

"Why? So that you could have worried and shared in his guilt? I think he was trying to save you from the agony he was going through. He wasn't trying to cut you out of his life. He made a mistake, yes . . . but it doesn't make him this big ogre. That's not how you knew him."

Molly sat silent for several minutes, then sighed. "Yes, you're right, but I do feel betrayed."

"I think that's probably natural and it may take a long time to get beyond that. But don't dismiss your good years together. Take great joy in the knowledge that you were deeply loved."

Molly put her hand over Lizzie's. "Now when did you get to be so wise?"

"I've been taking lessons." She leaned over and gave Molly a quick hug.

"I've been a real grouse to be around, haven't I?"

"People have noticed you've not been your usual self and we've been concerned."

"I've even stopped talking to Claydon."

Lizzie couldn't hide her surprise.

"Oh yes. He's in the front seat of his old Corvette. His ashes are. I keep the urn there and most nights I'd go sit beside it and tell him about my day and what's been going on in Ashton Corners. But not lately. Maybe it's time to give those ashes a decent burial. Or scattering. What do you think? Scattered throughout that maze he so enjoyed installing." She looked at Lizzie. "I think he'd like to be there."

Lizzie wasn't sure what to say. She hadn't known Claydon was still around.

Maybe a scattering would be cathartic for Molly. "I think that's a fine idea."

Chapter Twenty-one

◇◇◇

And if I were right, what on earth was he up to? Well, whatever it was, he wouldn't get away with it.

FRIENDS IN HIGH PLACES
—MARNE DAVIS KELLOGG

L izzie pushed herself to run at peak speed the next morning. The weather was perfect for a run; the wind had finally died down, the temperature pushed midfifties, and a slow dawn promised sun for most of the day. She ran along Sidcup Street and marveled at the Christmas decorations appearing in yards and along rooftops.

One house had a gathering of five deer in various sizes, sure to be covered in clear lights at night. Next to it, and not to be outdone, a small wooden sleigh with Santa as driver was being pulled along by one enormous reindeer. It looked slightly out of place with the large elderberry flowering behind it. And not a hint of last Saturday's snowfall. The house across the street, a restored clapboard painted in a subtle shade of sand and taupe, had an angel with trumpet in residence on the white front porch.

She ran a few blocks farther, then veered along Ulysses and over to Rosemont, looking at the windows of the variety of small businesses on that block, just two streets over from Main. She must remember to take a walk one night and just enjoy the lights after dark. Maybe Mark would join her. Mark. She quickly refocused her thoughts.

She gave a chuckle as she turned onto her street and saw what the Beauchamps had done to their front porch. The country-style house had a traditional porch railing running across the front of it, and on that railing at the far right side sat an angel, halo slightly askew, one knee drawn up, leaning against the corner post.

Lizzie chuckled as she continued down the block. The drapes were still drawn at Nathaniel's, she noticed as she slowed to a saunter to cool down. She headed along her driveway and past her car, turned back to it, dropped down on one knee and peered under the Mazda. Feeling slightly foolish, she went inside to be greeted by the cats.

They stayed close to her as she made a protein shake for breakfast, followed by an espresso, and then headed to the shower. When she went into her bedroom to get dressed for work, the cats had curled up on the bed, backs touching. She pulled on a purple V-necked jersey T with three-quarter sleeves and khaki jeggings, decided on gold ballerina flats, and added a green scarf. She turned back to her closet and pulled out her concert outfit. The long black skirt looked just fine but she took it to hang on the shower curtain railing for the day, hoping to eliminate any unseen wrinkles.

At school, she started her day in the classroom of a fourth-grade teacher, making notes on two of her more challenging students. Things seemed to be improving, she thought with some relief. She had two more classroom observations scheduled before lunch.

When she settled at the table in the staff room, she checked her cell phone for any messages. Bob Miller had left a message to call him. She excused herself and went into the hall to make the call. Bob answered on the first ring.

"I've been hoping you'd get my message," he said by way of a greeting. "I went to check the county records this morning and no Derek Alton listed, so I asked my friend to do a search of electricity records. That may take a day or so, unfortunately, 'cause my contact has to do it on the QT, so to speak."

"I was hoping you might have some good news," Lizzie said, feeling let down.

"Well, girl, it just so happens that I might. And it's my nosy sister, Lucille, who may have the news. She called me today and said there was something familiar about the picture of Alton that she saw in the paper and it's been nagging at her. She'll get it eventually. She's got a good memory, unfortunately; never forgets anything you want her to forget."

"Thanks for the heads-up. That could be

promising. I guess I'll see you at the reception after the concert tomorrow night?"

"Yup. I know this'll give Lucille enough material to keep her meddling for a long time coming, though. Gotta go, girl. Break a leg, as they say."

"Thanks, Bob." She tucked her cell away and went back to eat her lunch.

Sally-Jo slid into the seat beside her and Lizzie shared the info from her phone call.

"What do you think about that?" Sally-Jo asked.

"Well, Lucille's lived here all her life. I'm wondering if she recognized Derek and maybe Ken Wicks was right after all. I wish we could think of another way of checking."

"What can I do?"

"Let's divide and conquer the staff room. Ask around and see if anyone recognized Derek. If Ken did, surely there's someone else, too. You take that half"—she pointed to her right—"and I'll go that direction and we'll meet back in the middle."

Sally-Jo finally smiled. "Good. It's better to be doing something about it rather than waiting for Officer Craig to pull out the cuffs."

By the time the bell rang for afternoon classes, they'd spoken to everyone.

"No luck," said Lizzie. "What about you?"

"Nada. They're mainly in their twenties and thirties, though. They might not remember him even if they saw him. Derek was what, in his late forties? We might have better luck with some of the older staff members. Why don't you try the admin staff and I'll keep any eye out for teachers?"

"Does my list include the vice principal?"

"Yes. Why?"

"Did I tell you what she wants me to wear for the school pageant next Friday?" Lizzie asked in an appalled voice.

"Not yet . . . Spill."

"An elf costume. As in, Santa's helper."

Sally-Jo burst out laughing. "Sorry. That's just so not you but I see her point. It is in keeping with the pageant."

"Thanks, you're sadly lacking in the moral support category. Oh well. She won't put it to rest so I guess I'd better just face her straight on. Have a good afternoon."

"You, too. If we don't talk before, I'm looking forward to your concert."

Lizzie nodded her thanks as Sally-Jo took off down the hall at a brisk pace. And rounding the corner from the other direction was none other than Vanda Striker. Lizzie squelched her initial reaction to slide back into the staff room and maybe hide out in the restroom. Instead, she waited.

"Do you have a minute, Vanda? I need to ask you something."

Vanda smiled in anticipation. "Absolutely. Did

you get your elf costume? Mrs. Farnshaw told me she'd measured you and was almost finished sewing it."

Lizzie steered her down the hall toward the office. She had Vanda's room booked for the next hour anyway.

"Yes, I've got it." *Unfortunately.* "Actually, I wanted to talk to you about the murder of Derek Alton last week. Did you hear about it?"

Vanda had turned an unhealthy shade of pale, or maybe it was the sunlight streaming through the back door, Lizzie thought.

"Uh-huh, I did read something about it in the *Colonist.*" She turned to Lizzie. "That's right, it happened at your house, didn't it? What a terrible thing for you to witness."

"Yes, it was. So you'll understand why I'm trying to find out if anyone knew Derek. I'm wondering what he was doing in town."

Vanda stopped and turned to Lizzie. "I thought he'd come to do a signing or some such thing. Something to do with his book, anyway. Your book club, wasn't it?"

"No. That was just tacked on because I happened to meet him at the Book Bin. I figure he must have known someone in town and was here to visit them. The question is, who? And Ken Wicks said he thought Derek looked familiar, that he might have lived here at one time. Does that ring a bell? Did you recognize him?"

"How would I recognize him when I didn't get to meet him?"

"I meant, his picture in the newspaper."

"Those pictures are always so grainy, but no, I didn't know Derek Alton. Sorry I can't help. I've got to run. Let me know if there are any snags with the pageant, you hear?" Vanda strode down the hall a few feet then turned abruptly. "Did Derek Alton say what his new book is about?"

"No. We didn't get that far in our talks."

Vanda appeared relieved. She nodded and walked off.

Now, what was that about . . . if anything?

Lizzie made it to the choir dress rehearsal early, hoping to find Lucille Miller and help prime her memory. The rehearsal, like the concert, was being held in the St. John's Episcopal Church sanctuary. The risers had been set up in the nave while chairs and music stands were arranged for the small string orchestra. There were a few fiddlers already in their chairs, tuning their instruments. The harpist had yet to show.

Lizzie dropped her music bag on a pew and chatted with a couple of altos standing in the aisle, since she couldn't spot Lucille. The church felt chilly and she was glad she'd worn her light fleece top. Lizzie heard Lucille before she saw her. That laughter was unmistakable and it sounded like someone had just told a good joke. Lizzie excused herself and joined Lucille at the back of the church, as she hung up her coat.

"You may want to keep that on awhile. It's chilly in here," Lizzie warned. "Can I ask you something?"

Lucille spun around. "Lizzie, dear . . . just the person I was going to look for. You first, then I have one for you." She squeezed Lizzie's arm.

Lizzie cringed inside, pretty sure she knew what Lucille's question would be about. Rather, whom. Oh well. "Bob said you might have recognized Derek Alton's picture. Has anything about him come to mind?"

Lucille shook her head. "No, and it's not from lack of trying." Lucille pushed a few strands of her shoulder-length, silver-streaked blonde hair out of her eyes. She was all in gray tonight—a light, flowing top down to her thighs and dark gray pants. *A very flattering look for her,* Lizzie couldn't help but think.

"I'm sure I don't know the name," Lucille went on. "I'm pretty good with names. But that face, I don't know what it is, but there's something. But maybe it's that I saw his picture in the paper a long time ago when he won the award and it stayed with me. He's a very good-looking man. Or was."

Lizzie nodded, trying not to let her disappointment show.

"Now, tell me what's going on with Bob and

Molly. I know something's up. Bob would never agree to come to our concerts when I asked him, and now Molly asks, and he accepts. Is there some hanky-panky going on?"

"I really don't know, Lucille," Lizzie tried to convince her. "Molly bought the ticket for Bob as a Christmas gift. That I do know. She wanted to thank him for all the help he's been. That may be all there is to it. You'll have to ask one of them."

"And what is it with Molly these days? She's wearing the most outlandish outfits around town. What has gotten into that gray head of hers?"

Lizzie shrugged. "She's just having a bit of fun." Lizzie flashed a broad smile at Lucille and started toward the front of the church.

"I usually am good with names and faces, you know," Lucille tossed after her. "Although I'd thought I'd seen Xenia Henshaw before, too, and turns out I was wrong."

"Xenia Henshaw?" Lizzie stopped in her tracks. She went back to Lucille.

"That's right. When she moved here, oh, about sixteen or so years ago, I was sure she had lived here before. Had a husband, even. When I finally asked her about it, she told me I was totally wrong, on both accounts." Lucille shook her head and picked up her music folder and water bottle, ready to go.

Lizzie wasn't sure what to say. "Well, thanks anyway."

Stanton Giles clapped his hands for attention and invited the singers to take their places on the risers at the front of the church.

After two hours of less-than-stellar performing, Giles wrapped up the rehearsal with a reminder that poor dress rehearsals meant great concerts. The soprano standing next to Lizzie muttered under her breath that there was always a first time.

"Well, if Stanton feels that way, we should also," Lizzie said.

The soprano shrugged. "Well, he may say that but he's ticked off."

"He's frustrated, all right. But we've been through this before. It will be all right," Lizzie stressed. However, she left feeling down. Preconcert jitters, investigation blues, it was really too much for one night.

Although she sang along with the practice CD in her car, Lizzie's mind was on Xenia Henshaw during the drive home. Was she hiding something? Like having lived here before? And if so, had she also lied about not knowing Derek? And was there a connection to his murder?

Chapter Twenty-two

◇◇◇

It was a clear morning with the sun not yet high over the horizon . . . everywhere around was an unbroken carpet of thick snow. The world looked very pure and white and beautiful.

THE ADVENTURE OF THE CHRISTMAS PUDDING—AGATHA CHRISTIE

It took longer than usual for her computer to finishing loading, and Lizzie impatiently tapped her fingers on the desk. She really should take the thing in for a cleaning out of old files, or maybe she needed more memory. Whatever, she didn't have the patience to wait these days.

Finally, Google appeared and Lizzie tapped in Xenia Henshaw's name. There were several pages of hits, most of the items having to do with real estate listings. In one article, Xenia had been named Business Woman of the Year in Ashton Corners. That was five years ago. A short bio had been worked into the story but didn't tell Lizzie anything about her life prior to her moving to town.

She ran through each of the items, hoping to find some more information, but they all said much the same thing. Either it was Xenia's standard response or the info was lifted from earlier postings. She found an obituary, obviously not the same person. And a hopeful listing under "People" that promised a biography, too. When she clicked on it, Lizzie was faced with fifteen small photos of Xenia Henshaw. She chose one that opened onto a page featuring a short sales pitch about Xenia and at the bottom, the promise of more.

She clicked on it and a more in-depth biography appeared, outlining her involvement in the Chamber of Commerce, the FallFest committee, the First Baptist Church, and various other civic pursuits. No mention of where she came from or what she'd done before moving to Ashton Corners. The few tabs at the side linked directly to property listings.

Totally frustrated, Lizzie clicked off the computer for the night, filled the cat's dry food dishes and headed to bed, where she was joined by Edam and Brie after a few minutes. Her mind refused to shut down, though.

Two people thought they recognized Derek, one of them suggesting he'd actually lived in town a long time ago. Xenia Henshaw also scored on the recognition scale. Did it mean anything? She tried to be objective. Had she ever had that feeling about someone? She thought not. She wished she could discuss it all with Mark.

Mark. Would he even bother showing up for the concert?

• • •

The Prius was back in Nathaniel's driveway as Lizzie made her way home from her run the next morning. It hadn't been there when she'd left. Awfully early for a visit. She was longing to go ring the bell, find out what was happening in his life these days, but she couldn't think of a good enough excuse.

She picked up the phone as soon as she got in and dialed Paige.

"Good morning, best friend in the entire world. I need to pick your brain," Lizzie said.

Paige laughed. "What's left of it is yours. Why don't you come over? We may be able to find an oasis of calm in the chaos of my life. The girls are hyper since we put the tree up last night, and Brad's gone shopping."

"Sounds ideal," Lizzie laughed, thinking, *Not.* However, it had been a couple of weeks since she'd seen Paige's daughters, one of them her goddaughter, and she looked forward to it.

"I'm going to shower and have breakfast. How about a midmorning coffee in an hour or so?"

"I look forward to it. Really. I do. A lot." Paige rang off.

Lizzie flipped through the morning paper as she ate her hot oatmeal standing up at the counter. She took a few minutes to comb both of the cats and then dashed upstairs to take a shower. She was out the door just a little bit later than she'd promised and was knocking on Paige's door shortly after that.

Paige welcomed her with a hug and a mug of coffee. "It sounded like you needed this. I know I do."

"So you said." Lizzie laughed as she hung her jacket in the hall closet and followed Paige into the kitchen. She just managed to set her mug on the table before being attacked by two small, blonde-haired girls, screeching and giggling as they each grabbed onto a leg.

"Auntie Lizzie, our tree's all ready for Santa," yelled five-year-old Jenna.

"Yup. He's coming tomorrow," Cate said with all her three years of authority. She tugged at Lizzie's hand. "Come, see."

"He's not coming tomorrow," Jenna said, shaking her finger at Cate. "He's coming . . . soon."

Lizzie allowed herself to be pulled into the living room by Jenna while Cate rode staunchly on her left foot. They all fell in a heap on the tan-colored Berber carpet in front of the tree.

"Wow," said Lizzie in appreciation. "It's humongous. I'll bet your daddy needed a ladder to put that angel on top. Or did you do it, Cate?" She grabbed Cate and tussled with her while Jenna leapt on her back.

Paige came in, clapping her hands for attention. "Y'all are worse than a house full of boys. Now, let Auntie Lizzie get up and you girls go get dressed. Then you can go and play in the basement until your daddy gets back."

The girls looked at each other, giggled and gave Lizzie a final push backward before running off up the stairs.

Lizzie lay where she'd landed, staring at the ceiling. "Nap time."

Paige set both coffee mugs on the glass-topped coffee table. "Okay, I'll be the shrink. You be the patient. What's on your mind, young lady?"

"I'm confused, doctor."

"Nothing new. End of consultation. That will be two evenings of babysitting service, please."

"Yikes, your rates have skyrocketed." Lizzie laughed, pushing herself up off the floor. She flopped down on the couch with Paige. "But seriously, I am confused. One of the teachers told me he thought Derek Alton had lived here a long time ago. And then last night, Lucille Miller said his picture did look familiar. And also, she'd thought the same thing about Xenia Henshaw when she moved here years ago."

"Not so strange. Haven't you ever thought you've seen someone before? Do you think the two suspicions are related?"

"Well, the two situations are very similar. Is there a connection or is it coincidence? Or, am I trying to force a connection in this? Xenia was interested in coming to the book club and hearing

Derek speak. She said it was because she liked his books. That's the only connection."

"But something not sitting right?" Paige took a sip of her coffee.

Lizzie sighed. "I just don't know. I guess I was hoping if I told you, you'd spot the crux and say something most profound."

"Sorry, no profundity here today. I do have some dirty dishes, though."

Lizzie made a face. "You're still planning on coming to the concert tonight?"

"Of course. The dishes will be washed by then. Besides, I wouldn't miss it. Will it be great?"

"It better. Last night was a bust."

"Ah, bad rehearsal, good concert."

Lizzie finished her coffee, had another and stayed a couple of hours longer, talking to Paige. She left with a quick kiss for everyone. What if, she wondered, she just confronted Xenia about her past? What would she say?

Lizzie turned left on Yancy and headed into town. She parked in front of the Corners Realty but spotted the "closed" sign from the car. Odd, for a Saturday. She wanted to talk face-to-face, not via voice mail, so she decided to leave it for another day.

The phone was ringing as she entered the house. She grabbed it on the final ring before it went to the message.

"Is this Lizzie Turner?" a woman's voice asked.

"Yes, this is she."

"I was sorry to hear about the shooting at your house. I greatly admired Derek Alton's writing. Now, dear, I was just wondering if he talked to you about this new book he was writing. If he mentioned any of the characters in it?"

"No, he didn't. That would have been his topic for the book club meeting, but of course, he never made it there."

She couldn't properly hear the murmured response. "Who is this?" Lizzie asked.

"Oh, just a reader. Thanks anyway." She hung up.

Lizzie looked at the receiver a moment, as if to glean further information from it. She shrugged her shoulders and hung up, then went in search of her vacuum cleaner. She needed to get some serious housework done and leave enough time for her session with Andie, and a light snack before the big event.

Chapter Twenty-three

◇◇◇

"There are many things that are unbelievable," said Poirot. "Especially before breakfast, is it not?"

THE ADVENTURE OF THE CHRISTMAS PUDDING—AGATHA CHRISTIE

Lizzie straightened her long black skirt, after putting on her black shoes with the midheight heel that gave her the right amount of support for two hours of standing. She checked the mirror one final time. Black jersey wrap top, small, discreet silver studs in her ears. She grabbed her purse, her music binder and a light jacket and left.

At the church, the choristers made their way to the risers for a warm-up and quick rehearsal. They had an hour in which to get it right before the doors would be opened to the public. The orchestra was busy tuning, and spouses who had been talked into taking tickets at the door and handing out programs waited at the back.

Stanton Giles strode in, had a brief talk with the orchestra's concertmaster and then called for quiet. He led them through five minutes of warm-up before turning to the Britten.

Lizzie's fingers tingled. She always loved this part the best. As hoped, all of last night's mistakes had disappeared, heads were up out of the music watching Giles and cues were not missed. She knew the concert would be great.

After about half an hour, the stage director gave them final instructions and they filtered back to their assigned room to await the curtain.

Lizzie joined a small group of sopranos at the far end of the table discussing the latest George Clooney movie in town. She spotted Lucille, head buried in her music, mouthing words to herself, off in a corner. Finally, the knock on the door, and they went out into the hall to line up in order for the walk onto the risers.

From what Lizzie could see, the church was packed. People were scurrying to take their seats and the emcee went through his usual welcome and warning about turning off cell phones. Then they were singing. She felt transported, away from the audience, away from Derek Alton, away from Mark . . . eyes riveted on Giles, the music filling her body and soul. All too soon, it was over and the choir bowed on cue to a standing ovation, then filed out.

After turning in her music to the choir librarian, Lizzie made her way to the reception hall in the church basement and was immediately surrounded by friends.

"Great concert," said Brad.

Paige hugged her. "You looked and sounded terrific. And, Mark was here but left right after."

"At least he came," Lizzie said, smiling, although she was totally disappointed he'd ducked out.

Molly and Bob appeared at her side, with Lucille in pursuit.

"I so enjoyed it, honey," Molly said, giving her a warm hug. The dazzling greens, yellows and blues of her Indian sari looked festive although slightly out of place. *Just how many countries are on her agenda?* "I've always loved the Britten. What did you think, Bob?"

Bob shifted from one foot to the other. He nodded his head. "Yup, it was good."

"And which piece did you enjoy the most?" Lucille demanded.

Bob swallowed hard. "Umm, the last one."

Lucille snorted. "You'd probably say, 'Because it was the last one,' if I asked you why. So, I'm not going to." She gave his cheek a friendly swat and moved away.

"I don't mean to be rude," he said, "but maybe we could leave real soon, Molly?" He looked pointedly at Lucille's retreating back.

Molly laughed. "Of course, I just wanted to let Lizzie know what I thought. Let's go, then. We can have some eats at my place." She gave Lizzie another hug.

Bob did the same and they left. Lizzie looked for Paige but she was talking to someone Lizzie didn't know, so she didn't disturb them.

"Great concert," George Havers said, slinging an arm around Lizzie's shoulder.

Lizzie thanked him and gave his wife, Sandra, a hug. "It's so nice to see you again, Sandra. It's been a while."

"It has, but I've been reading all about you," Sandra said, suddenly serious.

"Yeah. There's that."

"It was such a good concert. I enjoyed it very much." She gave Lizzie's arm a squeeze and then maneuvered George toward the food.

After talking to Nathaniel, Sally-Jo and Jacob, and several teachers, Lizzie eased her way toward the door and made her escape. She was exhausted when she reached home. No cats when she opened the door. She found them asleep on her bed and it didn't take her long to join them.

Chapter Twenty-four

◇◇◇

"Let's lay out what we've got so far," she said briskly.

BURN—NEVADA BARR

Sunday morning. An espresso and the *Birmingham News*, both enjoyed in bed. Both cats content, curled up against Lizzie's legs. Soft classical music on the NPR station playing in the background. A good start to the morning. Lizzie had put her run on hold for the day. Eventually, she crawled out of bed, shrugged into her robe and padded downstairs to start breakfast.

Waffles it would be. She mixed up the batter and got it cooking in the Cuisinart griddle while making herself another espresso. The cats wandered in and checked their dishes, noisily attacking the food she'd left them. Lizzie leaned back against the counter and smiled. All was good in her world.

The shot shattered the kitchen door window and her serenity. It slammed into an upper cabinet door, just inches from where Lizzie stood. She dropped to the ground. The cats scattered. She eyed the cup in her hand and finished drinking. *At least I didn't spill my espresso. I must be in shock.*

She peered around the end of the counter, toward the back door, but couldn't see any movement. Just shards of glass all over the floor. The phone sat on the counter across the room, but she'd be out of sight if she stayed low. She took great care in setting her cup down on the floor and crab-walked over, pulled down the phone and dialed 911. She'd have to round up the cats and lock them in her bedroom before they got into the glass. She continued her crab-walk into the hall, dared to stand and sprinted upstairs. She found them huddled under her bed. After reassuring them, she closed the bedroom door and had made it to the bottom of the stairs as the sirens turned onto the street.

Nathaniel pounded on her front door, calling her name. She let him in and quickly explained what had happened. Officer Craig was the first one through the door.

"What happened? Are you all right?" She sounded concerned, Lizzie thought gratefully.

"Someone just took a shot at me. I was standing in the kitchen." She pointed the way.

"You just stay here with your neighbor while we check it out. And stay away from windows, you hear?"

Lizzie heeded and allowed herself to lean into the comfort of Nathaniel's arm around her shoulders. A few minutes later, Craig rejoined them. "I'm going to help search outside. I'll close your living room drapes and then you can go sit in there and wait. I've contacted the chief. He's on his way." She trailed a mixture of leaves and dirt into the living room and back out to the door.

Lizzie let out the breath she'd been holding, half expecting to hear someone shoot Officer Craig. She led the way into the living room and sat on the settee, her legs tucked up under her. "I could sure use another espresso."

Nathaniel chuckled, although it sounded strained. "I was thinking of a Jack Daniels, myself. I wasn't quite sure that what I heard was a gunshot, but I thought I'd better check. I did think, 'Oh no, not again,' though."

Lizzie glanced at the navy bathrobe Nathaniel was wearing, his multicolored striped pajamas poking out at the bottom, brown moccasin slippers on his feet. It looked like he was having a slow Sunday morning, too.

It didn't take long for Mark to make it over to her house. She heard his car door slam, and a few minutes later, he burst into the living room. He sat beside Lizzie and put his arm around her, kissing her forehead. "Are you sure you're not hurt?"

"I'm physically fine. My nerves are shot, though. So to speak."

"What happened?"

"I had an espresso while I was waiting for my waffle to be ready—Holy Moses, my waffle." She leapt off the couch but Mark grabbed her hand.

"Don't go in there. I'll check on it. Just sit down and wait here."

She nodded and obeyed. A couple of minutes later he was back. "Not edible, I'm afraid, but the griddle had cut off before igniting. So, you were waiting. Standing where?"

"Leaning against the counter facing the back-yard. And all of a sudden, I heard this loud noise and my window in the back door shattered. I dropped to the ground and crawled over to the phone."

Mark frowned. "I'm going to take a look. You

stay sitting here with Mr. Creely and try to relax. Do not go near any windows or doors, you hear?"

Lizzie nodded and shivered.

Mark looked at her a few more seconds and went back into the kitchen. Lizzie noticed with concern that his limp was more pronounced. Usually, she didn't give it a second thought. She knew he didn't, and as yet, he hadn't even explained to her how he was injured. She assumed it was during his stint in the army. A time in his life he wasn't ready to share with her. *He must be exhausted.*

She listened but couldn't quite make out what the officers were shouting to each other outside. She stood, hesitated a moment, and then walked over to the window, pulling the drapes back slightly to get a look outside. Four police cars, two with overhead lights still flashing, were parked at odd angles in her driveway. Mark's Jeep was at the curb. She could see Craig and two other officers checking the driveway and neighbors' yards. The neighbors were all probably getting an eyeful.

She glanced at her car. Had Andrea been right? Was someone was trying to kill her? She shuddered.

"Why don't you come back and sit down, my dear?" Nathaniel suggested.

"I'm too antsy. Sorry. Maybe I'll go upstairs and

get dressed. You really don't have to stay, Nathaniel. I do so appreciate your coming over, though." She put her hand on his arm and squeezed it.

He looked down at his own clothing. "You're right. I'll go on home and get dressed also. I'll be back in a little while, though. Or if they kick you out again, just come next door."

Lizzie gave a small, nervous laugh. "They'd better not. I want some answers."

She saw him out the door then ran upstairs, taking care not to scare the cats as she opened the bedroom door. "It's me, babies. I'm going to get dressed. You two just stay up here for a while. Everything will be okay." She moved over to the windows, keeping to the wall, and pulled the curtains shut.

She quickly pulled on black jeans and a pink long-sleeved T, adding a lightweight fleece zippered jacket and a pair of black Keds on her feet. It took just a couple of minutes to brush her teeth, add some eye shadow and lipstick and run a brush through her hair before tying it back in a ponytail. She felt energized from the action. Just sitting around waiting was getting her down.

Mark reentered the house through the front door as Lizzie reached the bottom step. He shook his head. "There's not much to go on. Maybe we'll find some casings in a yard, once we figure out the angle the shot came from. How are you feeling?"

"I'm a bit shaky but good to go. I want some answers, Mark. What's this all about?"

"I was hoping you could tell me. The first thing that comes to mind is Derek Alton's murder. Either the killer thinks you saw something . . ."

"That's what Andie thinks."

"What?"

"Andie Mason thinks the killer thinks I spotted him or her and is trying to silence me. But if that were the case, it's not someone from around here. Because I would already have told you who it was and you would have arrested them." She sat down with a thud, reluctant to hear the other part of Mark's theory.

"Or, maybe you didn't see the killer but instead saw something that might eventually click with you and you'll realize who it is. That's his or her fear."

Lizzie brightened at the thought. *She wasn't the target.*

"Or Alton wasn't the target. You were."

Lizzie shrank back into the seat and folded her arms across her chest. "There's no reason to kill me. Not because of Derek's murder and not because of any other reason."

Mark pulled over a chair and sat facing her, knees almost touching. "Are you sure? Can you think of anyone who's upset with you? Someone you've angered or who threatened you, even if it's totally off base?"

Her mind was blank. She shook her head. "No, I can't think of anyone."

"Someone from work?"

She thought back to the interviews and interactions she'd had at the school over the past few months. Nothing came to mind. The same for the literacy class, choir and jogging. "No. Nothing and no one. Nothing I do would elicit such an extreme reaction. I'm sure of that, Mark." She looked at him.

"What if it had something to do with you? Maybe a jealous former girlfriend?" She realized too late that she'd spoken the words out loud. Mark's eyes clouded over as he thought about it. Just how many former girlfriends were there, she wondered?

"That's unlikely, but I wonder about the job. Maybe someone's holding a grudge and might try something like that to get even with me. I come across all sorts of wackos, even here in Ashton Corners."

"You didn't warn me about the hazards of dating a cop," she said with a small smile. "That's quite a stretch, though, don't you think?"

He looked at her and smiled. "Probably. I shouldn't even float that theory. Doesn't do much for my romantic credentials."

Lizzie laughed. Despite the terror and the very real threat, she was so happy that they seemed back to normal. "You've got that right. But seriously, I don't think I'm the target. I can't be. I live a very ordinary life. Except for when Frank Telford was killed. But that murderer is behind bars."

"With his trial coming up next year. I wonder if someone doesn't want you testifying. What about the girlfriend?"

"I can't see her as a killer. And in any case, I'm not the only one who will be called to testify. What about Molly and Bob and Sally-Jo? Gads, the entire book club." Her imagination got the better of her for a minute. "Do you think it's part of a massive plot? You can't protect us all."

Mark reached out and grabbed her hand. "Whoa. Let's think small to start with. I can and will protect you. And I'll also have a chat with the girlfriend, just to be on the safe side."

Mark stood, pulling Lizzie up also, and wrapped her in his arms. "I've got to get back out there. What are your plans for the rest of the day? You're going to see your mama soon, aren't you?"

"Yeah, right after lunch. Then, I've got a lot of stuff to do around here, including getting that window replaced."

"I'll send Ozzie Verge along to keep an eye on you."

"Oh no, Mark. Is it really necessary? I don't like the idea of someone following me and I'm sure there's a lot more important police work to be doing."

"You've just had a shot fired through your window. The second in two weeks. Yeah, I think it's necessary. Don't worry, Verge'll stay in his car. Indulge me, Lizzie, and don't give me any grief on this, okay?"

Lizzie nodded. Reluctantly.

Lizzie found her mama sitting in her favorite chair, holding the Christmas ornament from last weekend. She wondered if Evelyn carried it around with her all the time. Did it take her to a place of good memories? She hoped so.

While her mama seemed more alert and even answered the odd question, Lizzie knew not to get her hopes up too high. It did give her the impetus to track down the manager before she left and ask about taking Evelyn Turner home for Christmas.

"I know it's important for you to have her at your place, Ms. Turner," said Mrs. Farthington, sitting back in her chair. They were in her office, a small but highly efficient–looking space melding her obvious taste for contemporary design with the comfort of her clients. The chair Lizzie sat in had a straight back but also loads of padding to soothe any tired body.

"I don't think you realize just the amount of attention your mama requires," she went on, "not necessarily physical, although she needs assistance in dressing and dining often. But she tends to wander when left on her own. And, you can't be with her every minute, I'm sure. She also gets agitated when she leaves Magnolia Manor and its gardens. And while you see some improvement in her demeanor and you're wanting a wonderful family Christmas, I don't see that as the outcome. I'm sorry."

Lizzie closed her eyes briefly and nodded. She'd sort of expected this and thought she'd just press her point, but now, she wasn't so sure.

"She is your mama, and if you insist, we will, of course, follow your wishes. But I don't think that it's wise."

"I understand, Mrs. Farthington. If I look at it from Mama's point, it's better she stays here. And so she will. Thank you for taking such good care of her."

Lizzie stood and they shook hands. She left feeling down but realized it was mainly because her fanciful thoughts of the perfect Christmas were strictly that. She did have an invitation to Molly's and she would stop by to see Evelyn before church on Christmas Eve and on Christmas Day for a visit. That was just how things were.

Chapter Twenty-five

◇◇◇

Mystic River is what I'm going down, without a paddle.

A VEILED DECEPTION—ANNETTE BLAIR

Lizzie quickly showered after her run the next morning and ate her breakfast of granola and fruit, made sure the cats were okay, then walked out the door, ready for the final week of classes before the Christmas break.

She couldn't see who the officer in the cruiser was but thought the build was different. Right uniform, though. They must have switched while she was inside. When she had parked in the lot at the school, she got a better look. Officer Craig. She walked over to the police car and leaned toward the open window.

"I'll be here until three P.M. today so it's really not necessary for you to hang around," Lizzie said in as pleasant a tone as she could muster.

Craig nodded. "Thanks. I've got a lot of things I could be following up on. You just call my cell when you're ready to leave, you hear?" She handed her business card to Lizzie. "And if you don't I'll be forced to stay by your side wherever you go. Just remember that."

Lizzie felt her spine snap to attention until she noticed the twinkle in Craig's eyes.

"Heaven forbid," she answered with a smile. "Point taken. I will follow instructions." *Okay, so maybe Amber Craig wasn't so hard-nosed after all. Just doing her job. That's what Mark had said. Maybe he was right. Maybe I should try being pleasant in return,* she thought as she walked toward the school.

Lizzie spent the morning in the library writing more reports. By noon, her brain called for fresh air but she wanted to check the staff room and see if there was anyone who hadn't been in on Friday when she and Sally-Jo did their questioning.

The first person she spotted was Wendy Innes, standing at the counter, refilling the coffeemaker. Lizzie grabbed her mug out of the cupboard and waited to pour herself some coffee. Wendy looked over at her and smiled.

"You've worked at this school for quite some time, haven't you, Wendy?" Lizzie asked.

"Oh my, yes. My entire teaching career and that's over twenty-five years." She laughed, a loud belly laugh that was her trademark. All her students loved making her laugh, just to hear it. What made it so unusual was her size. Lizzie guessed she shopped in the petite section at Sears.

"So, you've lived in Ashton Corners at least that long."

"Why, I'm a native, Lizzie. Born and raised here. My daddy owned the Remax Theatre, which is now the Centertown, on Main Street. Not very original, is it? Anyway, I spent my younger days in front of that screen—got in for free, of course—and the rest of my time daydreaming. My folks thought I wasn't good material for nursing or anything that required absolute fierce concentration, so they directed me into teaching."

Lizzie nodded. "Most people tend to come back here to settle after being away at college, don't they?"

"That they do. Now, what's got you thinking along those lines? You feeling warmhearted about our li'l old town?"

Lizzie laughed. "Actually, Ken Wicks and I were talking the other day and he's been here a long time, too. We were talking about Derek Alton."

"Oh dear. That's right. He was shot in your house. How dreadful for you. I imagine it still gives you qualms."

Lizzie nodded, determined not to add any details about yesterday's shooting. "Ken said he thought Derek might have lived here a long time ago but couldn't really be sure. So, I was wondering if anyone else knew if that were so."

"Ken's right, you know. But the reason he wasn't certain is probably because that's not the name Derek Alton went by back then. And he lived here only a couple of years, at that."

"You knew him? Derek Alton's not his real name? What is?"

"I think it was Harry or Harvey, something like that. I didn't really know him or his wife, not more than to nod at. We lived on the same block, you know."

"His wife?" Poor woman probably didn't even know her husband was dead. But why change his name? Was it a writer's pseudonym? But wouldn't his publishers know if that were the case? Mark hadn't mentioned it.

"Oh yes. I'm not really sure what he did, although I guess now I'd say it was writing. And she did office work someplace, I think. Anyway, they moved away and I didn't hear mention of them anymore, although I think he may have left a few broken hearts in his stead. The gossip at the time was that's the reason they moved."

"Would you happen to know where they went?"

"No, I never heard anything more about that. But you should ask Xenia Henshaw over at the Corners Realty."

"She knew them?" *And didn't let on!*

"Knew them? Why, sugar, Xenia was his wife."

"Are you certain? How do you know that?"

"Well, she sold me my new house, that was about ten years ago so I guess it's not so new anymore. She'd gone and changed her name, her hair and her large nose and lost a lot of spare tire

210

from around her middle. I'd only met her once or twice so I didn't catch on right away, but something niggled and then it came to me."

"So who else knows?"

"I have no idea. They didn't get it from me. I called her on it and she eventually admitted it, said she didn't want to be reminded of those terrible days, and I can respect that."

"Wow."

"Uh-huh. The coffee's ready. Let me pour you some."

Lizzie shook her head. "No, thanks. On second thought, I need to go see someone. Thanks, Wendy."

She was halfway to her car when she remembered Officer Craig. But if she phoned her, Craig would want to know where she was going, and when they reached the realty office, she'd probably want to know why. Lizzie took a quick scan around. She didn't see anyone dangerous-looking, especially no one with a gun. She'd do it on her own.

She pulled into a parking spot half a block from the office and hoped Xenia would be there, and be free. She glanced at her watch. She had about forty minutes. She opened the door to the office and found Xenia in the same spot as last time, scrolling through something on the computer screen.

"You're a very busy person, aren't you?" Xenia

211

asked. "I just wish you were coming through that door looking for a listing."

"As it is, Xenia, I'm looking for more information. Like why you didn't tell me about being married to Derek Alton."

The shocked look stayed on Xenia's face only a few seconds but long enough for Lizzie to notice. She felt a certain satisfaction in catching Xenia Henshaw in a lie.

"We aren't married."

Lizzie opened her mouth to respond but Xenia held up her manicured hand.

"We divorced about twenty-three years ago and I hadn't seen him since. I was as surprised as everyone else that he came to town. And his name wasn't Derek Alton at the time we were married, so what I told you was true: I didn't know Derek because he didn't exist." She sat back, a small smug look on her face.

Lizzie toyed with making a smart mark about semantics but decided not to. "What was his real name?"

"Harvey Warren. He changed it when he sent *Judgment* out to a publisher. He'd had so many rejects as Harvey; he hoped to get a fresh start. He even invented a new background, one that didn't include me. Of course, I'd had it by then anyway. We divorced just after moving."

Lizzie wondered if Mark was aware of this. If so, he hadn't told her. Of course, he hadn't told her much of anything lately. "In that case, I'm wondering why you wanted to come to the book club."

"Just as I'd said, I was curious as to how he was doing, what he was writing. For old times' sake, you know."

"How were you about the breakup?"

"How was I? How do you think I was? I'd struggled to keep going, working at a nothing job, while he just stayed home and wrote and gave a couple of night-school classes. That was when he wasn't screwing other women, of course. But it was my decision to leave him. Get that straight."

She stood abruptly, pushing the chair back into the filing cabinet, and walked over to the counter where the coffeemaker sat. She poured a cup, turned and offered it to Lizzie, who shook her head. Xenia shrugged, added some sugar and milk, took a small sip and walked back to the desk.

"And with all that, you still were curious about him, for old times' sake?" Lizzie couldn't keep the skepticism out of her voice.

Xenia shrugged again. "That was then. I changed back to my maiden name and Xenia's my middle name but I felt more like a Xenia—strong and ready for anything. I took the Realtor's course, got some experience and moved back here."

"Why come back?"

"I liked the feel of this town and I wasn't about to go back to my hometown. Too many bad memories and everyone would know the whole Harvey story. At least here, we hadn't done much as a couple so I thought people might not remember. So I made some changes to my appearance and here I am. A new person."

"Nobody guessed?"

"Well, obviously somebody did or you wouldn't have found out about it. But I kept away from the old neighborhood and anyone I might have known and put a lot of time and money into publicizing my new profile. Often people will readily believe what you tell them, you know." She was silent a few minutes, and Lizzie let her sit there thinking, wondering where her thoughts were wandering.

"I guess a part of me wanted to rub Harvey's nose in it," Xenia finally admitted. "Show him I was a successful businesswoman. That's why I wanted to go to the book club." She took a long sip and stared at Lizzie, her eyes challenging.

"How did you feel when you heard he was dead?"

"Shocked." She paused. "Yes, shocked, but that was all. There was nothing else left to feel."

Lizzie glanced at the clock that hung on the wall behind Xenia. "I've got to get back to school." She stood and was about to thank Xenia when she thought of another question.

"Did you see him at all while he was here?"

Xenia took her time in answering. "Yes. He stopped in for a few minutes on his way to your place, actually. He invited me to the book club and said I'd find what he had to say about his new book to be very interesting."

"What do you think he meant by that?"

"Knowing Harvey, it would have to be something with some shock value."

Chapter Twenty-six

◇◇◇

Okay, I've been stupid in the past. Not consistently stupid, but occasionally stupid.
DEAD RECKONING—CHARLAINE HARRIS

As soon as her afternoon meeting at school ended, Lizzie phoned Officer Craig and waited until the black-and-white cruiser pulled into the parking lot before going out to her car. All she wanted was a quiet evening at home, a treat since the literacy classes were over until the New Year. She neglected to tell Craig about her noon-hour excursion but did mention she didn't have to hang around all evening.

Lizzie gave a small wave as she entered her house. She needed something to eat. Her eyes strayed to the upper cupboard door that had been replaced, along with the back panel where the bullet had lodged after smashing through one can

215

of chickpeas, a box of rice crackers and a vacuum-packed bag of dried cranberries. An uncontrollable shiver snaked through her body. She pulled her eyes away and reached for the phone. Mark answered his cell phone on the third ring.

"I hate to bug you at work but I really need to know if you've had any progress on the shooting?" She couldn't quite keep the desperation out of her voice.

"Are you all right? Has anything else happened? Is Officer Craig still with you?"

Lizzie gave a small laugh. "Hadn't you told me that a trained investigator should ask only one question at a time?"

Mark let out a deep breath. "You got me. I had some trouble with that course at police training. Are you okay?"

"I suppose. I was about to make supper and I opened the cupboard and it all just seemed sort of overwhelming. I just thought if you had any news, it would help." Lizzie sat down hard on a chair.

"I get what you're saying but other than telling you the bullet we dug out of your cupboard matches the one that killed Alton, there's not much. I've got some leads we're checking but nothing definite as yet. Look, I'm going to take a break, walk Patchett and then stop by the Oasis for a quick bite. Why don't you meet me there?"

"Okay, but why don't I walk Patchett for you?"

"That would be a help. Can you do it now and we'll hook up around six?"

Lizzie glanced at the clock. "I can and will. See you then."

Hmm. Not bad. Maybe they were back on track. And also, she might get some more answers. Of course, she had information for him, too, although she'd have to leave out some of the details, such as how many times she'd talked to Xenia. She'd tell him what she'd learned though. She quickly changed into a black-and-white knit top and jeans, fed the cats, grabbed her car keys and stopped only long enough to tell Officer Craig about her destination. She noticed a slight lifting of eyebrows, then a nod.

After a half-hour challenging walk around a few blocks, Lizzie returned Patchett indoors, gave him some treats and refilled his water dish. She knew she was in need of dog-training classes. She'd assumed that filling in for Mark at the classes he couldn't make would do the trick. But Mark had made it to all of them so far. She wondered if there were any classes for the walkers only. Either that or she might soon have an arm pulled out of its socket.

She drove over to Main Street and parked in the side lot next to Mark's Jeep. Officer Craig pulled in behind her and met her halfway between their cars.

"I'm assuming I'll hear from the chief if he needs me again," she said, and she waited until Lizzie had entered the diner before driving off.

Mark followed Lizzie home after their dinner then waited until Officer Craig arrived before going back to the station. It had been a relaxed meal, with Mark discouraging any talk about the investigation. At least Lizzie felt her personal life had slid back into place. She did have an anxious moment, though, when she told him about her talk with Xenia Henshaw as they left the diner. He was not at all happy that she'd gone against his wishes, although the information she'd found out did please him.

Lizzie sat at her desk in her home office and made a list of people to talk to. Xenia Henshaw was at the top. She needed to find out if *Judgment* was based on fact. And, she wanted to know more about Derek's alleged affairs. Could he be Flynn, his own main character? And if so, who were the women? Was that the reason she'd had two female callers in the last week asking about Derek's new book?

She'd obviously have to start questioning the callers, if there were any more, to find out their identities. She scrolled back through the caller ID list on her phone to see if any of the names and numbers might be listed. She couldn't remember what days the calls came in and the list showed several unknown listings. Maybe they were blocking their calls.

She jotted down one number she didn't recognize. She'd try the reverse phone book, and if no luck, she would try calling it later.

As if sensing her thoughts, the phone rang and she almost dropped the receiver. This caller ID did show. Jensey Pollard.

"Hi, Lizzie. I hope I'm not disturbing anything."

"Not at all, Jensey. I was just catching up on some paperwork. Nothing that can't wait. How are you?"

"Fine. Just fine. But I was wondering the same about you. I heard this afternoon that you'd been shot at. What a shock that must have been. You weren't hurt, I hope."

"No, I wasn't. The shooter must not have been very good." She laughed.

"That's a relief," Jensey said. "And so soon after Derek Alton being killed. I wonder, I shouldn't say anything, but I wonder if that first shot had also been meant for you. Oh dear, such a stupid thing to say. I hope I haven't upset you?"

Lizzie sucked in her breath. "I don't know who would want to shoot me. It's more likely the killer thought I saw him or her. But I didn't."

"Her? Do you really think a woman might have killed him? In all the cozies, women usually choose poison as the method of murder."

But this is real life. "We can't make any assumptions."

"So true. Did he tell you anything that might be a clue? Do you think it might have something to do with his new book? I read somewhere that he said there might be some people not too happy with it."

"You read that? Where?"

Jensey sighed. "I can't remember right now. Maybe in one of the trade magazines. It was a while ago and I've forgotten most of the details. Did he talk about the new plot with you?"

"Like the last time you asked, the answer's the same. No, we didn't talk about it." Lizzie knew she sounded snippy but this was beginning to grate.

"Sorry, dear. I've got a lot on my mind these days. Business and all. I'm probably repeating myself all over the place. I'll let you go now. I just wanted to make sure everything's okay."

"Thanks, Jensey. I appreciate the call. I'll be in again before Christmas for some more presents." *And probably buy way too many books, to make up for my snippiness.*

Lizzie sat holding the receiver for a few minutes before finally putting it back in the cradle. She and Jensey were friendly enough but they never called each other at home. Highly unusual but very nice of her, Lizzie thought, tensing her shoulder muscles and holding them for a count of fifteen,

220

then slowly relaxing. She realized just how uptight she was. No wonder she bordered on rude. Time to give it a rest.

She wandered downstairs, poured a glass of water and leaned against the counter, trying not to think about the whole business. Brie sauntered into the kitchen and did a slow stroll through her legs until Lizzie finally bent down to stroke her back. She pulled out her brush and spent the next few minutes lazily brushing her. To top it off, she opened a new bag of treats, which brought Edam scampering down the stairs, arriving just in time for his own handful of seafood tidbits.

Lizzie picked up her copy of *Judgment* from the kitchen counter and took it into the living room. As she closed the drapes, she could see the police cruiser parked in front of her house, with Officer Craig standing beside the driver's door, probably stretching her legs. She curled up in the bucket chair beside the good reading lamp and started flipping through it again.

The phone disturbed her. She glanced at her watch to see that she'd been reading for over an hour. Another unknown caller.

She didn't recognize the woman's voice, but the question was becoming very familiar.

"I was just wondering," said the somewhat hesitant female voice, "if Derek Alton gave you any information about this new book he was writing?"

"No. Not to me but I'll ask around the book club. If you'll just give me your name and number, I'll get back to you."

"Oh no, that's quite all right. If you don't know, I'm sure no one does."

"Who is this and why are you asking?"

"Idle curiosity, my dear." The caller hung up.

Idle curiosity, my cheese straw! She'd start logging the calls.

Chapter Twenty-seven

◇◇◇

She patted my hand and gave a little laugh. "That's an excellent idea."

STATE FAIR—EARLENE FOWLER

Lizzie stopped by the Corners Realty on her way home from school the next day. If Officer Yost, today's escort, asked why, she planned to say she was thinking of buying a house. Which she did think about once in a while. Just not now. She'd spent most of the afternoon ducking Vanda Striker, but she did want to see Xenia Henshaw. After she'd finished her second reading of *Judgment*, she'd lain awake thinking about the plot, and thinking about the number of female callers over the past week, all with the same question. Why, even Jensey Pollard had asked about Alton's new book. Again.

She'd developed a theory but wasn't quite ready to share it with Mark. She now seriously believed that the callers were worried that Derek might write them into the new novel. But what did they have to hide? The affairs? Were these the same people she'd just finished reading about? Was it really based on his short stay in Ashton Corners and would the sequel be even more revealing?

She wasn't so sure Xenia would be that cooperative but she had to try. This time when she entered the realty office, someone else sat at the main desk. A young woman in her midtwenties, dressed in a baggy orange knit sweater, one hand rocking a baby carrier that sat on the floor beside her, looked up and asked how she could help. Turns out she couldn't. Xenia had taken the day off and was at home nursing a migraine. Lizzie thanked her and left. She knew where Xenia lived. She drove over to the west side of town where the houses were older but still well maintained. Xenia lived in a pale yellow clapboard bungalow. The side wraparound porch looked inviting, even though it lacked furniture. The two bushy cedars on either side of the front steps needed trimming.

Xenia answered the door on the third ring. She looked surprised and less than happy to see Lizzie, who knew she'd better talk her way through the door quickly if she wanted any answers.

"I'm really sorry to bother you at home but I just have to ask you a couple of questions. It won't take more than a few minutes," she promised.

Xenia let out a deep sigh but stepped back to allow Lizzie to enter. The interior didn't follow through with the warmth of the outside appearance. The entry needed a light turned on, which Xenia didn't do. Instead she opened a leaded glass door and led Lizzie into a blue and white living room. It looked like something out of a decorating magazine, but Lizzie shivered in the cool tones.

Lizzie sat in a wing-back chair covered in blue brocade while Xenia sank onto the white leather sofa, her thigh-length black sweater flowing out around her.

"I'm really not much up to talking today," Xenia said, putting on some dark sunglasses that had been on the end table.

"I promise this will be fast. You'd said Derek, or Harvey, rather, had affairs when you lived in town before. Did he ever talk about them?"

Xenia's bottom jaw dropped open. "What? You've got a nerve asking a question like that."

"Not really. You brought the topic up last time we spoke. I just wondered if you knew the names of any of the women. It happened so long ago, I thought you'd be well over it. Surely you didn't carry a grudge after all these years?"

Xenia played with the bottom fringe of her sweater. "No, of course not. He meant nothing to me now. He did have several short affairs. That was his style. He needed an ego boost, I guess. I put up with it for a while but then I couldn't take it anymore."

"And that's why you divorced?"

"What do you think? Of course it was."

"You said you'd loved *Judgment*?" Lizzie asked. "Do you think he would use himself as the main character and write about his affairs?"

"Actually, you could say I wasn't quite truthful about that. I had no desire to read it but I needed a logical excuse to go to your little club."

Lizzie's eyes narrowed at that comment.

Xenia sat with her own eyes narrowed, obviously giving the question some serious thought. Finally, she replied. "But to answer your question, it's possible. He'd been struggling with his writing. He just couldn't do characterization. Couldn't get into the heads of his characters. At least, that's what the rejection letters all said. So maybe that's how he overcame the problem. He wrote from his own viewpoint. What a bugger."

Lizzie raised her eyebrows.

The phone rang. "Excuse me while I take that. I'm waiting for an important client call."

She left the room and Lizzie heard a door shut farther down the hall and then the ringing stopped. She stood and wandered around the room, glancing at book titles in the small bookcase next to the sofa. *Judgment* was tucked in between two nonfiction titles. So, what else had she lied about?

Or maybe she just hadn't gotten around to reading it. Possible.

A small circular end table sat next to the bookcase. A clear Rubbermaid container sat on it. Lizzie glanced at the handwritten white label. "Book Club." Surprised, Lizzie took a closer look. The container had cookies in it. She opened the lid and looked at the peppermint chocolate chip cookies, the kind Derek had said he carried everywhere with him. She quickly closed the lid and wondered about the label. Why bring cookies to the book club?

Lizzie heard a door close and footsteps getting closer. She managed to sit back down just as the door opened.

"I'm sorry about that. Realtors are not allowed sick days. They need to be available to clients twenty-four/seven."

Lizzie made sympathetic sounds. "If you have a chance," she said, "I wish you'd read *Judgment* and let me know what you think of it. Especially if you think it's based on reality. I can lend you my copy."

"I'll think about it. I hadn't wanted to read anything of his. I really haven't wanted to know what was going on in his mind, not for a long time now."

Lizzie drove home slowly. Xenia sounded like she was telling the truth. It didn't seem like she had anything to hide. She was forthright in her opinion of Derek and in sharing how she felt about him and the breakup of their marriage. Or so it seemed.

But what about those cookies? Derek's favorite and the only kind he would eat. He had said he always brought his own supply. Although, if his ex-wife thought he would be visiting, it's possible she would have made some for him. But they weren't even friends anymore, so why would she? And the book. Why borrow Lizzie's copy when she had her own? Clearly, she didn't know this woman at all.

The next morning, Lizzie did her usual early run, Officer Craig following in the cruiser. As Lizzie passed Nathaniel's place at the start of her run she did a double take. The silver Prius sat parked in the driveway. Awfully early for a visit. She soon forgot about it until on her way back she glanced at Nathaniel's front window. A gray-haired woman appeared briefly, and either she liked casual wear or she had on a robe. The Prius hadn't moved.

Lizzie thought about it while she got ready for school. Surely, she'd been mistaken. The robe was merely a colorful long sweater. Maybe he'd gotten a new housecleaner and it was a smock. That had to be it. But his house must be very clean for the amount of time that Prius spent in his driveway. She was dying to know what was going on but not about to burst into his house and ask. She'd have to come up with a plan.

With just three days to go, the school gym had been blocked out for the individual classrooms to practice their pageant numbers. Lizzie's schedule would revolve around these rehearsals as she tried to put together some fill material to talk about between performances. She sat on an uncomfortable plastic chair next to the door. A couple of the mamas who had volunteered for general duty sat close by, critiquing the kids and discussing the latest sale at Walmart. When their own children were onstage, they sat in rapt silence.

By noon, half of the classes taking part had finished and Lizzie had pages of notes. She knew what her evening would be spent doing. At lunch, she suggested to Sally-Jo that they go to Tessa's Tex-Mex around the corner for some tacos. She was dying to get out of the school.

"Did you finish *Judgment*?" Lizzie asked as they waited for the Creole chicken tacos they'd both ordered.

"Three chapters left to go. I'll finish it tonight. If, as you think, it might be a fictionalized version of Ashton Corners and some of its more desperate women, I had no idea what's been brewing underneath the genteel exterior. So, what else have you learned lately that you're holding back?"

"Hah. I've learned it's true that Derek Alton used to live here, before he wrote *Judgment*. He changed his name when he sent the book out to publishers."

"How do you know that?"

"His former wife, Xenia Henshaw, confirmed it."

"Get away. Married? She was his wife? Give details, girl!"

Their food arrived, and between bites, Lizzie continued. "They were married back when he was Harvey Warren. She returned to her maiden name after they divorced and then moved back here and reinvented herself."

"Wow. Did she admit it?"

"Eventually."

"Do you think she killed him?"

Lizzie shrugged. "Hard to say. She says no and there's no proof."

"I truly don't believe a woman scorned, especially if multiple times, is likely to forgive and forget," Sally-Jo finally said.

"But it was over twenty years ago. You think she's still carrying a grudge?"

"Or maybe even a torch. Some women just like to lead tormented lives. That could be part of the reason she moved back here. You know, memories around every corner, that sort of thing."

"That's a pathetic thing to do, isn't it?" Lizzie asked, washing the last bite of her taco down with a long drink of sweet tea.

"Who's to say this woman is normal? Or not?

229

We don't know her. She could be really good at putting up a façade. Just look at all the serial killers who became serial because no one could imagine them doing such a thing. We believe what feels good."

"Wow, you're very philosophical today. You could be right. However, Xenia has an airtight alibi for the time Derek was murdered. She was showing a house to a client."

"She could have hired someone to kill him. She probably can afford it."

Lizzie sat thinking. "Okay, say you're right. But why try to kill me, too?"

"To stop you from nosing around?"

"Sounds like a drastic way of doing that, don't you think?"

"Uh-huh. But that's the only way it could work, if she's the killer. What's nagging at you?"

"Those cookies. If she still hates him, why bake his favorite cookies? Not only favorite, but also the only kind he can eat? And why plan to bring them to the book club?"

"Maybe the container originally had something else in it that she was planning to bring."

"Like what?"

Sally-Jo shrugged. "Not a clue."

"If she was planning to bring cookies for us all, why do that? She didn't know any of us, didn't know we eat as much as we discuss. She had no reason to bring food."

Sally-Jo shrugged. "I'm all out of ideas. I'll tell you, though, I'm so relieved we're finding out he has a past here in town. It makes me look so much less likely a suspect, don't you think?

Lizzie reached across the table and squeezed Sally-Jo's hand. "Yes, it does. But back to the cookies. What if she was planning on poisoning Derek by making the switch at the meeting?"

"What? We'd all get poisoned in that case."

"Not if she managed to pass the plate to him or fake it in some way."

Sally-Jo was silent for a few moments. "Hard to prove."

"The proof is in the cookies."

"I have two words for you. 'Chief Dreyfus.'"

Andie was waiting on her doorstep when she arrived home. Lizzie told Officer Craig she'd be home for the rest of the day and evening, while Andie did her usual inspection of Lizzie's car. Officer Craig watched in silence and slowly shook her head. She told Lizzie her replacement would arrive shortly and be there for the next shift.

"So, how is the studying going, Andie?" Lizzie asked after they'd taken their jackets off and gotten settled. She passed Andie a glass of orange juice and poured one for herself.

Andie groaned. "I tried what you suggested last week and I thought it was helping but I did a self-quiz last night and I suck." She made a gagging gesture.

Lizzie sat looking at her for a few moments before suggesting, "Maybe you're trying too hard at this point. If you thought it was a good study method and you were learning, you probably were. Once you added the pressure of the quiz, you tensed up and forgot. Maybe we should try some relaxation techniques, too."

"Oh yeah . . . like what?"

"Some deep breathing and maybe some positive visualization. You know, imagine your end goal—a good grade on the exam—and how you'll feel getting it. Then try to study with that feeling in mind."

Andie eyed her suspiciously. "You think that stuff really works?"

"It does for me. And it certainly can't hurt. The deep breathing is a good technique to try anytime you're feeling a bit tense. And it's easy. Sit up straight and we'll try it."

Andie sat up and her black T with red splotches slid up her tummy. She pulled it down and mimicked Lizzie, drawing her breath in until her tummy pushed out. She made a face but continued to do nine reps.

By the time they'd finished the exercise, they were both totally relaxed.

Chapter Twenty-eight

◇◇◇

It was going to be a long night.
DROPPED DEAD STITCH—MAGGIE SEFTON

The doorbell rang and Lizzie quickly put the open bottle of wine down on the counter. She'd asked Mark to stop by on his way home from work. She planned to tell him about Ellen Germain and also about her Xenia Henshaw theory, but now that he was here, she was having second and third thoughts. For starters, he'd be mad that she'd done as much as she had. For seconds, he'd think she was nuts. Neither option pleased her.

She glanced in the hall mirror as she passed by and paused long enough to retwist her hair and pin it up. She noticed Edam hovering on the top stair, having revisited his intention of walking down at the sound of the bell. "It's okay baby, just Mark."

When she opened the door, Mark quickly entered, closed the door behind him and gave her a big kiss.

"That's such a great way to end a long, tiring day," he whispered into her neck.

She pulled back slightly and gave him a quick kiss, feeling a bit guilty that his day wasn't yet over. "How about a glass of red wine while we talk? Or, I have some Coors in the fridge."

"Talk, huh? Fine. Red wine would be good."

She led him into the living room, where she'd already closed the drapes, gave him a gentle shove backward onto the settee, poured them both some wine and then sank down beside him. They each took a couple of sips and then she leaned back and decided to just get it over with. Ellen Germain would be the easier story to tell, especially since all she really knew was that Ellen had attended the same college as Sally-Jo and might therefore have known Derek Alton. Pure speculation.

Mark had pulled his notebook out and jotted some points then tucked it away and reached for Lizzie. She grabbed his hands, took a deep breath and filled him in on her visit to Xenia Henshaw. It didn't take long.

"And just what was Officer Yost doing at this time?"

"I had said I was thinking about buying a new house," she said, her cheeks turning an embarrassing shade of red. "But you know what's really interesting about all this is a Rubbermaid container of cookies that was sitting on an end table in the living room. It had a hand-printed label on it that said, 'Book Club.' So I assumed she'd been planning to bring the cookies to the meeting."

"This is leading somewhere, isn't it?"

"Of course. Remember I told you that Derek Alton said he'd be bringing his own cookies? Peppermint chocolate chip cookies. Well, that's what was in her container. And being his ex-wife, she would have known all about his allergies, right?"

Mark sat, glass in hand, staring at Lizzie and obviously processing what she'd just told him. "That's a fairly popular cookie. Lots of people, me included, like them. You think she was going to take them to the book club and substitute them for the ones Alton brought?"

"I do. But it doesn't mean a thing unless they're either strong enough to give him a whale of an allergic reaction or she was meaning to poison him."

Mark didn't say anything for a few minutes. It was better than him laughing outright at her, but not much. Finally he sat forward.

"There could be any number of innocent explanations, Lizzie."

"Or not."

He finally nodded. "I guess I'm going to have to get a warrant and have some of those cookies tested. That's what you were hoping, isn't it?"

"Yes. I mean, it could just be a nice gesture on her part but I sort of doubt that. And, since she did know all about his traveling with his own cookie stash, what a great way to just knock the guy off."

"Motive?"

"I don't know. Maybe she's still seething that he left her. Or she feels all those affairs he had made a laughing stock of her."

"That's not too likely since she's built up such a successful real estate business."

"You're right. But he did pay her a visit on his way over to my place. What if something he said to her just made her go off the deep end?"

"And pick up a rifle, follow him and shoot him?"

Lizzie nodded and took another, longer, sip of her wine.

"It must have been a hell of a conversation. She has an alibi but I'd better check it out more thoroughly." He also took another sip. "So how do the cookies fit in? She would have prepared them before that point."

"Maybe they'd talked when he first arrived in town and something he said at that point made her want to make up a batch of his cookies and tamper with them. She called about coming to the book club the day after I met him in the store. He would have had time to call her."

Mark didn't have an answer for that.

"And there's more, but not about Xenia Henshaw. I've been getting phone calls from women wanting to know if Derek mentioned anything to me about the content of his new book. It's supposed to be a sequel to the first, *Judgment*, and if, as I suspect, it was based on people in

Ashton Corners, then there might be a few women with secrets they don't want revealed. Even if it is fiction. Xenia Henshaw might be one of them."

"Did he tell you about the new book?"

"Only that it was in the early writing stages. It would be good to read the manuscript. Did you find a copy of it?"

"I'd have to take a look at the inventory. We did go through his computer but I was interested only in emails that might have pointed to someone he knew here in town."

"Okay. Could we maybe go to your office and see if the manuscript is on the computer? Is that where it is now?"

Mark groaned. "I was so hoping for an evening away from work." He downed the rest of his wine. "I guess we might as well get this theory checked out." He stood and held out a hand to her.

"I'd imagine you'd like to be in on this," he said with a grin, "and since you've have read the first book, it would be a good idea to have you check this one. Even though it's against my better judgment."

Lizzie glanced at him quickly to see if he'd meant the double entendre. He grinned. He had.

Chapter Twenty-nine

◇◇◇

Truth obliged her to acknowledge some small
share in the action . . .
SENSE AND SENSIBILITY—JANE AUSTEN

L izzie felt oddly contented as they drove to the
police station. It was nice not to have a police
escort but rather to be sitting beside one. The main
one. She also loved driving through town on a
clear night at this time of year. The Christmas
lights twinkled from the store windows, main-
taining the totally white lights theme agreed upon
by the downtown business association.

The city had gone all out, decorating the
massive fifty-foot fir tree in the town square in a
dazzling display of colors—being the only ones
allowed to deviate from the theme—while white
lights were strung along the band gazebo. The
Ashton Corners police station had even decked
itself out in white lights strung along the roofline.

"Nice," Lizzie said, nodding at the lights. "I
hope you didn't have to climb up there and attach
them."

Mark laughed. "Nope. It's a town building. Town
responsibility. Now, you haven't seen my lights at
home yet. We're about overdue for a dinner there
and I'm curious what you'll think of them."

"Dinner sounds great. And you've aroused my curiosity about the lights."

"That's not all I'm hoping to arouse," Mark said softly, as he exited his Jeep.

Lizzie grinned and slid out her side. He grabbed her hand and held it until they entered through the side door. A uniformed officer sat behind the main desk, concentrating on his computer screen. He snapped to attention when he saw it was the chief who'd entered.

"Still quiet, Henson?" Mark asked.

"Yes, sir. I'm just trying to input some of those old reports, sir."

"Great," Mark answered as he steered Lizzie to his office. "We're trying to get totally computerized but there are a lot of the old cases that are still sitting in boxes in the back room. Anyone with the time is encouraged to dig in and start entering the data."

"I guess it's all confidential stuff or else you could probably get some volunteers in to help," Lizzie said.

"Are you offering?"

Lizzie gulped. "Hadn't planned on it. Just suggesting."

"Well, I try to get some of the part-timers to do it but I know some of them feel it's a waste of their already short hours here, so we all take a turn."

"Hmm. Where's Derek's computer?" Lizzie asked, glancing around the office.

Mark pointed to a table in the left corner, just over from the door. He walked over and switched it on, removing his coat while it booted up. Lizzie added her jacket to the coatrack on the other side of the doorway.

"Okay. I'll just enter the password . . ."—he keyed it in—"and I'll let you hunt for the manuscript. I'm going to check my phone messages."

Lizzie nodded and sat, scrolling through the programs, looking for what appeared to be appropriate. "This is so frustrating. He has a file called 'Notes' but I need to find what he's written so far."

Mark grunted and went on with his own search.

"Can we print out the notes?"

"Yeah, it's hooked up, ready to go."

She clicked on the icon and then got back to her search for the manuscript. "Here's something called *Reconciliation*." She clicked on it but the file was blank.

"That's funny. There's nothing in it. And I can't see any other files that might be a manuscript. It must be this one. *Reconciliation*. Comes after *Judgment*, I'd say."

"That sounds about right," Mark agreed. "You sure there isn't a manuscript under another title?"

"No. Just his older titles and they're all listed in the 'Book' folder."

Mark scratched his cheek. "I wonder what that means, if anything."

Lizzie walked over to the printer and scooped up the pages. She sat in the chair opposite Mark's desk and started reading them through carefully. "Listen to this. It's notes for his new book and it looks like he uses code words for all the people."

She stood up and started pacing. "This is exciting, Mark. What if these words, these characters, are real people here in Ashton Corners? Any one of them might have had a motive to kill Derek if they thought he was about to expose some deep, dark secret. And by the number of calls I've been getting asking about him, I think this is the key."

She handed the pages to Mark and he read through them. "You could be right. I'd like a list of all your callers and anyone else you've encountered when you've been nosing around, even though you weren't supposed to."

Lizzie faked a pout. "Ah, but if I'm right, you'll be pinning a medal on me. Maybe even a badge."

Mark snorted.

"Unfortunately, my callers are mostly named 'anonymous' but I'll see what I can do. Maybe you could contact his agent and ask if Derek had sent the new manuscript to him, or even just how it was coming along?"

"Good idea. I'll contact him tomorrow, and if he has a copy, I'll ask him to send it here."

"And?"

He sighed. "And let you read it."

● ● ●

Mark had decided to call it an early night and Lizzie, although somewhat disappointed, understood. She read for a while after getting home, then went up to her bedroom. Brie sat on the floor, patiently staring at her catnip-stuffed cloth mouse that was attached to a long elastic and stick. Lizzie took the hint and started whipping it around for her. Edam crept into the bedroom and stayed well out of the way. Finally, Brie tired of the game and sat on the mouse, giving Lizzie the opportunity to get ready for bed. The phone rang as she stood brushing her teeth. She quickly rinsed her mouth and made a dash for the phone in her bedroom, catching it on the fifth and final ring before it went to the machine. She couldn't place the voice that answered her hello, but it was female.

"Is this Ms. Turner?"

"It is and who are you?"

"Ms. Turner, I'm so sorry to be calling at this late hour but I needed to ask you a question." She paused. "Did Derek Alton mention anything that he might be writing about in his new book?"

"No, he didn't. What did you say your name was?" Lizzie tried to sound casual about asking the question, not wanting to scare off the caller. She studied the top of her fuzzy pink slippers, sticking out from the cuff of her pink-and-orange-striped pajama bottoms.

"I'd heard it was a sequel to *Judgment.* If that's

so, you're sure he didn't talk about his characters or any such thing?"

"Really, no, he didn't. We didn't get to have that book club meeting, as you know. Now, will you tell me who you are and why you're asking?"

"I think not, dear. Thank you anyway. You have a nice evening, now."

The dial tone rang in Lizzie's ear. Frustrated, she hung up then went directly to the caller option. Herbert Trendy. And a number! *Eureka.* She rushed into her office, grabbed a pen and wrote both down. *Gotcha, Mrs. Herbert Trendy.* And tomorrow, I'll find out why you want to know.

She went to bed humming.

Lizzie was up even before the crack of dawn. It was still dark out as she got dressed for her run. She fed the cats and exited while they were busy eating. Officer Verge sat talking into his cell phone, cruiser parked across the street this time. Lizzie went over and waited until he rolled down his window after hurriedly finishing his call.

"Good morning. Hope it wasn't too uncomfortable a night for you."

The officer, looking embarrassed, probably at having being caught on the phone, shook his head and offered a small smile.

"I'm going for a run along the river and over to Glendale Park. There's a trail about fifty feet into the park, which I'll take. If you cut over to the entrance, I'll join you there about two minutes after I'm out of sight."

"Can't do that, ma'am. I'll have to go with you."

Lizzie shook her head in amazement. "Officer, I'm out early and taking a route I haven't done in several weeks. Surely this invisible gunman won't think to be around yet."

"Oh, I'm sure you are right, ma'am. But do you know what the chief would do to me if he ever found out?"

"I won't tell him. Promise."

"Sorry. If you're going somewhere I can't see you, I'm there running with you."

She shook her head. "Okay. Just trying to make life more tolerable for you."

"And I do thank you for that, ma'am." He turned the key in the ignition, which Lizzie took to be her signal to start running.

She started slowly, as usual, which also allowed him to pull a U-turn and fall in behind her. She went along Charles and then at the third intersection, turned right for ten blocks before turning again, left, onto the path that paralleled the Tallapoosa River. The dawn was making its entrance as she reached the edge of Glendale Park. She heard Officer Verge sound his car horn and she jogged on the spot until he walked over to her.

She looked him up and down, taking in the jacket and heavy gun belt, along with the Gore-

Tex boots. "You sure you can run dressed like that?"

"Don't you worry about me none. I've been trained to pursue a suspect dressed liked this. You just lead on, ma'am."

It was almost a challenge, and Lizzie took off at her fast pace not looking back until she reached the path that jutted to the left and through the park. But she could hear the rattle of his belt and knew he wasn't too far away. She slowed to turn and looked back. Officer Verge was about ten paces behind. She was impressed.

They made it through the park and back out the main gate, along the road, until they were back at his car.

"Nicely done, Officer."

He grinned. "Told ya, ma'am. But I think I'll drive the rest of the way." He tipped his ball cap and got into the car.

Lizzie grinned and retraced the last few yards back to the park entrance, then turned to run along Main Street and loop back to her place.

As she put together a breakfast of poached egg and toast, she pondered how best to approach Mrs. Herbert Trendy. She could wait till later in the day and phone. And Mrs. Trendy could hang up. Or she could stop by after school. And Mrs. Trendy could shut the door, or even not open it. Or, she could stop by on the way to school, surprise her totally at this early hour. Her chances of getting a foot in the door seemed much stronger.

She ate quickly and ran upstairs to shower and get dressed. She didn't have any appointments scheduled; her time was her own these last few days, and although she would use it doing the endless reports and planning, she could go for a more casual look. She chose gray cords and a black cotton shirt, with a pale denim jacket to top it off.

The cats had already claimed their spots on the bed and were busily grooming each other. She wished them a happy day, grabbed her tote and left. She'd found Trendy's address and used Google Maps to get directions. She was all set. Except for Officer Verge. What the hey, she'd just tell him she had to visit someone on the way to school. Mark would never make the connection, if Verge was feeding him addresses and other intel.

She grinned to herself, feeling a touch like Mata Hari. She no longer needed to check under her car, either.

She pulled up in Trendy's driveway, although she'd wanted to leave the car down the street a bit so that Mrs. Trendy wouldn't see it if she peered through the curtains. But Officer Verge might be suspicious of that move. She looked at the house, watching for rustling curtains, and seeing none, wondered if anyone was up yet. She glanced at her watch. Eight twenty. *Here's hoping.* That was the only snag. If she weren't up, she'd be forewarned. There was a hitch to every plan.

The cruiser waited at the curb in front of the house. That was good, Lizzie thought. Mrs. Trendy might see it and, thinking the police were at the door, open it without question. Lizzie was smiling when the door did open.

"Mrs. Trendy? I'm Lizzie Turner and I really do need to talk to you, right now."

Trendy's mouth dropped open. The two large rollers on top of her head shook ever so slightly. She looked down at her mint green chenille robe and furry mint green slippers. Lizzie moved her own foot subtly inside the door before Trendy thought to close it.

"It's really early, Ms. Turner. I can't think what would bring you here this early in the morning. I'm not even dressed."

"You don't need to be dressed for a talk. It won't take long. I promise."

Trendy stood looking at Lizzie for a few moments, then sighed and moved aside. "Okay. Come along in."

Lizzie followed her into the living room, to the right of the door. The room felt warm and rosy, probably because of the mauve pink walls and the country-style furniture upholstered in swirls of pink, purple and aqua on a white background. It looked like a room Mrs. Trendy would be comfortable in. The equivalent of a chenille bathrobe.

"Is there anyone else at home?" Lizzie asked, figuring a husband lurking upstairs might make Mrs. Trendy less chatty.

Her back stiffened. "I'm a widow. Why do you ask?"

"I was just wondering if we had privacy. I won't beat around the bush. I want to know why you were asking about Derek Alton. And don't bother denying it was you who phoned my house last night."

Trendy stood and walked over to the window, drawing the curtains. She gasped. "Why did you bring the police?"

"He's not there for you. Believe me. You did know Derek, didn't you? Or should I say, Harvey Warren."

Again, Trendy looked startled. Her black hair, what wasn't done up in rollers, ended just above her shoulders and was a mass of waves and curls, framing a face that sagged under both eyes, and a double chin. She dropped back down in her chair and pulled her robe tighter around her slender body. "What do you know about Harvey Warren?"

"I know that was his name when he lived in Ashton Corners over twenty years ago and before he became a famous writer, at which time he changed his name. And, I know that he was very cozy with some women in town."

Trendy nodded. She wrung her hands. "I . . . I

248

just can't bring myself to tell you. I can't let anyone know."

Lizzie leaned toward her and spoke in a gentle voice. "Mrs. Trendy, I've no wish to spread any gossip or tell anyone something that might damage your reputation, if that's what you're worried about. I will have to tell the police, if it suggests you might be a murder suspect, though."

Trendy gasped. "I did not kill Harvey—I mean Derek. I didn't. You have to believe me. And you might as well call me Nola." She sighed and stared out the window, into the past. "I knew he was in town and I heard he'd be speaking to your book club. But I went out of my way to avoid seeing him. I had no idea that Derek and Harvey were the same person until I finally read *Judgment* about three years ago. I saw his picture on the cover. He'd changed a lot. He used to have glasses. Maybe he used contacts these days. And he now has a beard. It took a minute or so but I knew it was him. I was totally shocked, especially when it mentioned on the jacket that the book was set in a small Southern town. So much of it sounded like Ashton Corners, I thought. And I got to wondering if he might have been basing some of it, at least, on people here."

"Did he try to contact you?"

"No, thank God." She was almost in tears. Lizzie felt badly but had to press on.

"What made you think it was Ashton Corners?"

Trendy took a deep breath. "Some of the descriptions. You probably wouldn't connect it if you weren't looking for it, but I was. Especially after I'd read about the . . . the affairs the main character, Flynn, had."

"Did you recognize some of those women?"

"I thought so but I wasn't positive."

"Were you one of them?"

The tears started and she pulled a tissue out of her pocket. She nodded. "I was newly married and my husband, he was a salesman for Rallest Chemicals and traveled a lot, and I was so lonely. I decided to take a night-school class at the high school and Harvey was the teacher. He told me I had talent and offered to help me. Well, one thing led to another . . . and we had an affair. It only lasted a month, though, and then I saw him with another of the students and knew it was her turn. I was so ashamed, I quit the class, never wrote again and also didn't tell anyone about it."

"Really, it won't get spread around," Lizzie assured her, thinking how much it sounded like Sally-Jo's story.

"It can't. I'm a grandmamma. Who wants stories like that going around about their granny?"

Lizzie felt badly for her. She sounded like a really decent woman who'd given into temptation and now lived in fear of the truth getting out.

"I'm not certain if I have to tell the police about this. I need to think about it. Can you tell me the names of anyone else he was having an affair with? I'm just looking for someone who may have been in contact with Derek recently."

Trendy thought a few minutes then shook her head. "I'm sorry. No, wait . . . I'm pretty sure Karen Goodrow had a relationship of some sort with him. I saw them kissing in the park one day, behind a tree. I hurried off before they saw me. And Cassie Noonan. She was in the night-school class. Of course, I don't know their married names. Cassie went to Ashton High and was a couple of years behind me but I didn't know Karen at all before the writing class."

"Does any of this help?"

"It might." Lizzie stood. "I should get to work now. I'm truly sorry for making you feel so badly, Nola, but I really thank you for being so candid."

Trendy stood and gave her a shaky smile. "You know, I do feel better for having finally talked about it. Confession must be good for the soul." She gave a thin laugh. "If you read the book and didn't make the connection to Ashton Corners, that's also a relief to know. I think I'll finally put this all behind me."

At the door, Lizzie impulsively gave Trendy a quick hug and left the other woman smiling as she went out to her car. Lizzie gave a thumbs-up to Officer Verge and got in her car. History seemed to repeat itself with Derek, Lizzie thought as she drove off.

Chapter Thirty

◇◇◇

No, no, dear lady. I'm sure everything you did was for the best.

A RARE MURDER IN PRINCETON
—ANN WALDRON

Vanda Striker leaned over the front counter in the main office, her back to the door, arms waving. Lizzie took that as a signal to quietly back out and disappear. The school secretary saw Lizzie as her savior and waved at her. Vanda pivoted and her face lit up.

"Lizzie. Thank God you're finally here. I have a major calamity about to happen and I need to attend to it right away. I'd like you to take charge of the dress rehearsal this morning, please." She had just the right amount of begging in her voice to make Lizzie agree, although she resented the dig at the hour of her arrival. She was ten minutes early, for pity's sake.

"Of course. What's going on?"

"Santa Claus is in the hospital. His wife called about a half hour ago to say he was admitted last night. Now I'll need to find a replacement real quick."

"What happened to him?" Lizzie asked. She could see Betsey, the secretary, roll her eyes toward the ceiling and clamp her mouth shut. This oughta be good.

"Seems like he was putting up the outside lights at their house and the ladder got away from him. He landed in the holly bush and was in such a rush to get out of there, he tripped and hit his head on the wooden sleigh in the yard. He's not seriously hurt or anything, thank goodness, but he is out of commission for a few days. You'd think she could have let us know last night and that would have given me plenty of time to start calling around." Vanda finished with a huge sigh.

"I guess his wife was pretty worried about him. It would have slipped her mind until she saw it on the calendar or something this morning," Lizzie ventured.

"I know you're right and I should feel sorry for the poor guy, but this pageant is jinxed. He's the second Santa we've gone through, what with Ken having to leave early on vacation. In fact, he got his neighbor to stand in. This guy has been playing Santa for years now, even has his own costume, which was just great. I don't have a clue where to start looking."

Vanda turned back to the secretary. "Would you please check in the directory and on the Internet and see if there's a Santa Claus society or association or some such thing in town. I just need a contact and I can go from there."

Lizzie suggested, "Why not call the man's wife

back and ask if she or he can suggest someone?"

Vanda stared at Lizzie a moment, her mouth slightly open, as the words pushed through her self-created stress zone. "Why, that's brilliant, Lizzie. Thank you so much. I'll do that right now. Of course, she's bound to know of someone. I should have thought of that myself." And with that, she fled down the hall in the direction of her own office.

Lizzie watched in amazement. She'd never seen Vanda so stressed before. Unflappable Vanda Striker. Wow. She gave Betsey a shrug and followed in Vanda's direction, making a beeline to the gym. She wanted to check that everything had been set up for the day's pageant rehearsals. Several rows of chairs had been placed theatre style for the various teachers and whoever else might stop by to watch. Although it wasn't open to the public, often mamas would trickle in for a sneak preview. Also, the entire school would be watching today, since they were putting on the program, the classes wouldn't be able to sit in the audience tomorrow.

Satisfied, Lizzie glanced at the large clock hanging to the left of the stage. Rehearsals would begin, in order of the program, in twenty minutes. She wondered what was left for her to do. She'd received a copy of the schedule yesterday in her mailbox, as had all the teachers. They all knew their roles.

She pulled out the file folder with her notes and comments. She'd been working on them, polishing them as she watched various classes practice, and she hoped they'd work. It was the timing that concerned her. If a class went overtime, Lizzie would have to edit her comments on the fly; she would need to add filler if the reverse happened. Her main role was to introduce the teachers and the classes, along with a little spiel about what they'd be doing. She pictured herself on the stage, in her elf costume, and shuddered.

The classes started arriving in time and sat in order of performance. With all the shuffling it took longer than expected, but the level of excitement was high. Lizzie smiled and took her place at the podium, set up on the extreme right of the stage, ready to welcome them all.

By the time the final class had performed, there were still twenty minutes before lunch. All had timed out rather well, Lizzie thought. But still no sign of Vanda. She went in search of her and found her hunched over her desk, phone receiver to her ear.

Lizzie gave her a thumbs-up sign when she finally glanced over; Vanda nodded and waved her out of the room. Lizzie took that as a sign to mean she was off the hook and decided to go home for lunch. She wanted to be out of sight, out of mind, for an hour. An hour all her own and she'd spend the rest of the time trying to figure out what the code names they'd found in Derek's notes meant.

The cats did not come running when she opened the door, a sure signal they were tucked in asleep somewhere, probably on her bed. She ran softly upstairs to check, and sure enough, that's where they were.

She went down to the kitchen, pulled out the tuna salad wrap she'd made for lunch, filled a glass with water and set them on the kitchen table. She glanced out the window and felt a small spasm of fear. Maybe she shouldn't sit in full view. Nonsense. There was a police car out front, and besides, she didn't believe the killer was after her.

Maybe if she kept telling herself that, it would be true.

She found her notes, sat down and ate while she read through them. She sat thinking about the plot of *Judgment*. She'd enjoyed the writing style—smooth and yet snappy but with an undercurrent of sarcasm. Overall the story had left her feeling down. The main protagonist was a male, mid-thirties, a visual artist with a well-developed ego but small bank account. Although married, to a travel agent, he put a lot of time and energy into casual affairs with women in the town. Most of them didn't know how to play by his rules and explosive scenes would take place throughout the book. However, the final of his conquests was the affair that lasted the longest. He didn't know why because he readily admitted he didn't love her. He laughed it off. After several months, she told him she was pregnant and he demanded she have an abortion. She offered to divorce her husband, suggested the artist should divorce his wife and they'd marry. She threatened to kill herself, which again he laughed off. At this point he simply packed up and left town with his wife. No one knew where they'd gone. Leaving his lover poised to kill herself, rifle barrel stuck in her mouth. The end.

Lizzie shook her head. "The Lady, or the Tiger?" all over again. Did she kill herself or not? And, who was she? Someone real, from Ashton Corners?

Lizzie wasn't quite sure why the book had won an award but admitted she often couldn't understand what others saw as winners. She did have definite thoughts on the inspiration for the plot and characters. Although Ashton Corners was not identifiable in any way, Derek certainly was, from what she'd learned about him. Derek Alton as Flynn, writer and artist.

And even more so, was the book he was working on indeed the sequel to this? Nothing more could happen to the final lover, but what did he have in store for the others? Were they the code words she'd found listed in his notes at Mark's office? She glanced at the clock. She had to get back to school and, she was sure, another meeting with Vanda Striker.

Chapter Thirty-one

Murder will out.
"THE PRIORESS'S TALE"—CHAUCER

A note awaited her in her mailbox in the school office. Vanda Striker would be out of the school for the remainder of the afternoon. She would see Lizzie first thing in the morning. Hooray! Lizzie decided to play hooky, also. Although that wasn't truly the case, as she had to go down to the school board office and pick up some books she'd ordered that had arrived there. They'd never make it through the internal mail drop before school vacation started the following week.

She found the parking lot at the downtown location surprisingly empty. Either Christmas holidays had started early at the mother ship or other things were afoot. She gasped at that thought. Today was the staff Christmas luncheon being held at Bennie's Bistro just down the street. She'd been invited, although she couldn't remember if she'd RSVP'd. Hopefully she had and sent her regrets.

She gave a quick heads-up to Officer Verge and ran inside to the Curriculum offices on the second floor. She checked her mailbox and read the note that books she'd ordered were on the floor behind the counter. She read the labels. Great—her Rapid Reads. That Canadian supplier wasted no time. She hoisted the two boxes off the ground and made her way back out to her car. Officer Verge jumped out of his cruiser and relieved her of the boxes while she searched for her car keys, the ones she thought she'd slipped into her jacket pocket but were actually lying at the bottom of her purse. Boy, she was losing it.

He stashed the boxes in her trunk and, after hearing that Lizzie would be heading home for the rest of the day, got back in his cruiser and waited to follow.

She arrived home just as Andie came sauntering down the street. Andie stooped to look in the window of the cruiser and scoped out the driver before turning onto the driveway. Lizzie stood at the trunk of her car, an amused look on her face.

"Does he meet with your approval?" Lizzie asked.

"I just wanted to make sure his eyes were open and he's not dozing on the job. I hope you're still checking your car in the mornings. I don't trust those guys to stay awake all through a night shift."

Lizzie chuckled. "I have the utmost confidence

in them all. Now Andie, if you don't mind, I'd like you to tote those two boxes inside for me."

Andie shrugged. "Sure." She passed her backpack over to Lizzie and picked up both boxes at the same time.

"Oh, you shouldn't have done that. It's bad for your back. One at a time, Andie," Lizzie chided.

Andie leaned against the car. "I already have a mama." She added under her breath, "Sort of."

Lizzie bit her lip. Best not to laugh at a serious Andie. "You're so right. I apologize. I'll open the front door and you can leave them at the bottom of the stairs, please."

Andie stood after depositing the boxes. "I could truck them upstairs. I don't mind."

"Thanks, but I'm going to sort them down here first. Now, how's the studying going?"

Andie groaned as she retrieved her backpack from the floor where Lizzie had placed it. "If I flunk out of English Lit, will I have to drop the book club?"

Lizzie found that both pleasing and disturbing. The thought she might not pass was upsetting, as it was Lizzie's job to make sure she knew the work. But the fact that she wanted to stick with the book club was heartening.

"No, you won't, but let's make sure you pass the exam. What's giving you the most trouble?" She led Andie to the kitchen table, poured them both some iced tea and slid a plate of sugar cookies in front of her as Andie routed through her backpack. Her choice of clothing didn't reflect her despondency, Lizzie noted. The black long-sleeved T looked like an artist's splatter board. Her black jeans sported red and yellow circles highlighting the torn parts. And on her feet were the bloodred New Rock boots she'd been lusting after for months. Perhaps an early Christmas gift?

"This passage that starts on page 127"—she opened her book and pointed it out—"I still don't have a clue what the guy's saying, ya know?"

"Well, tell me what you think about him. What's he like as a guy?"

Andie went into a well-thought-out description that pleased Lizzie and gave her hope. Andie seemed pleased by it, too.

"Okay, so what do you think his response would be to what's happening? Think of him as one of your friends. You know pretty well what they'd say or do. So what about our fictional guy?"

Andie sat playing with her pencil, eyes focused on the wall across the kitchen. The silence became longer and drawn out. Lizzie feared she'd lost her when suddenly Andie explained what she'd been thinking.

"Not his words, of course, but that's what he's been getting at. Very good, Andie."

Andie beamed. "Yah, I guess. That made it so much easier. You think if I look at all the characters in that way, it'll become easier to understand?"

"I'd say so. Now, any other specifics?"

They spent the next two hours going over passages and possible questions Lizzie had found from old exams. By the time Andie left she seemed more confident. Lizzie hoped it would last until her exam on Monday morning. She reiterated that Andie didn't need to show up for the book club meeting later but Andie insisted she needed a break and promised not to stay too long.

Lizzie was hoping Molly would come but wasn't so sure. After storming out of the last meeting, even though she did apologize and seemed to be on good terms with Bob at the concert, Lizzie wasn't assuming anything. She'd just wait and see. She started tidying the place then took a quick dinner break, thawing a piece of frozen catfish and then baking it in a Creole sauce in the toaster oven. She added some leftover veggies to the plate and sat to eat when the fish was done.

By the time Sally-Jo arrived, Lizzie had the place ready. She'd vacuumed the entire main floor, washed down the powder room and put some empty serving dishes out on the counter. Sally-Jo put her armload of goodies down on the table and shrugged out of her heavy jacket.

"There's a chill to the air tonight. Maybe we'll have it cold for Christmas," Sally-Jo muttered.

"A cozy fireplace Christmas would be nice," Lizzie agreed, thinking it was too bad she didn't actually have a fireplace. She helped Sally-Jo add some double chocolate cookies to one of the serving plates. The doorbell rang and moments later, Stephanie waddled into the kitchen followed by Jacob.

"We're so glad you were able to come out, Stephanie," Lizzie said.

"Me, too. I was going nuts in there. This child just doesn't want to leave me," Stephanie replied, laying her right hand on her swollen belly. She reached over for a cookie and bit in. "Oh, mama, this tastes so good. Sorry for not restraining myself but I just cannot resist baking these days."

"No problem," laughed Sally-Jo. "They're meant to be eaten."

Jacob reached over and took one also. "In that case, I'm happy to help out."

Jacob answered a knock on the back door and Andie entered. "Yo, Lizzie. Whoa, Steph . . . you're as big as a horse."

"Thanks, Andie. I hope that's good."

Andie didn't appear to have an answer. She just stared at Stephanie's belly.

"Here, Andie," said Sally-Jo, thrusting two plates of cookies into her hands, "please take these into the living room and place them on the end table. In fact, y'all just move on into the living room now. We're done in here." She finished filling the glasses with tea and picked up the tray to follow them in.

Lizzie bit back a grin. Sally-Jo certainly seemed a lot more determined tonight. Maybe it was the thought of facing the relatives next week or maybe she'd finally stopped worrying about still being on the suspect list. Maybe they could ease that fear even more tonight.

Bob and Molly arrived as they were getting seated. Lizzie was so pleased to see Molly and also to see that she'd taken great care with her appearance. The old Molly was back. She said a silent prayer of thanks. Molly, looking elegant in a mauve cashmere sweater and matching pants, took a seat next to Lizzie while Bob hung up their jackets.

He sank into the wicker chair next to Stephanie, who sat on the straight-backed kitchen chair Lizzie had provided just for her comfort, and gave her a wink as he asked, "You still hanging around here? I thought we'd be visiting you in the hospital by now, young lady."

Stephanie sighed and Lizzie watched her belly rise and fall. "I sure do wish that was so, Bob. I'm getting right tired of waiting. My body is so sore all over I just want this to be over. I thought tonight might help take my mind off it."

"Well, you can't have the baby until Christmas Eve," Andie wailed. "It would be sooo cool. And then he could play the baby Jesus in the manger concert at the church next year."

Lizzie was surprised at Andie's enthusiasm. She wouldn't have thought it of her.

Bob said, "I hate to burst your bubble but a one-year-old's not likely to lie in any manger for a concert, not so far as I remember anyway. Only if you tie him in."

Stephanie laughed. "Not that it would happen anyway because this here baby's a girl."

"Huh. You got that in writing or did you have one of those scans?" Bob asked.

"No. I just know it's a girl. We've been bonding already." Stephanie gently rubbed her belly.

"Let's hope that's so, then," Molly added. "Now, before we begin, I need to apologize to y'all. I am truly embarrassed by my behavior the last time we were all together. My manners just went all out the window."

"Don't worry about it," Jacob said. "We've already forgotten. That is, until you brought it up again." He grinned.

Molly couldn't help but answer his smile with one of her own.

Lizzie smiled, too, hoping they were back on track. "Well, my reason for calling this meeting tonight is to compare notes about *Judgment*. I take it y'all have read it?"

Everyone nodded.

"Good. I'll lay out what I've learned about

Derek Alton and how I'm thinking it all ties into this book." She told them about what she'd discovered since their last meeting, including the search for the new manuscript. "I haven't heard from Mark, Chief Dreyfus, as yet so I'm assuming he hasn't heard back from the agent. So we're no further on the new book. Except for this list of words. I wonder if they could be code names. They don't make sense otherwise, unless they were meant to trigger some thoughts. I'll read them out: 'citron,' 'ending,' 'xenolith,' 'neglect,' 'julep' and 'veritas.' What do y'all think?"

Bob said, between taking bites of his cheese straw, "It sounds like a long shot but that's what they could be. If so, what are you thinking they refer to?"

"Well, if *Judgment* was based partly on his escapades in Ashton Corners, then there are a lot of women out there who were depicted in the book. Or maybe others who missed being in the first go-round are now awfully anxious this is their turn. That would explain all those women calling me and refusing to leave their names. Maybe these are codes for those names."

"If he was going to mention anything that could possibly identify them, then the married ones in particular would be very nervous," Bob said.

"Nervous enough to kill him?" Stephanie asked.

"Could be," Bob agreed. "Anyone got any ideas about who those names refer to?"

Lizzie made a list as she spoke. "The only names I have are Xenia Henshaw, Karen Goodrow, Cassie Noonan and Nola Trendy, along with a lot of unidentified callers."

Molly had written them down, too. After a few minutes she said, "Well the first letter could refer to the person's first name. For instance, 'xenolith.' That's got to be the oddest word on the list. It could refer to Xenia Henshaw, in which case the last letter in the code word would be the person's surname."

"You've got a mind like a steel trap," Bob said, and Molly turned pink.

"And 'neglect' could be Nola Trendy," Lizzie added. "It makes sense, Molly. 'Citron' for Cassie Noonan. But nothing for Karen Goodrow."

"Y'all know who 'julep' would be then, don't you?" Sally-Jo asked. "J. P.?"

Lizzie's eyes grew wide as it dawned on her. "Jensey Pollard. I didn't have her on the list because she was too obvious. We know she knew Derek because I met him in the Book Bin. But she told me she hadn't known him before that. Of course, she could be lying. Or it could be another J. P. entirely."

"What could be her motive?" Jacob asked, taking a cheese straw from the plate Andie passed around. "And what about you, Lizzie? We haven't been seriously looking at who would want to shoot you."

"That's because it's unlikely anyone would. I haven't made any serious enemies and surely the killer must realize by now that I know nothing or he or she would be in custody."

"You're probably right but I see the chief's not taking any chances. You still have your escort."

"I'm going to suggest that end. I'm sure the officers are hoping by now that someone will shoot me, just to make their shift more interesting."

Molly gasped. "Oh, don't even suggest that, honey."

"No, really. I honestly and truly don't believe I need protection." *I hope.*

"I have a question," Jacob said. "If he was Harvey Warren when he lived here but he wrote as Derek Alton, how do all these women know to call and ask about the book?"

"Good question," Lizzie agreed. "Probably like Nola Trendy. She recognized his photo on the book jacket."

"I'm afraid I'm going to need a hand standing up," Stephanie wailed. "I really need to use your powder room, Lizzie."

Jacob and Sally-Jo both launched out of their chairs and gave her a hand. Stephanie waddled down the hall and they all found it hard not to stare. Lizzie spoke to get their attention refocused.

"Any suggestions?"

"Re-read, re-think and re-solve . . . how's that?" Bob suggested.

"Wow," Andie exclaimed. "That's cool."

They all agreed and tucked into another cheese straw, passed around this time by Sally-Jo. They'd all steal glances toward the doorway, and after a very long time, Stephanie came waddling back in. Lizzie breathed a sigh of relief. She'd envisioned a water-breaking crisis or some such thing. Although it would be better if it happened with them all around and able to help.

"I'm sorry but I gotta go home and lie down. Baby's getting tired." Stephanie looked exhausted.

Jacob leapt up. "I'm ready. Andie, I'll give you a lift also if you like."

"Don't forget our Christmas party is next Thursday night. And only a small gift for the name you drew," Lizzie reminded them.

"Looking forward to it," Jacob said and opened the door for his passengers.

The three left followed by Sally-Jo and then Bob and Molly.

Lizzie fell asleep trying to picture who in Ashton Corners might be on that list. The problem was, she kept rejecting faces that came to mind. Other than Xenia Henshaw and Nola Trendy, she had no idea what type he went for. Well, Sally-Jo. But that only broadened the possibilities. She needed to narrow them down.

Chapter Thirty-two

◇◇◇

If I hear or see anything else I'll report back.
And don't forget, this is between us two.
WARNING AT ONE—ANN PURSER

The school halls were teeming with parents streaming toward the gymnasium, with the aid of some teens from the high school who were helping out as ushers as part of their community involvement marks.

Lizzie could hear Vanda Striker as she burst into the staff room calling out Lizzie's name only to be told Lizzie was in the restroom changing her clothes. Vanda pounded on the door and Lizzie opened it a crack.

"Do you need any help?" Vanda demanded.

Lizzie could hear she was tight as a wire. This was so un-Vanda. What was going on with the woman? "No, I'm all right. I'll be out in a minute. Why don't you sit and take a break. I'm sure everything's coming along as it should." She looked down at her costume. She looked like a frog. A frog with a short skirt of green leaves. Ugh.

She should never have agreed to wear this. Mrs. Farnshaw had done a fine job of sewing it. But the design was totally ridiculous. She worried about hurting the poor woman's feelings, though, so she reminded herself to keep her thoughts to herself.

She left her sanctuary in the restroom with great hesitation. Fortunately, the staff room had cleared, as all teachers needed to be with their classes, trying to keep the lid on the excited kids and make sure they were ready.

"Oh, don't you look just . . ." Vanda faltered. "Oh my, . . . I'm sorry, Lizzie. It's not really what I had in mind. But the children will love it. And that's what counts. Here, don't forget this bracelet of bells."

She slid it over Lizzie's right hand. "It will make so much more noise if you wear it on your right."

Lizzie groaned. She looked at Vanda, who appeared about ready to cry. Too dramatic a reaction to a silly costume. "Vanda, what's wrong?"

Vanda shook her head and sniffed. "No, I can't stop to think about it, Lizzie. This day is for the children. We're going to make sure it's one they remember." She stood and straightened her skirt and walked to the door. She turned back to Lizzie as she went through the doorway. "Ethan is leaving me."

Lizzie stood with her mouth open. The very proper community leader, Ethan Striker, was leaving Vanda? What was that all about? Poor Vanda. No wonder she was such a basket case these days. She felt badly but knew there was nothing to say right now and a show to put on.

She stuck her head out the door and looked both ways. Still filled with parents and the curtain would go up in ten minutes. She had to get to the back of the stage. Just suck it up and walk proudly down the hall. *Oh boy!*

She managed to slip in the front door of the gym and get backstage without having to talk to anyone. The stagehands, all teacher's aides and office staff, were just as excited as the children. She peered out between the curtains and saw the students were being seated, class by class, with the youngest at the front. The first class to go on, Elvis Everett's first grade, was lining up, ready to go on. She looked back out front and spotted Sally-Jo, who gave her a thumbs-up and grinned. *Easy for her.*

At the appointed hour, Lizzie stepped up to the microphone and signaled for silence. After several moments, everyone obeyed. She launched into her opening remarks and then introduced the first class to thunderous applause.

Two hours later, even louder applause mingled with cheers signaled the finish of the pageant, only ten minutes overtime. Lizzie felt totally exhausted. How could a two-hour pageant feel more like eight hours? Children and parents mingled over juice and cookies set up at the back of the gym and Lizzie made her escape. She quickly changed back into her clothes and stuffed the costume in a bag to take home and launder. It would be placed on Vanda's desk first thing Monday morning.

She made her way through the teachers congratulating her and also the many humorous remarks, to Vanda's office. No sign of her.

Lizzie glanced around. No Sally-Jo, either. She made her way back to the gym and mingled for a while, talking to parents and children, then she left. She had planned to do some decorating before tonight's special choir practice.

When she got home, she hauled the two large Rubbermaid containers out of the closet in the office and struggled to bring them down the stairs. One problem: She didn't have a tree. But she could finish decorating the mantel and shelves.

Maybe tomorrow.

Supper would be a chicken spaghetti mix. She pulled the chicken breast out of the freezer and nuked it while boiling the pasta. She found the pesto container and checked the best-before date . . . it still was usable.

After supper she stuffed her music into the music bag and said good-bye to the cats. On the drive over to the church, she did her usual warm-up, keeping the windows closed.

She hadn't seen any of the choir members since the concert and was looking forward to recapping with them. This special practice had become a routine part of their yearly schedule. The choir offered to sing at the midnight Christmas Eve service as payment for the use of the hall for rehearsals. Most members were able to make it, although the odd few would be out of town with family or just unable to get away.

Lizzie loved the service and was happy to be part of it. It had quickly become part of her Christmas ritual. She loved the music and the air of total joy and well-being everyone felt when leaving the church.

Tonight, Stanton Giles was ready to go as soon as they all had taken their places. "First of all, I'd like to thank you for a wonderful concert. I've had so many compliments about this choir. You did an outstanding job." He folded his hands as in prayer and touched them to his forehead in thanks. "Now, this is a new mass but also not too difficult, so between tonight's practice and the extra one next Wednesday, I'm sure there won't be any problems with it. David Willcocks is known for his love of more traditional choral anthems and I find this ties into the Christmas message. Let's start with a warm-up."

They spent the hour and a half without a break and went through the mass several times, learning their parts as sopranos and altos together, then as tenors and basses, then all four voices together, as well as the anthem "Hymn to the Virgin" by Benjamin Britten.

As they left the church, Lucille Miller hooked

her arm through Lizzie's and walked out to the parking lot with her. "I see you still have your police escort, dear. I sure hope all the danger is long past."

"Thanks, Lucille. I'm pretty sure it is. It's just convincing the chief about it."

"I'm sure. Speaking of the chief, how are Bob and Molly getting along?"

Lizzie bit her tongue. It wouldn't do to tell Lucille to mind her own business or, better yet, to ask Bob. "As a matter of fact, we had a book club meeting last night and they were congenial, but then of course, that's Bob for you. He's friendly and helpful to us all."

"Hmm."

"See you next Wednesday," Lizzie said, grateful they'd reached her car. "Have a good weekend."

"Thank you, dear. And you, also. By the way, your discretion is admirable although frustrating."

Chapter Thirty-three

◇◇◇

"So how do you want to do this?" he said.
THE PROFESSIONAL—ROBERT B. PARKER

Lizzie looked out at the dreary sky on Saturday morning and wondered if she'd be caught in a rainstorm while running. Oh well . . . she needed to wash her hair anyway.

She got dressed and raced the cats downstairs, taking time to give them each a little attention before filling their food bowls. She changed the water and tied her shoes. She went through her stretches, grabbed her cell phone and keys and stepped outside, taking another look at the sky.

Officer Craig got out of the cruiser as Lizzie walked down the driveway. She was dressed in running gear.

"I thought I could use some exercise," Amber Craig said as Lizzie took in her outfit. "That will give us a chance to talk, too."

Lizzie glanced at her sharply but Craig was staring down the street. What did she want to talk about? Hopefully she wasn't going back to the questioning mode. Since being shot at, Lizzie hadn't been bothered by questions about Derek and her. Maybe the grace period had ended. She hoped not.

They started toward town at a leisurely pace. After about three blocks, Lizzie glanced over at her. "Are you ready to ramp it up?"

Craig nodded and grinned. They kept up a good pace for about forty minutes, taking them through town, across the square and around the gigantic Christmas tree, along Main Street and past the equally large Santa's sleigh and reindeer parked outside the entrance to Glendale Park. Lizzie led the reverse to her run earlier that week, cut into the park, turned right on the first path and out to the pathway along the river, then back toward home.

As they neared Pruitt Street, Lizzie slowed her pace and eventually they walked the last block.

"That was good. I needed that," said a slightly breathless Officer Craig. "Now, I wanted to talk to you about tonight. You know it's our staff Christmas party at the Black Tomato restaurant? They have a nice-sized private banquet room and we can even go out on the deck, if the weather's warm enough."

Lizzie nodded, wondering where this was leading. She knew all about the party plans, and also knew it was officers only, no partners or spouses, although she was sure there were several in that latter category who were pretty steamed about it.

"I'm inviting you."

"What?" Lizzie almost tripped over her own feet.

"Not as my date. But you need to come to it so we can all be there. Otherwise, someone, and it might turn out to be me because we're drawing straws, will have to babysit you and miss the dinner. Now, that's just not fair, is it?"

"No. But you could all go and no one babysit me."

"Not going to happen. The chief is still adamant you might be in danger."

"Does he know about this conversation?"

"No. I'll enlighten him once I have your agreement."

"Well, no one will be happy, will they, if a civilian is there? I thought that was what tonight was about. Only staff members so you could spend the evening discussing police stuff as much as you like."

"That's the theory. But I think it's time to change the pattern. We do nothing but talk about police business all frigging day long, every day we're on duty. Besides, I have this guy I'd like to bring."

"You have a boyfriend?"

"Of course. You sound surprised. I do have a private life, too, you know. And, I'd like to get back to it."

Lizzie was overjoyed; not that she believed anything was going on between Mark and the officer, but she had thought Officer Craig had eyed Mark longingly now and again.

"I can't imagine Mark being so rigid he wouldn't change the format," Lizzie said. They'd reached her house and stood outside the cruiser talking.

"Oh, it's not him. I'm sure he'd be happy to but it's the Sarge and Yost. They've been working there way too long, and not only are they set in their ways, I think they take a perverse pleasure in telling their wives they can't attend. So we all go along with it."

"I'd be the crack in the mold."

"That, too," Craig said with a big grin.

"Sure, why not!"

"That's great. I'll let the chief know and he can decide if we need the straws for your escort." She winked and unlocked the cruiser and got in. She rolled down the window. "Do I have time to go home and change? You won't skip out on me and you'll keep your curtains drawn?"

"Absolutely."

"Well, go inside so I can say I saw you safely in."

Lizzie laughed and went up the driveway. She glanced at her car. It had been left unattended for a while but she was putting aside all those thoughts. No one was after her. And, she was going out partying tonight.

She took her time in the shower, enjoying the hot, revitalizing spray, then dressed for a morning that included grocery shopping and a new mystery book. She wondered if she should ask Jensey again about knowing Derek. Was she really "julep"? It would have to be a quick stop, though, because she planned to visit Molly in the afternoon.

This was the day Molly had originally been planning on hosting a large dinner party, partly to celebrate what would have been the sixtieth year of her marriage to Claydon had he but lived beyond the thirty-four years they had together.

She'd abruptly changed her mind about the party after learning of his secret. Lizzie thought Molly might be in a deep funk today. She planned to pick up a bouquet of flowers and something sinfully tasty to go with an afternoon tea, to bring over.

Even though the cats had been fed before her run, they followed her downstairs, hoping for a handout of dried treats. They both wound around her legs while she fixed herself a breakfast of poached egg on Kamut toast, and even after she'd indulged them, they continued following her.

She grabbed two brushes and knelt down to try a two-handed session. Unfortunately, Brie, on the left, got the feeble attempt. She spoke to them the entire time, filling them in on her plans for the day, and asking for suggestions on what she should wear to the party. Finally, they took more of an interest in each other than the brushes, and eventually played a game of tag racing upstairs.

Lizzie washed up her dishes and grabbed her handbag and jacket. Officer Craig was indeed back outside and Lizzie let her know of her day's plans.

"You're still up for tonight? . . . Haven't backed out?" Craig asked before rolling her window up.

"Absolutely. Just trying to decide what to wear."

"It's a dress up night but nothing formal. I can't wait to see some of these guys out of uniform and jeans, their second uniform. Enjoy your shopping."

Lizzie nodded and went to get her car.

Her first stop was the Piggy Wiggly on Ulysses. The lot was about half full and she parked close to the street so that the cruiser could see it without entering the lot. She managed to get everything on her list within twenty minutes, stopping only once, briefly, to chat with a neighbor.

Lizzie found a parking spot in front of the Book Bin. The cruiser had to park two cars behind her. The bell over the door announced her entry and Jensey glanced up, a look of surprise on her face.

Lizzie had been thinking about Jensey and her interest in Derek's newest book. The other women she put down to concern about the kiss-and-tell aspect. Of course, it was most natural that Jensey as a bookstore owner would more than likely be interested in something that could be another bestseller, especially since Derek had visited Ashton Corners. Yet, it could mean something else entirely, if she was "julep."

"Hi, Jensey. I'm in need of another mystery fix. Anything new in the last couple of days that you'd recommend?"

Jensey cleared her throat and joined Lizzie at the front rack of new arrivals. "Well, there's this new Avery Aames. I think you're reading her series, aren't you?"

"Yes. This'll be great, thanks." She quickly selected three other books and took her purchase to the counter. "By the way, I know you said you didn't know that Derek Alton had once lived in Ashton Corners."

"Of course not. I'd have heard if a bestselling author had lived here. We all would." Her hand shook ever so slightly as she accepted the ten-dollar bill from Lizzie.

"That's because he changed his name when he started getting published. Before, he was Harvey Warren and he lived in town with his wife."

Jensey looked a bit pale and her hand shook even more when she handed back her change, but her voice was strong. "Doesn't ring a bell. How odd to think he'd maybe shopped at the same Piggly Wiggly or even gone to the same church. I surely didn't recognize his picture on the book jacket."

Lizzie picked up her purchase. "Well, knowing that and having read *Judgment*, do you think it could have been set in Ashton Corners?"

"It wasn't recognizable, if that's the case. I think all writers must use a bit of their lives in their books but it doesn't mean everything is based on something truthful."

Lizzie nodded. "Yeah, you're probably right. Well, thanks for the books. Have a busy week-end." The door opened and four customers walked in, as Lizzie waited to leave.

That didn't get her any new information but it did get her a new book she'd been waiting for. Lizzie wondered how long Jensey had owned the

Book Bin and would she have been as aware of the budding young author, Harvey Warren, if she didn't own it at that time? Or had she been lying through her teeth?

She glanced at the dashboard clock. She'd better get a move on if she wanted to spend some time with Molly before preparing for the big night out. She glanced at the bouquet lying on the backseat and took a deep breath inhaling the aroma of the freshly baked cinnamon pecan twirls she'd picked up at LaBelle's Bakery.

After a quick lunch and a change into some casual black pants, Lizzie drove to Molly's. She'd been right, she realized when Molly answered the door. It was a depressing day for her.

Lizzie handed her the bouquet and gave her a big hug. "I thought we might have a tea party this afternoon and talk, if you want to talk."

Molly sniffed. "It's thoughtful of you to remember, honey. I've been trying my darnedest not to think about Claydon but it's there just beneath the surface and I know it's got to be faced at some point. The tea is all made. So if you'll just go and serve it up along with these delicious-smelling twirls, I'll find a vase for these beautiful blooms. Thank you so much." She gave Lizzie a quick kiss on her cheek.

Lizzie put two of the twirls on a china side plate and chose two tall crystal glasses from the cupboards for the iced tea. She set them out on the kitchen table, along with some colorful Christmas paper napkins, and sat waiting for Molly to return.

When she did come back, Molly held a tall glass vase and quickly cut and arranged the flowers, placing the vase on the table, close to the window.

"They're beautiful. It's so nice to have fresh-cut flowers in these days of floral arrangements everywhere you look. They really do well at Christmas. I'll bet the cut flowers don't sell quite as quickly. They're so available all year round and . . ."

She stopped talking and looked at Lizzie. "I had thought today I'd be celebrating the years I'd had with Claydon, but instead, I'm still trying to reconcile the man I thought I knew with the swindler he turned out to be." She looked on the verge of tears but held up her hand before Lizzie could answer.

"No, it's all right. You were right. I do focus on the good years we had and the fact that he did love me. It's just the odd thing will set me off." She took a sip of tea. "Maybe I should have gone ahead with the dinner party after all. After all, I could have worn my new cheongsam. It's the most beautiful shade of blue."

Lizzie smiled, much relieved to hear Molly talking herself out of the blues, even though it did sound like she might be slipping back into exotic dress mode.

• • •

Lizzie couldn't decide between the purple crepe with one shoulder bared or the black jersey sheath. Fancy but not formal. They both fit the bill; in fact they were the only pieces in her closet that would be suitable. But which one?

She grabbed the phone. When Paige answered, she said, "I need a quick fashion phone consult."

Paige laughed. "Oh goody. A date with Mark?"

"More like with the entire Ashton Corners Police Department." She explained and then described her two choices to Paige.

"You want something that will totally grab Mark's attention, even if it means putting your life at risk because he won't be focused on protecting you. Are you still worried about the shooter?"

"No. I'm sure that whatever that shot was about, it wasn't about killing me. Even with a police escort, it could have happened. If someone had been stalking me, the opportunity had presented itself a few times." She thought of her stubborn decision to run through the park, even though it was a short distance. Totally foolhardy, but she'd been determined not to let fear get the better of her.

"That is such a relief. So, go with the purple one-shoulder dazzler. There's nothing like a bare shoulder to hook a guy. He'll be like butter. Especially if you wear those pewter sandals with the three-inch heel you splurged on last time we went therapy shopping."

"The purple and pewter it is. And what do you have planned for tonight?"

"We have a babysitter on tap and we're going out to a house party just down the street. It should be an early evening but it'll be fun to get dressed up for a change and even, dare I say, go out without the girls."

"Well, be sure to wear something that will totally grab Brad's attention."

Paige laughed. "You give good advice. Give me a call tomorrow . . . I want a complete report, please."

Lizzie had a quick shower then fed the cats before getting ready. She did her makeup, slid the dress on over her head, fixed her hair and pulled the sandals out of the closet.

The doorbell rang at precisely six and she ran downstairs, shoes in hand. She put them on before opening the door.

Mark stood there, all dressed in a dark suit and light blue shirt. No tie. He grinned when he saw what she was wearing.

"Craig told me what she'd done and I told them all I was pulling rank, so I'm your escort."

She stepped aside so he could come in. "You're not upset with her?"

"Hell, no. I've been trying to figure out a way to get dates included without stepping on anyone's toes. She's found the perfect way. There's no going back now. Shall we go?"

She grabbed her jacket and he helped her with it then turned her around in his arms and gave her a deep, long kiss. No doubt in her mind he wasn't upset.

Chapter Thirty-four

◇◇◇

Old sins cast long shadows.
HALLOWE'EN PARTY—AGATHA CHRISTIE

Lizzie woke on Sunday morning feeling extremely contented. The evening had been almost perfect. She'd enjoyed the good food, the camaraderie among the staff, and Mark's attentions even though he had to dance at least once with all the females from the department. She even enjoyed the little game one of the office clerks had devised to give out small presents to everyone. She'd been happy with the singing angel tree ornament while Mark had gotten a key chain shaped like a pair of miniature handcuffs. All thoughts of the horror of the past couple of weeks disappeared and the officers enjoyed a well-deserved diversion.

Mark had been almost reluctant to leave her at the door but Patchett needed walking, and although Lizzie volunteered to help, she wasn't really dressed for it.

She plotted her day as she pulled the Sunday edition of the *Birmingham News* out of the mailbox and made herself a cup of espresso. Carrying both, she headed back to bed and stayed there for another couple of hours.

It was hunger pangs that drove her down to the kitchen. She thought about waffles and froze as she revisited the events of the previous Sunday. She shook her head to clear the unwanted memories and opted for a poached egg on toast instead.

After breakfast, she played with the cats until they lost interest and needed refueling at their dishes, then she ran the vacuum through the house before showering and getting ready to visit her mama. She drove into the parking lot of Magnolia Manor at one P.M., just when the residents would be heading back to their rooms or into the spacious great room after lunch. Her mama sat alone in the sunroom at the end of the hall, clutching the cockatoo, her eyes closed.

Lizzie greeted her and pulled a chair close to her. She put her hand on her mama's and sat quietly, staring outside at the spacious green lawn, at the wooden pergola covered with butter bean vines and the hedge with the winterberry shrubs. After about twenty minutes, Evelyn Turner stirred enough to snap Lizzie to attention.

Evelyn held the cockatoo up to the window and smiled as the light played off it. She then reached out for Lizzie's hand and squeezed it. Lizzie thought her heart would burst.

"I'm so very glad you like it, Mama. Do you know, it's Christmas next weekend. Sunday, as a matter of fact. I'll be stopping in on Saturday before I go to sing at the late service at St. John's Episcopal Church and then I'll come by Sunday morning and we can unwrap gifts together, okay?"

Evelyn whispered, "Okay."

Lizzie almost forgot about the new gift she'd brought until it was time to leave. She handed over the gift bag and waited while her mama pulled out a snow globe with a couple of carolers dressed in eighteenth-century costumes in its center. "This can sit beside your Christmas tree."

They walked back to Evelyn's room and set the snow globe on the bureau beside the small ceramic tree. Lizzie reached into the bottom drawer and brought out a small gift box, dressed up with wrapping paper, which held the tiny lights. They inserted them together, a ritual they'd had since Evelyn had lived at Magnolia Manor. Evelyn then turned her chair facing the tree and she sat down looking toward it. Lizzie gave her a kiss and said good-bye. She waved at a couple of residents who were walking together arm in arm along the hall toward her. On the drive home, the sun slid behind some clouds and Lizzie wondered if rain showers might be in the forecast but she made it home and it was still dry.

Lizzie noticed the car parked in front of her house as she pulled into her driveway. Officer Yost noticed it, too, and was out of his car, at the driver's window, when Lizzie approached.

"Ma'am, this woman's name is Vanda Striker. Do you know her?"

"Yes, Officer. We work together."

He passed Vanda's driver's license back to her, touched the tip of his hat and went back to his car. Vanda exited hers and turned to Lizzie.

"I'm sorry to bother you and oh my, I'd forgotten all about your protective detail here. I just wanted to talk, if you had some time." Vanda looked so forlorn, Lizzie was glad she didn't have anything planned.

"Come on in, Vanda. I'll make us some tea and we can sit and talk."

"I first of all wanted to thank you for all you did on Friday," Vanda said as they sat in the living room. "I should have done it then but I just felt I needed to leave. But you really did carry the whole thing, despite that costume." She gave a small laugh.

Lizzie nodded but didn't interrupt.

"And, I'm sorry for that outburst. It's not like I go around telling everyone the horrid details of my life. But it just came out. I guess because I was still so much in shock."

"And are you feeling any better now?"

"It's hard to tell. I don't know what 'better' feels

like but I'm accepting of it. It just came as such a shock. After thirty-five years he up and tells me there's someone else, someone younger, and our marriage is over. I didn't have a clue that was coming. Guess I've just had my head buried in work so long now." She took a deep breath and straightened her shoulders.

"I will be okay, though. I'm strong. I didn't make VP in the school system by just waiting for opportunities."

Lizzie was happy to hear that because she'd been feeling like a louse, thinking about asking Vanda about Derek, but she had to take this opportunity. Vanda had asked about him, but did she know his real identity?

"Vanda, I can't even imagine what you're going through but I do know you are a remarkable woman and I believe you will make it come out right." She sipped her tea. "I'm sorry to ask you this now but how well did you know Harvey Warren?"

Vanda looked totally shocked. She seemed at a loss for an answer but finally replied, "I have no idea who you're talking about." She grabbed her handbag that she'd set down on the floor and stood. "I really should be running along now. I'm sorry I just burst in on you but thank you for letting me talk. I don't have many girlfriends but I guess I might need to cultivate some in the future. I should get going."

Lizzie had a quick flash on a girls' night out with Vanda, and quickly dismissed it. She respected her as a colleague and even liked her but doubted they had much in common besides work. And perhaps, Derek Alton.

Chapter Thirty-five
◇◇◇

It's possible to solve a mystery and still not know all the answers.
SPANISH DAGGER—SUSAN WITTIG ALBERT

The final two days before Christmas vacation. Lizzie felt like cheering as she got ready to go in to work the next morning. Not that she disliked her job; she just felt so in need of a total break for a while. Two weeks less a day would be great!

She glanced in Vanda's office but the lights were off so she went to the staff room only to be greeted with congratulations and thanks from the various teachers grabbing their morning coffee. The school sounded strangely silent without the students. It was as if the building itself took a deep breath and settled peacefully for the break.

Sally-Jo rushed in and headed straight for the coffeepot. "Morning, Lizzie. I am so deliriously thankful only two more days of work. Outside the house, that is."

Lizzie leaned against the counter and sipped her

coffee. "Did you spend the entire weekend getting ready for your guests?"

"Yesterday was the great house decorating marathon. You don't know my family, Lizzie. If I don't have every speck of space decorated, I'll be in for lectures galore about a traditional Baker Christmas. I spent a small fortune at Clifford's Home Hardware for stuff I'll probably never use again."

"Until the next time they all descend on you."

"Wash your mouth out, Lizzie Turner! But you're right. I'll invest in some large plastic storage bins in the New Year and tuck them away. Fortunately, Jacob came over and helped me pick out a tree and actually get it up."

"Are you going to introduce him to your family?"

Sally-Jo grimaced. "I hate to turn them loose on him, especially since, though separated from his wife, he's still married. Who knows how much they'll embarrass him and me. But they need to know about him."

"Uh-huh. That sounds promising."

Sally-Jo's cheeks colored slightly. "Yes. Now, I'd better get started on my paperwork or I'll be in here all week. Why don't you drop by tonight if you're not doing anything?"

"What, you have more decorating to do?"

"You'll see."

Sally-Jo squeezed by Ellen Germain in the

doorway. Ellen looked around the room before helping herself to some coffee. She moved next to Lizzie.

"Could we take a walk?" Ellen suggested. "I really do need to talk to you."

Lizzie agreed, hoping she wasn't having more trouble with those twins in her fifth-grade class, and grabbed a jacket. "Oh, oh," she said when they were outside. "I'd forgotten about my shadow. We'll be tailed by the police but try to ignore them."

"The police." Ellen shuddered and glanced nervously at the cruiser. "I've already had a visit from them. I'm thinking it was either Sally-Jo or you who told them about me being at the college where Derek Alton taught."

It wasn't a question but Lizzie felt compelled to answer. "It was me. You must know they're looking at every connection from his past."

Ellen turned right when they reached the sidewalk and set a fast pace. "I know. I'm not blaming you. I just wondered if you knew anything about the investigation?"

"Do you have something to worry about, Ellen?"

Ellen took a deep breath but continued walking, looking straight ahead. Lizzie didn't like to pry, but after all, Ellen had initiated this talk.

"Did you have an affair with him?"

Ellen stumbled but quickly recovered and kept

walking. At the end of the block she abruptly stopped and looked back toward the school. "They'll find out, won't they?"

"Who?"

"The police. They'll just keep on digging and then it will become public knowledge and everything will be ruined."

"I don't know what to say, Ellen."

Ellen took a deep breath. "I was in his class and we did have an affair." She started walking again. "He took pictures and videos."

Lizzie hadn't expected to hear that. She was flabbergasted.

"And," Ellen stopped walking again but continued staring ahead, "he was blackmailing me."

"What?"

Ellen turned to Lizzie, a frantic look on her face. "He saw my wedding picture in the paper. My husband's family is well-known there and has money. Derek contacted me and said he hated to do it, but he was desperately in need of money. I had no choice. If I didn't pay him . . . well, you can imagine. When my husband was transferred to Montgomery I thought it would just end but Derek kept tabs on us and I continued paying."

"Did you see him while he was here?"

She nodded. "Yes. That was part of the reason he came. I'd told him I'd had enough. I was tired of living a lie and trying to cover up where the money was going."

"What happened?"

"He said I'd be fired after the pictures got out. And my husband would leave me. But I'd made up my mind. He came to town to convince me in person to keep on paying." She started crying. Lizzie put an arm around her shoulders.

"But why would he do that? Was he really that much in need of the money?"

"Why? Because he was spiteful. Because I threatened to turn him in to the police. I guess that's what really pushed him. But I didn't kill him, I swear."

Lizzie wasn't sure what to do with the information. She wished she didn't know it. But she did. And Mark needed to know. Even though it would catapult Ellen to the top of the suspect list.

"Where were you when Derek was killed?"

Ellen sobbed. "I'd taken the day off. I'd been so upset from talking to him the night before. I spent most of it in bed, hiding, and then later in the day I went for a long walk through Glendale Park."

"Did anyone see you?"

"I don't know."

"I'm afraid you're going to have to tell the police, Ellen. They need to hear your story even though it looks bad. You know that, don't you?"

Ellen nodded through her tears.

"I promise I'll try to help in any way I can. I believe you didn't kill him and I'm going to find out who did. Let's go back and wait for Chief Dreyfus." She called Mark on her cell phone as they headed back to the school. She wanted him to be the one to hear the story.

Mark came back into the school after seeing Ellen seated in the back of the cruiser and driven off to the station by Officer Yost. Lizzie waited in the staff room.

"I know it looks bad for her," she said before he could speak, "but I don't think she's the killer."

Mark looked amused. "No? Why not?"

"She's too emotional to plan a cold-blooded killing. She's the type who might pick up a butcher knife and stab him in the kitchen during a fight but I really can't see her plotting to shoot him. And where would she get the rifle?"

"It's not so hard to do when you're desperate. I'll have to look deeper into her background. Maybe Ellen Germain was a markswoman or maybe she used to go hunting every weekend with her daddy. It's not inconceivable."

"Okay, I will keep quiet on the topic. But after all, Derek was playing around with quite a few of Ashton Corners's females. Xenia Henshaw confirmed he'd been fooling around during their marriage."

"Was this before or after the cookies? I thought I'd asked you to stay out of it."

She decided to ignore that. "Speaking of cookies, have you gotten an analysis back yet?"

He shook his head. "Do you have any information that Derek might have been blackmailing someone else, too?"

"No, but maybe one of the women?"

"These anonymous women whom I may not be able to trace?"

"Yes. Them." Lizzie leaned back against a table. She'd not told him about Nola Trendy and was still hoping she wouldn't have to. "On another topic, do you think you could drop the ghost detail? I really don't think I'm in any danger. I'm certain that shot was either a random sniper or meant to divert you in the investigation."

"Random sniper? We have those in Ashton Corners? And what makes you so sure you weren't the real target?"

"Because there hasn't been another attempt. There have been opportunities, even with that cruiser on my tail. If someone were dying to kill me, so to speak, it would have happened by now. Don't you think?"

Mark appeared to be thinking it over. "I don't like it but you may have a point. And, I can make use of my officers in other ways." He looked intently at her a moment. "It's done if you agree to certain things."

"Such as?" she asked warily.

"No active searching for the killer."

"And what would passive searching be?"

"Internet, phone calls . . . just try not to make yourself a visible target. And, secondly, I want to be kept in the loop about any passive searches. I want a list of who you've spoken to, searched for on Google, asked questions about . . . everything. And I want a report each day, end of day."

"How end of day?"

He sighed. "You're not going to make this easy, are you?"

"I just want to make sure I understand you so that I won't be accused of not going along with the agreement."

"Five P.M. every day."

"Agreed."

"I'll go have a longer chat with Ms. Germain now."

"You'll let me know how that goes?"

"As much as I can, you know that, Lizzie. I'll be in touch." He gave her arm a squeeze and left her there to put together a plan for passive investigation.

Chapter Thirty-six

◇◇◇

Be careful of what you wish for, Gretchen thought.

DING DONG DEAD—DEB BAKER

L izzie turned quickly and glanced around the school parking lot. She had the distinct feeling someone was watching her, but aside from a teacher parking his car, she was all alone. For a few seconds, she regretted having asked Mark to remove the protective cruiser.

She shrugged it off and gathered the casserole dish from the backseat, clicking the alarm system on as she walked toward the school. Final day before vacation and the annual staff Christmas luncheon in the staff room at noon. Her potluck contribution was a red lentil casserole she'd actually made from scratch a couple of days before and stashed in the freezer. She'd added sprigs of fresh parsley to complete the Christmas color theme. It wasn't often she felt the urge to cook but after seeing the photo of the casserole in *Southern Living* magazine, she wanted to try it out.

She left it on the counter in the staff room and went down the hall to Vanda Striker's office. Still dark. In the main office she checked the bulletin board and, sure enough, Vanda had taken the two days off. There was also a note that Ellen Germain would not be in. Everyone else seemed to be assembling for the feast day.

She had nothing left to do so she offered to help anyone who needed it. She was snapped up by a sixth-grade teacher and was asked to help sort workbooks for the next term. At noon, they both followed the wonderful aroma down the hall and into the staff room, which had been transformed into a Christmas tableau. Garlands of greenery had been draped along the edge of the counters, tinsel dangled from curtain rods, and poinsettias festooned coffee tables, bookcases and the fridge top.

Word had not turned into gossip about either Vanda or Ellen, for which Lizzie was thankful. The chatter revolved totally around Christmas plans, who was flying out to where, who had relatives coming in, how many gifts still needed buying and the like. By the time they were into cleanup detail, Lizzie felt energized and eager to get home and finish decorating. Finally, the Christmas spirit had arrived.

She stopped by Clifford's Home Hardware on her way to pick up an extra extension cord and while there, on a whim, chose an artificial holly wreath to hang on her door.

The cats were tuned in to the plans and sat awaiting her at the front door. She deposited her purchases and sprinted upstairs to change. She snuck a quick peek out the bedroom window but didn't see anyone lurking about. *Silly of me.* The cats sat poised on the end of the bed awaiting directions.

She laid out her plan of action, grabbed the first bin of decorations she'd returned upstairs to the office, and the cats followed her back downstairs. She poured a glass of acai juice from the fridge, drank half of it and went back upstairs for the second bin.

She took her time emptying the bins, pausing over the nativity scene and its memories of her daddy fashioning the stable out of an old Arturo Fuente cigar box. The porcelain figurines were in mint condition, although the shepherd had lost his crook when she was still a child. She could almost picture her daddy's big hands gently adding the pieces to the stable, tucked into the cotton snow on the mantel in their old living room.

The phone pulled her out of her reverie and she was pleased to hear Mark's voice. She glanced at the clock. Four thirty already.

"I was just leaving the office and going to walk Patchett. I thought I might come by after and we can . . . discuss the case some more." She could hear the suggestive tone in his voice.

"As much as I'd like to talk about the case all evening, I'd really appreciate it if you could help me choose and transport a Christmas tree." *You have a Jeep, after all.*

"Sure. We could start with that. See you in about an hour."

What about supper, she wanted to ask? Should she assume he'd eat on the way or plan something? Maybe she'd have some almond butter now to stave off hunger and just see how it played out.

Lizzie grabbed her jacket and scarf when Mark arrived and ran out to the Jeep. He drove to the other side of town and a lot that sold Christmas trees as a fund-raiser for Big Brothers Big Sisters.

"I didn't even know this was here," Lizzie admitted.

"I buy from them every year. They have some good quality trees here and it's a good cause. Now, how tall were you thinking?"

Lizzie stood on her tiptoes and stretched her right arm skyward.

Mark laughed. "Let's say six feet for your space."

"All right. That sounds manageable. I'd really like a pine." They wandered along the rows until Mark stopped and pulled out a nicely shaped Virginia pine.

"Perfect," Lizzie said. "How much?"

The attendant appeared like magic and quoted her fifty dollars. She was tempted to try and barter but she thought about the kids and knew that the few extra dollars could help.

Mark managed to bundle the tree onto his roof racks and tie it down. They headed back to her place and struggled to get it into the house. After securing it in the stand, Lizzie added water and stood back to admire it.

"It fits so well. Very good choice, Mark. Thanks."

He turned her to face him, wrapped his arms around her and said in a low voice, "Do you know the only thanks I need?"

She didn't trust herself to speak. "What?"

"Supper. I'm starving." He kissed her lightly on the lips.

"Humph. Actually, I am, too. Let's raid my freezer. You never know, we might get lucky."

"That's sort of what I was hoping," Mark said as he followed her to the kitchen. She noticed he took a thorough look around the room and peered outside. When he was satisfied, he leaned over her shoulder while she checked the fridge. She frowned and bent to sort through the items in the bottom freezer instead.

"Hmm," he said. "Not a whole lot of choice. How about grilled cheese sandwiches?"

Lizzie stood, almost knocking Mark over. "I can do that. And they'll taste just great with some wine." She pulled a bottle of Shiraz from the top cupboard and handed it to Mark.

He unscrewed the top and found a couple of glasses in the cupboard, filling them and passing one to Lizzie.

"To Christmas," he toasted.

She joined him, "To Christmas. Speaking of which . . ."

"Let me go first," he said. "I'd like to spend Christmas Day with you." He looked at her expectantly.

"Um, that's pretty much what I wanted to say but I'd like you to spend it with me at Molly's. I usually visit my mama in the morning, then go to Molly's for the afternoon and turkey dinner. Would that be okay with you?" She waited expectantly, hoping the arrangements would work for him.

He took a few moments to think about it. "That doesn't leave us much alone time."

She felt a tensing in her stomach, hoping he'd understand how important it was to her to have some time with both her mama and Molly on Christmas Day. She took a sip of wine and waited.

"Not wanting to plot this too heavily, but how about after you sing at the Christmas Eve service, we go to my place and walk Patchett, maybe even give him his gift, and then head over to your place? We could visit your mama and Molly after our Christmas morning together."

She couldn't remember seeing such a look of insecurity on Mark's face before. Like all his hopes and expectations were out there, ready to be blown away if she chose to do so. She realized he couldn't imagine how happy that suggestion made her feel.

She put her wineglass down on the counter, removed his from his hand and placed it down also and threw her arms around his neck. "I'd love to do that, Mark. It would be a perfect Christmas."

He kissed her until the tingle in her toes reached the top of her head. Both cats jumped up on the counter, not wanting to miss out on some attention. The head butt from Brie drew Lizzie back into the present and she glanced at the cat, then at the stove, and shrieked.

Mark turned around and grabbed the fry pan, flipping the crisp grilled cheese sandwiches into the sink.

"Oh my God. They're ruined. This kitchen's becoming a disaster area for me," she wailed.

He put an arm around her and grabbed the phone, dialing with one hand. Before placing an order for Chinese takeout, he kissed her on the forehead.

"Fifteen-minute service, guaranteed," he said, hanging up. "Now, let's just leave this until later and we'll finish our wine in the living room." He handed her a glass and gently shoved her in the direction of the settee.

By the time the food arrived, they still had most of their wine waiting, and had to untangle to open the door. Mark took care of the food while Lizzie set the kitchen table for two.

"Your holidays start tomorrow, right?" Mark asked between mouthfuls of General Tao's chicken.

"Uh-huh. Why, do you have an assignment for me?"

"Well, you could walk Patchett in the late afternoon, if you don't mind."

"Sure, but I was thinking something more along the lines of trying to shake some names of Derek's lovers out of Xenia Henshaw."

Mark stiffened. "We had an agreement, Lizzie. I don't want you talking to her, really. Not until I get the analysis back. Promise me you won't do that."

Lizzie sighed. "Yes, I promise. But maybe there's somebody else I can just casually talk to for you?"

"That would be a 'no.' Why don't you try some Christmassy pursuits instead? Like asking me for a gift list and then spending the day trying to fill it." He grinned.

"Huh. Who says I haven't already found your gift?"

"So, I can go ahead and buy what's on my list for myself?"

She tried to keep a straight face. "Well, not for another week. I'd like to take a look at the list anyway. Just for fun."

"Who would you want to talk to, just out of curiosity?" he asked.

She waved him off until her mouth was empty. "I'd like to go back to Calvin Knox. I know he's a remote possibility but he sounded like there was still a lot of anger inside him. Did you check his alibi?"

"Yes, he was at work, although he made a delivery for the store around noon."

"How long did it take him? Could he have made it here in that amount of time?"

"He tacked his lunch break onto it, so yes, he could have. But how would he have known where to find Derek? Whoever shot him either had to know his plans for the day or had to have been following him since he left the hotel. Knox doesn't fit either of those scenarios."

"What if he hired someone to tail him?"

"A private eye? We don't have many of those in Ashton Corners. And I've already checked with the two we do have to see if either had a job keeping an eye on Alton. Neither did."

"Hmm. So, probably not Calvin Knox."

"Doesn't look like it. Besides, I don't think he could afford it. But he's not off the list."

"What about Sally-Jo, is she off the list?"

"No, but she's at the bottom. Until the killer is behind bars, that list stays intact. I'll add to it but not subtract."

"So, we're back to the women in his life."

"Seems the most likely. Lizzie, I know you're anxious to help, but please, just don't. I'm not able to do my job properly if I'm worrying about you all the time."

Should she tell him about feeling like she was being followed? Probably not. He might put it down to foolishness or, on the other hand, reassign a car to tail her. Neither appealed to her.

"I'd also like to point out, I'm off duty right now and I'd really like to get through a meal without discussing the murder of Derek Alton."

"Too late for that," Lizzie said. "But, we can probably find something to do that will take our minds off him." She ran her fingers lightly up his arm.

He grabbed her hand, set aside his food and pulled her toward him for a kiss.

Chapter Thirty-seven

◇◇◇

"Oh dear," she murmured. This was the last thing she needed.

THE TEABERRY STRANGLER
—LAURA CHILDS

L izzie woke feeling totally energized and ready to get on with her day. She dressed quickly, fed the cats and was out the door within ten minutes. She looked around but couldn't spot anyone else out at that hour. She turned right and planned to do her usual route in reverse. She did notice the Prius parked in Nathaniel's driveway yet again.

Her curiosity sensors were quivering but she decided Nathaniel would have to talk to her; she couldn't just come out and ask whom it belonged to. Maybe a relative was moving in to keep him company, or even take care of him. He was aging. Maybe he wasn't too well. She hadn't seen him much in the past couple of weeks and hadn't really given too much thought to him, what with everything going on.

Maybe she should stop over today and make sure everything was okay. She felt badly that she'd been so wrapped up in her thoughts of murder that she might have missed something right under her nose.

Just before turning into the park, Lizzie stopped abruptly and turned, searching for movement. That feeling of being watched was back. She wondered if it was wise to take the park path but, seeing nothing, decided to go for it.

Her senses tingled as she ran toward the main roadway at the entrance. She'd worked her imagination up real good. *Stop it. No one is watching you. No one is around.* Only the squirrels, she added as two ran across her path.

By the time she got home, she'd managed to shake the fear and chided herself for being such a wuss. She did some cooldown stretches, blended a protein drink, which she drank standing at the counter, and went upstairs to shower.

Over breakfast, she made a list of her plans for the day. Christmas shopping was at the top. Contrary to what she'd told Mark, she hadn't bought any gifts as yet. Not for anyone. She'd offered to take Stephanie to her doctor's appointment at two P.M. and she had to finish decorating the tree. Well, start decorating it, actually. Not much got done the night before. She smiled at the memory.

First stop in town was at Justine's Frocks, where she picked out a poncho for her mama. The deep rose color was her favorite and she knew the soft cashmere would appeal to her sense of touch. She was leaving the shop when a mother-of-pearl hair comb on a shelf near the door caught her eye. *Very Spanish senorita.* Molly would love it, she was sure. She left feeling pleased that two gifts were now off her list.

She'd drawn Bob's name in the book club gift exchange, and although she was tempted to buy him an Agatha Christie, she thought that better left for Molly to do. She'd stop by Clifford's Home Hardware on her way home and pick up some handy-dandy new tool. But she wanted to have gifts for Stephanie, who was to be at Molly's for Christmas dinner, and Andie, too.

She veered into Creamy Delights and was immediately caught up in the fragrances of the shop. Some luxurious body cream would be a treat for Stephanie, she was sure. She found some, thick and wonderful smelling, called Mango Memories. Pricey but certainly something Stephanie wouldn't be able to buy herself. Not for a long time. She wondered if Andie would like something from the shop.

She realized just how hard this gift would be to choose. She had no idea if Andie was into creams and fragrances. She wouldn't dare choose any item of clothing, especially since her own tastes were nowhere near punk or gothic. Books were a possibility but since they spent so much time with them, she wanted something totally different. She let her eyes wander over the counters and displays. Nothing leapt out at her as the "perfect gift."

She sighed and hoped inspiration would hit before Christmas Day.

She couldn't resist stopping at the Book Bin, which meant, of course, another book. Maybe something for Mark but she had no idea what his tastes in reading were. Odd.

Lizzie waved at Jensey who was surrounded by desperate shoppers. Two high school girls were also working the floor helping to relieve the pressure. One asked if Lizzie needed any help but she declined. When she'd chosen a book for herself, the first in a new mystery series by Jacklyn Brady, she took her place in line at the cash register.

Jensey looked harried but smiled at Lizzie when it was her turn. "Business is good," Lizzie commented.

"It will be like this all week. This is what keeps me going until spring," Jensey answered in a soft voice. "Are you all set for Christmas?"

"Just finishing off my shopping today."

"You're off school now?"

"Yes, for two wonderful weeks."

"Nice for you. Are you singing at the Christmas Eve service at St. John's again?"

"Yes. Will you be at the service?"

"Absolutely. It sets the whole tone for the season."

Lizzie stared at Jensey for a moment, wondering if she should slip in a question about Derek, but they'd been over it all before and she didn't want to harangue her in front of her customers. Next week when things calmed down, she'd be back in.

She dashed home for a quick lunch. She had some time to spare so she pulled out the strings of lights and set about adding them to the Christmas tree. Edam and Brie appeared without warning and batted the lights around as Lizzie tried to finish the job without having the tree pulled over. She then distracted them with treats before running off to pick up Stephanie.

She managed to read a few chapters of the new Jacklyn Brady book while she waited for Stephanie's appointment to end.

"Would you like to stop by the Oasis for a drink before going home? My treat," Lizzie said as she helped Stephanie maneuver back into the car.

"Oh, that's real sweet of you, Lizzie, but I don't think I can manage getting in and out of this car too many more times. I'm just so tired of being so humongous. I can't wait for this baby to get here."

"What did the doctor say?"

"Same as last week. 'Any day now.' Easy for him to say." Stephanie looked like she might erupt in tears.

"All right, I'll take a rain check for an afternoon

escape after the baby's born. We'll get Andie to babysit and just have a quiet break. I'm sure you'll need it."

Stephanie chuckled. "I'm already looking forward to that. Thank you. I really am sorry to be such a bother and I'm sorry I'm not helping out more with this murder thing."

Lizzie glanced at her in surprise as she started the car. "Why, there's nothing you could be doing. It's all up to the police now. Don't you worry about it."

"Well, I know you're right but I also feel just so badly about your being shot at."

Lizzie reached out and touched her hand. "Thank you for that, Stephanie, but the police have it all under control. See, no police cruiser following me anymore. For all we know, they may be closing in on the murderer right now." She glanced around as she said it, suddenly aware how vulnerable they were in that parking lot. And that feeling of being watched had returned. She gave her head a slight shake.

"I'll get you home and settled right quick. You're planning on coming to Molly's for Christmas dinner, aren't you?"

"Oh yes . . . if I'm still around. It's been a long time since I've been part of a really happy Christmas celebration. I'm really, really looking forward to it." She clapped her hands like a small child.

"And everything else is all right?"

"You mean the calls? I haven't heard a thing from my ex-boyfriend since I told him I was going to the police about harassment. That was a good idea. I think he got the message. At least, I hope so."

"Well, you remember to call right away if you hear from him or if you're feeling spooked at all."

"I will. Thanks."

They pulled up in front of the small two-story building where Stephanie rented the basement apartment. Lizzie helped her out of the car and on the short walk along the sidewalk, holding her purse while she unlocked the door.

"Can I get you something to drink? Help you tuck in?" Lizzie asked inside.

"No, I'm just fine. I'm going to go lie down on my bed for a short nap. I have some soup that Molly brought over ready to heat up for my supper. And Andie's coming by later with a DVD for us to watch. Something with vampires in it." She grinned. "Not that it'll be good for my blood pressure."

Lizzie gave her a hug and let herself out. She glanced at the dashboard clock. She had a little over an hour to get home, feed herself and then get off to choir practice. She started humming "Silver Bells" as she planned her meal, something with three food groups for a change.

Everyone had made it to the practice. Everyone who would be singing at the Christmas Eve service, that is. Lizzie glanced around at the smaller but still well-balanced group. Just enough sopranos, altos, tenors and basses for a full sound. Lucille winked at her.

After the warm-up, Stanton Giles took them on a run-through of the service since many of them were not members of the congregation. He spent more time on the parts the choir would be leading, and after the break, he concentrated totally on the mass setting and the anthem.

She felt invigorated by the time the practice was over and headed home eager to finish decorating her tree. After adding the final ornament, a crystal ballerina her daddy had bought her, which always had the place of honor near the top, she threaded some wide red velvet ribbon around the tree then stood back to enjoy her masterpiece. She had Christmas music playing on the CD player, a glass of wine at her fingertips and, as she settled onto the couch, two cats instantly attached to her lap.

Eventually she dislodged the cats and searched for the list of code names that Derek had been using. She found it on the counter by the telephone. She now had some new names to add. And she had two code words without names: "ending" and "veritas." The connections glared at her. Ellen Germain had to be "ending."

The other name came as a shock. She only knew one person whose name started with a "V." Was Vanda Striker "veritas"? How had she missed that? She thought back to their conversation about Derek. It hadn't really raised any red flags. Maybe that's why Vanda hadn't sprung to mind. But what was her secret? Surely not an affair with Derek Alton? It boggled the mind.

She'd already denied knowing him. Lizzie would just have to come right out and ask her. Was that what had really led to the divorce?

Chapter Thirty-eight

◇◇◇

I wanted to know. I didn't want to know.
LIE DOWN WITH THE DEVIL—LINDA BARNES

On her way back from her morning run, Lizzie let her mind wander through all she still had to do in preparation for Christmas. She was so deep in thought she almost missed the movement on Nathaniel's front porch as she passed by.

She glanced over in time to see Nathaniel, in his bathrobe, in conversation with a well-groomed gray-haired woman. It looked like they were saying good-bye. Lizzie noticed the silver Prius next. The same Prius she'd seen so many times lately parked in his driveway.

She almost tripped and focused on the sidewalk until she turned into her driveway. She tried to watch the tableau without appearing to stare but knew she'd failed when Nathaniel looked over at her and, after a few seconds, gave her a slight wave. She waved back and ducked into the house.

Why did she feel like she'd just been privy to something? She shrugged it off and did some stretches before mixing a protein shake. The front doorbell rang after she'd showered and was looking for some breakfast ideas in the fridge.

She opened the door to Nathaniel. He looked sheepish and handed her a plate of freshly baked buttermilk scones.

"I thought we might enjoy these. Do you have a cup of coffee to go with them?"

Lizzie nodded and led the way into the kitchen. "These smell delicious. I'm sure glad I had a long run this morning." Oops, she mentioned it. Now it was his turn.

He cleared his throat. "Yes, I saw you coming back. And I imagine you saw Lavenia and me taking our leave of each other."

Lizzie looked at him. *So formal. So sweet.* She nodded.

"Ahem. Well, you see, we've become quite fond of each other. I'm not quite sure how it happened but there it is." He looked helpless.

Lizzie smiled. "Where did you meet her?"

"We met at the public library. We both attended a talk entitled "New Perennials Being Introduced to the Region" last month. We sat next to each other and started talking and, well, it's just so nice to have a woman back in my life. And I don't mean any disrespect to Charlaine. She'll always be my special love. But, you know, I've been lonely."

Lizzie set his cup of coffee in front of him and added a dish of butter next to the scones. "I think that's just wonderful, Nathaniel."

"You do?"

"Of course. You're a real catch, you know. And you should have someone in your life. Now, I hope she appreciates your baking."

He chuckled. "Oh yes, and she has some very good recipes up her sleeve, also."

His chuckle turned into something more conspiratorial and Lizzie actually blushed.

"What are your Christmas plans, Nathaniel?"

"Well, I was going to drive down to Naples to spend a few days with my daughter. In fact, I still might. Lavenia is supposed to visit her son and his family in Boston. So, we'll probably just continue with our plans. You'll be spending it with your mama and Molly?"

Lizzie nodded.

Nathaniel looked at the clock. "Speaking of which, I have some errands to run. Got to buy some stocking stuffers, you know. I'll leave around noon tomorrow. I'll pop around to say good-bye."

"Good. I want to give you your present."

He chuckled. "Ah-hah . . . I look forward to that."

Lizzie set about vacuuming the main floor after he left and had just put the machine away when the doorbell rang again. This time it was Andie on her doorstep.

She bounced in and Lizzie felt relieved. She'd been hoping Andie's spirits would lift as soon as exams were over.

"I think I might have passed everything, Lizzie. Not aced but at least passed," Andie said jubilantly.

"That's great. You've worked hard so you deserve to pass. What do you have planned for your holidays?"

Andie shrugged and eyed the plate of scones and looked back at Lizzie. Lizzie nodded and Andie chose the largest one, opening it to slather butter inside. She took a huge bite and collapsed in the chair.

"Would you like a tea?"

Andie shook her head then reconsidered. "Do you have any cola?"

"No, but I have acai juice."

Andie scrunched up her nose. "No thanks, water will do."

Lizzie poured a glass for her and sat across the table. "What do you usually do on Christmas Day?"

"Oh, my folks sleep late, we open presents, and then go to the country club for turkey dinner. Only this year, they're flying to Nassau for a few days."

"And you're not going with them?" Lizzie was shocked.

"Nope. I can't stand the thought of a beachy Christmas and they don't really want me with them in their 'exotic locale.'" She made a face. "It's okay. I'm staying at Gussy Gilbert's. There's just her and her mama so I can bunk in the spare room. It'll be okay." She snagged another scone.

Lizzie tried to read Andie. The cool exterior was so nonchalant, but she knew Andie was a deeply emotional girl. She'd like to have a long talk with Mr. and Mrs. Mason but knew it wasn't her place nor was it likely to do any good. They made sure she had the essentials, even special tutoring when her grades hovered at the failing mark. But it seemed to end there. Not a warm, loving family.

"Why don't you come over to Molly's in the afternoon for Christmas dinner? Do you think Gussy and her mama would mind? I'll be there, and Stephanie and Bob. And Chief Dreyfus. Molly makes a turkey dinner that's to die for."

Lizzie saw Andie was tempted. A small smile tugged at the corners of her mouth as she struggled to remain cool. "I'll have to check with Mrs. Gilbert first. They're kinda expecting me."

"Okay." Lizzie wondered if Molly might stretch the table to include Gussy and her mama. She'd be sure to ask.

Lizzie was the first to arrive at the book club Christmas party. Molly took a minute from arranging the trays of goodies she'd baked to relieve Lizzie of the wine and cake she carried in. Then she gave Lizzie a big hug.

"I thought everyone would enjoy this French croissant. I found it in a Wolfgang Puck recipe book and just had to try it out. Taste one, tell me what you think, honey."

Lizzie bit into the flaky texture and sighed. "Heavenly."

Molly's smile lit up her face. She was wearing a stunning cream-colored silk cheongsam with orange and gold Chinese embroidery. Lizzie felt frumpy beside her, even though she'd thought she'd looked festive in a red silk tunic with black leather and rayon leggings.

Molly watched Lizzie taking in her outfit. "Oh, don't you go worrying none, honey. I'm just having some fun here. This is the final one of my armchair travel outfits, and I thought this was the perfect night to wear it."

The others arrived almost as a group. Everyone was dressed for Christmas; even Andie had ditched her usual torn jeans and black T for a lime green cotton blouse and, from the look of it, brand-new jeans. At least there were no holes in the jeans. She looked as excited as a small child.

It didn't take long for the food and wine to flow. Lizzie noticed that Bob seemed to be sticking very close to Molly and that she wasn't objecting. Stephanie chose a solid-backed chair and stayed put except for numerous visits to the powder room off the library.

Sally-Jo looked more relaxed than Lizzie had

seen her in a few weeks. With her family arriving the next day, that was a surprise. Jacob hovered around her so maybe that accounted for it.

Lizzie thought fleetingly about Mark, wondering if he were still at work. She hadn't heard from him all day and had decided not to bother him even though she was dying to know if he'd made any progress. She'd had to leave a message when she made her five P.M. check-in call.

As if reading her mind, Bob asked, "What mischief have you been getting yourself into lately?"

"No mischief. I gave Mark my word that I wouldn't go questioning anyone else. And I will keep it. I hope. But, there is another person on the suspect list that y'all haven't heard about yet."

Jacob grunted. "I hope that means some have been eliminated." He glanced at Sally-Jo.

"Derek has been blackmailing her for several years now. In fact, she's the reason he came to Ashton Corners," Lizzie explained.

"Hah." Bob slapped his knee. "Blackmail's a top motive. And if it was worth paying him off, it might have merited a murder, too. Do you know her? Do you think she could have done it?"

"I don't know her that well but she doesn't strike me as being a cold-blooded killer."

"Does she have an alibi?" Jacob asked.

"No, like most of the suspects."

"Why was he blackmailing her?" Stephanie asked. She looked exhausted but in a party mood, wearing a tight-fitting white stretch T, green pants and a white scarf with tiny Santa Claus and reindeer patterns all over it.

Once again, Lizzie wondered how much to share. She felt strangely at odds talking about others' secrets and yet, those secrets could have led to murder. She explained as briefly as possible.

Bob whistled. "That's pretty serious, I'd say."

"I sure hope they catch the killer before Christmas," Molly stated, passing around the plate of shortbread. "It's supposed to be a season of peace and goodwill."

Lizzie nodded. "I sure hope so, too." She was also hoping that Mark wouldn't be distracted by the investigation over the holidays.

The evening passed quickly with the highlight being the sharing of gifts. Lizzie loved the pewter bookmark in the shape of a Siamese cat from Jacob, and Bob was pleased with his miniature LED flashlight shaped like a fish, which made Lizzie feel that the hour she had spent trying to decide on just the right gift had been well worth it.

Lizzie was the last to leave. She felt exhausted even though Molly, forty years her senior, looked like she was still raring to go. It pleased Lizzie to see this renewed energy but it tired her out even more. She headed home and to bed.

By Friday afternoon, Lizzie was really getting into the spirit of the season. She knew she should put all thoughts of the murder out of her mind until after the Christmas weekend but she stopped by the station to tell Mark about solving the mystery of the code names. He was standing at the front desk talking to a man when she entered. Mark glanced at her and waited until the man had stopped talking before turning to Lizzie.

"Lizzie, this is Derek Alton's agent and we've just been talking about his new book. Lizzie Turner . . . Quentin Underhill."

They shook hands and Lizzie was about to ask if he had the new manuscript when Mark gave her a discreet shake of his head. Now she really wanted some answers but it looked like Underhill was on his way out, so she decided to wait.

The short—well, shorter than her five-foot-eight—man looked to be in his forties, with blond hair just touching the collar of his chartreuse shirt. She'd bet the color was out of a bottle. He kept rocking back on his heels the entire time he said his good-byes, which turned into a long speech about how much he appreciated the police and all they were doing.

Lizzie could tell that Mark was doing his best to remain unperturbed. When Underhill finally left, Mark let out a long sigh.

"That guy was really getting on my nerves. Just too slick, and that little end speech?"

The officer sitting at a computer behind him let out a chuckle.

Mark suddenly grinned. "Yeah, he was kinda funny. Come into my office and I'll fill you in." He put his hand under Lizzie's elbow and guided her into the inner sanctum and then his office. He gave her arm a final squeeze before walking around his desk.

She sat opposite him. "So, give. What did he say about Derek's book?"

"He confirmed that it was the sequel to *Judgment* and, from what Alton had told him, very explosive. More than a few people would not be happy."

"Wow. So, is Underhill a suspect?"

"I'd like him to be but he was in New York at the time, in a meeting with a publisher."

"He could have hired a hit man."

"I'd like to pin something on him but it won't be murder. I'd say Alton was worth a lot more to him alive than dead. He wasn't a big enough name to drive sales up significantly since his death and there was already a bidding war over this book, apparently. Now that's dead, so to speak, since there isn't any book as yet."

"Nothing?"

"Just some more notes, which his agent handed over. He indicated there wasn't even enough here in order to hire a ghostwriter to do the book."

"That's too bad, or really good, for someone. Well, you've got enough suspects already, haven't you?"

"You've got that right. What's on your mind?"

"I've been going over this list of code words along with the names of women who've asked about him or had some connection. I think I've matched them all now. Here, have a look."

She handed over the list and watched Mark's face as he read it over.

"That's good, Lizzie. I'll go through Alton's notes and see if anything matches or indicates what he planned to write about them." He glanced at the list again. "Xenia Henshaw. For an ex, she's sure turning up a lot. I got the results back on the cookie. It was loaded with powdered OxyContin. That's a pain-relieving opiate."

"Do you think she'd planned to bring them to the book club, substitute hers for his and, what, kill him?"

"Maybe not kill. But make him deathly ill, at the very least. I'm going to bring her in and see how she explains this." He pointed at the report.

"I'd love to be here when you do that."

"Not going to happen, Lizzie. You've already done enough. I want you to leave the rest to me."

"You're such a tough guy," Lizzie said as she leaned across his desk and gave him a quick kiss.

He was right. For now.

Paige finished setting the table and called everyone to sit down. Her two exuberant daughters, Cate and Jenna, had been vying to sit on Lizzie's lap and tell her about what they thought was under the tree for them. Lizzie stood gratefully and shepherded them to the table.

"I can see this household is seriously lacking in Christmas anticipation," she said, taking her seat opposite the two girls.

Brad grinned. "As if you're not excited, also, Lizzie Turner. I know all about the Christmas you opened and then retaped all your gifts under the tree." He passed her a serving dish of balsamic root vegetables.

Lizzie glared at Paige. "You told him! I thought that was our secret."

Paige shrugged. "Sorry. We didn't cross our hearts." She turned to Brad. "Lizzie is just a big kid at heart at this time of year. We all know that."

Cate said, "I want to stay up and say hi to Santa but Mama won't let me."

"Your mama's wise," said Lizzie. "She knows Santa's shy and might leave without giving you gifts if he sees you."

"Oh. Okay. I'll go to bed. What did you bring me Auntie Lizzie?"

Brad answered. "That's not very polite, sweet pea. If Auntie Lizzie forgot to buy gifts this year, she'd feel very foolish right about now."

Lizzie smiled. "Oh, there might be something in the trunk of my car. I thought it best to get supper out of the way before adding more excitement."

"Bless you," Paige said as she took her seat at

the head of the table nearest the kitchen. They had renovated the house soon after buying it, just before Jenna was born, and after many rounds with the architect, they had opted to stay with the traditional layout rather than the open concept Paige had initially wanted.

After supper, as promised, Lizzie brought in a large shopping bag of gifts. She let the girls eye them and set them under the tree, and when they'd finished, they presented her with three gifts—a large gift bag from Paige and Brad, and a small one from each of the girls.

"This is wonderful . . . thanks so much. I'm going to take them and open them with my mama tomorrow afternoon, if that's okay with y'all."

The girls bounced around the room. "Yes, it is, Auntie Lizzie," they chanted.

Once the girls had gotten interested in their toys, Paige asked Lizzie about the case. "Where's your police escort? You didn't ditch them, did you?"

"No. I told Mark I didn't really think I was a target and would he please remove the shadow . . . so he did."

"Huh. I thought he had better sense than that."

Lizzie looked at Paige in surprise. "Yeah. But nothing else has happened to me. I think I was meant to be a diversion, to get Mark looking elsewhere for Derek's killer."

"Yeah, but," Paige mimicked, "the reason no one's taken a potshot at you could be because of that black-and-white police car following you around town. Did you think of that?"

Lizzie looked at Paige and decided it was time to switch gears. Paige could be very stubborn at times, like now. "The suspects in Derek's murder are all local."

"What? That's not good news. I'd hate to think someone I knew was capable of that. So, who's on the list? Anyone I know?"

"I'll tell you but it goes no further. Not even to Brad."

Paige nodded and crossed her heart with an extra kissing of two fingers and a swat at the air thrown in. It was so natural, they'd done it hundreds of times as kids, that Lizzie was momentarily overcome by a blast of the past. She swallowed hard.

"Okay. So, Xenia Henshaw, Realtor and ex-wife of Derek, formerly Harvey Warren, is at the top. There's also a teacher who was being blackmailed by him . . ."

"Not Sally-Jo!"

Lizzie shook her head and continued, "Followed by any number of Ashton Corners females, whose names I won't divulge because if they're not murderers, their indiscretions are none of my business. But you do know one of them."

"Oh, Lizzie. You didn't have to add that. Now I'll be looking at every woman I pass on the street, wondering." Paige huffed. "Well, what about the guy from River's End? The writer?"

"He has a solid alibi. He could have hired someone but I don't think he could afford it and it seems like he's gotten on with his life, even though he still carried a grudge. Now, Derek's agent has just entered the picture, and although he's just passed along information, I'm wondering if maybe he was double-dealing Derek or something like that."

"Or Derek meant to ditch him?"

"Yeah . . . there are all sorts of possibilities. I'm not sure if Mark has him on his radar as a suspect, though."

"I'm sure you'll enlighten him. You know, for all of the Mr. Creep that it sounds like he was, Derek Alton didn't deserve to be murdered, so it's sad."

"It is, and this is Christmas, so let's leave sad topics behind."

Brad entered the living room carrying a tray with three glasses of cognac and Lizzie wondered if he'd been listening, or else his timing was perfect.

"Wonderful. Thanks, Brad," Lizzie said, choosing the glass nearest her.

"So, Lizzie . . . what's your Christmas Day look like?" Brad asked.

"The usual. The morning with my mama, then to Molly's in the afternoon for turkey dinner. She's also invited Stephanie Lowe, if she's not in the hospital giving birth, and Bob Miller." She took a sip. "And Mark."

"Aha! Good on Molly."

"Well, actually, Mark invited me to spend Christmas with him so I suggested he join us instead."

Paige's eyes almost popped out of head. "He wanted to spend Christmas with you? Alone? And you're dragging him to Molly's? Your first Christmas together?"

"You know I can't not go to Molly's."

Paige sighed. "You're right, of course. And it will be good for him to see what he's getting into."

Lizzie threw a pillow at Paige and settled in to enjoy her drink and listen to the excitement the two girls stirred up when they joined the adults.

As she was getting ready for bed later, Lizzie thought about Paige's comment about Mark and Christmas. It would be good to make him totally aware of her life forces. Her routine with her mama and the fact that Molly played such a major role in it all. Brie stretched up her side and she picked her up for a cuddle. And, of course, her cats.

Chapter Thirty-nine

◇◇◇

"Guys," she said, when their chatter came to a pause, "there's something I'd like to talk to you about."

STRING OF LIES—MARY ELLEN HUGHES

Another sunny Christmas Eve morning. Lizzie shook her head, silly to feel sad about the sun! She loved sunny mornings. They energized her, helped her look forward to the day, put a smile on her face. But she'd been hoping for snow. Ever since the small snowfall last week, her appetite had been whetted and the optimist in her had held out hope.

Oh well. Just a few hours until Christmas Eve. That was an exciting thought. Even in the darkest years after her daddy had died, Christmas Eve always kept its magic and gave her a bright spot to focus on.

She tucked her running clothes in the closet and, fresh from the shower, pulled on some jeans and a light green hoodie. She quickly made her bed and gave the room a thorough tidying, just in case she'd be sharing it later.

Edam and Brie were already waiting at their dishes when she entered the kitchen. She filled their bowls, changed the water and brushed them as they ate. She made an espresso and read the paper on the sofa while she sipped the dark brew. The cats joined her, and after she'd finished, she relaxed with them awhile, stroking their silky fur.

The phone made her finally move. It was Mark.

"Happy Christmas Eve," he started.

"And to you. I'm so glad you called."

"That's what I like to hear. Any reason in particular?"

"Not really."

He sighed. "That's nice. Now, I have some news I thought you'd like to hear. Alton's notes made mention of some contractual changes he wanted. I don't think his agent had meant for me to see that. However, when I called him about it, the agent admitted they were going through some heavy negotiations and that's why the work was stalled. Derek refused to write anything until he either got a better deal with the publisher or the agent cut his commission."

"That explains a lot but also might give the agent a motive, wouldn't you think?"

"I did think, but his alibi is airtight and he swears he didn't know that Derek was coming to Ashton Corners. So, even if he'd hired someone to kill him, they'd have had to be tailing him all along. And why wait to take him out at your place?"

"So, you have been giving that angle some thought."

"Only because I knew you'd go right there. Quentin Underhill is not our killer."

"What are you going to do next?"

"Try to flush out the person."

"Really? How?"

"This manuscript is of interest to so many, I thought that next week I'd let word out that I have a copy of it and hope to make an arrest shortly."

"Hmm. What do you think the killer will do? Run? Try to steal the manuscript? Shoot you?"

"I hope either of the first two." She could hear him sigh. "I probably won't have time to stop over at your place before the church service tonight but I'll wait for you outside after it's over."

"Absolutely. I'm looking forward to it."

"Me, too."

Lizzie's toes tingled at the suggestive tone of his voice.

Lizzie wanted some fresh flowers to take her mama in the afternoon, so after some housework, she drove to Blooms 'n Roses and also picked up a small bouquet of white roses for herself. On a whim, she stopped by the Book Bin. Jensey seemed run off her feet while her two high school hirelings hung around the cash register, talking to each other. By the time Jensey was free, Lizzie was almost ready to leave.

"Did you have a chance to give any more thought to Harvey Warren, Jensey?" Couldn't hurt to push a bit.

Jensey's smile froze on her face. "No. I already told you, Lizzie. And just what are you insinuating, anyway? I don't appreciate this one bit."

Lizzie almost took a step backward. Ouch. "I'm sorry if this upsets you, Jensey. It's a natural question to be asking . . . I'm asking a lot of the Ashton Corners women about him. I didn't mean to offend you."

"Well you did, and here I thought you were such a nice person. Anyway, I have lots of customers as you can see. I need to get back to them."

She turned her back on Lizzie and sought out a couple in the historical mysteries section. Lizzie felt like she'd been slapped. Something was bothering Jensey.

Maybe it was just the tension of the Christmas rush. She'd probably be apologizing tonight at church for being so brusque.

Lizzie had a quick lunch then changed into a pink tank top with a silk chiffon blouse top and gray jeans, grabbed the flowers and another small gift bag, and went to Magnolia Manor.

Her mama appeared to be waiting for her, dressed in a pale blue long-sleeved blouse and navy slacks, sitting in the tub chair beside the window. A good sign.

Lizzie showed her the flowers, white lilies with red and white Gerbera daisies and some holiday greens and red berries thrown in for effect, and put them in a vase of water. She talked about her plans for the evening. She left out the details of her sleeping arrangements but emphasized she'd be at the Manor in time for Christmas lunch with Evelyn. She'd hoped for some sign of glee but told herself it would mean a lot to her mama tomorrow.

She passed over the gift bag and waited until Evelyn finally decided to look into it. She pulled out the poncho and seemed to get lost in the color. By the time the tea cart stopped outside her door, Evelyn finally seemed more animated and they enjoyed tea and a cookie together.

When Lizzie left, it was with a promise to be back for lunch the next day. Evelyn squeezed her hand. Lizzie kissed her forehead and left. After a quiet early evening with the cats, a glass of red wine and a good book, and Christmas music on NPR in the background, Lizzie got ready for church. They had to be there an hour early for a short practice.

Lizzie made sure she had all of her music in her binder and took one last look in the mirror. She'd chosen a silver satin tank top and three-quarter-length black crepe skirt, even though the choir gown would cover all. She was thinking of afterward.

She made sure the cats' dishes were filled, explained she'd be home much later and left.

Several cars were already in the parking lot. It

looked like she'd be one of the last of the choir arriving. Oh well. She'd been warming up in the car. She parked at the far end of the lot, leaving the spaces closer to the church available for the congregation, many of whom were elderly. She grabbed her stuff and locked the car. She heard someone call her name and turned to see Jensey Pollard standing at the back of Lansing Dry Cleaners, the next building over on Charles Street.

"Oh, hey, Jensey. You're here early."

"I have a good reason, Lizzie. Do you want to hear it?"

Lizzie glanced around. Something in Jensey's voice had her feeling uneasy. She was totally alone in the lot, aside from Jensey. *This is foolish; it's Jensey. She's probably wanting to apologize.*

"It's okay, Jensey."

"No, it's not. Nothing will be okay again. And you've ruined it, Lizzie."

Lizzie saw the rifle at Jensey's side, pointing to the ground.

"What are you talking about?" She couldn't take her eyes off the gun.

"You've figured it all out, haven't you?"

"No. I haven't figured out anything. What are you talking about?"

"Derek . . . no, Harvey. And me." She suddenly brought the rifle up and pointed it at Lizzie. "Walk over here, real quick now. Don't say anything that might attract someone."

Lizzie dropped her bag but hung on to her binder. She walked quickly toward Jensey, who motioned her along the small alley between the backs of the stores. She told Lizzie to stop when they were about three stores in. Lizzie tried to maneuver to the side so that the tiny light shining in her face would be in Jensey's instead.

"Just stop moving. Back up against that wall. Now, tell me all you found out."

"Believe me, Jensey, I know nothing specific. I have lots of speculation. Mainly about Xenia Henshaw and if she killed Derek. But also about Derek, or rather Harvey, and the many affairs he had. I'm wondering if he was blackmailing any of the women and maybe that's what got him killed. And there were a lot of women."

"Shut up!" she shrieked. "Are you trying to hurt me even more? I know Harvey had many lovers but I was the one he truly loved. He told me so. Even though . . ." She sobbed and seemed distracted. Lizzie gauged the distance between them but thought she'd need a lot of luck to make it to the gun before Jensey could fire it. Better to keep her talking.

"Did you kill him?"

"Yes. Yes. Yes," she screamed. "He admitted he'd written about me, about us, about what happened, in *Judgment*. And that he'd be continuing the story in his new book. He laughed when I asked if he was sure I couldn't be identified. He actually said it might do me some good to come out from under my rock and show everybody that I could have some fun. Fun! There isn't a day goes by when I don't think about what happened and just shrivel up inside."

That must have been some breakup. "Jensey, you have a wonderful husband. Derek was a womanizer and not a very honorable guy, from what I keep hearing. Why do this to yourself? He wasn't worth it."

"What will my 'wonderful husband' do when he learns that his wife had an affair and an abortion? What will the whole town think? I killed my child. I killed it because Harvey told me to do so. He wouldn't marry me. I couldn't tell my 'wonderful husband' it was his because . . . well, he would have known. And what made it even worse, I found out later that I couldn't have any more children."

The tears were streaming down her face. Lizzie dared to hope she might lose concentration and lower the gun. Instead, she squared her shoulders and sniffed.

"I chose to be a murderer instead. So, now I've also murdered the person whose fault it was. And you know he had it coming. I don't feel badly about it, at all."

"Why shoot at me?" Lizzie whispered. Now she was scared. Her hands were shaking, and she almost dropped her binder. Maybe she could throw it at Jensey and deflect the rifle, or at least distract her long enough to run. But where? She couldn't possibly reach the parking lot before she was shot. She thought she saw movement at the end of the alley but couldn't be certain.

"I did it to make the police think you were really the target, so they'd stop looking for someone tied to Derek. I hadn't meant to hurt you . . . or I would have. I'm a good shot."

"And now?"

"Now, you're too close. You know everything. You knew when you were in my store today. I could tell. Or at least you were so close to getting it that I couldn't take the chance you'd catch on and tell the police."

"What are you planning to do now?"

"I'm going to have to shoot you. I like you, Lizzie. So, I'm really sorry. But you know, once you've murdered someone, you become hardened to it. Makes the next one easier. Forgive me, Lizzie."

She raised the rifle to her shoulder and Lizzie flung her binder at Jensey's face. The shot grazed Lizzie's left shoulder and threw her back against the wall. She felt a surge of rage race through her body and she charged Jensey, hitting her full force. They toppled to the ground, Lizzie on top, using her right arm to try to pin Jensey's arm holding the rifle.

A few seconds later, she felt herself being lifted

off Jensey and Mark's voice penetrated her brain. He gently pushed her to one side and bent down to grab the rifle and flip Jensey over, handcuffing her. She started screeching and crying.

Mark went back to Lizzie just as two officers came running along the alley. He had his flashlight out and saw her bleeding arm. He pulled out his cell and phoned for an ambulance.

"Can you walk?"

She nodded. "Yes, of course."

He walked her gently to the parking lot and sat her down on one of the cement pilings.

"It's snowing, Mark." Despite the pain, her face lit up as she lifted it to let the flakes settle on it.

"So it is." He sat down beside her and took her hand in his. "Lizzie, I don't think I've ever had such a fright. I saw your car and your bag on the ground. And I could hear some yelling from the alley."

He wasn't the only one frightened. She squeezed his hand. "I thought I heard two shots. But I was only shot once."

"I fired at her but she'd already swiveled from your throwing whatever it was at her."

"My binder. Could you look for it, please? I have to return my music."

Mark shook his head and smiled. "You've just been shot and you're thinking about your music?"

The ambulance tore into the lot and killed its sirens. Within minutes, Lizzie was lying on a stretcher with her vitals being checked out. A small crowd was assembling. The paramedics finished taking her blood pressure and then moved the stretcher into the ambulance. Lizzie saw Jensey being loaded into a police cruiser. Then Mark appeared in the open door.

"She'll be just fine," the paramedic said. "We'll take her to Jefferson Hospital and they'll patch her up. Are you riding with us?"

Mark looked over at the cruiser. "No." He looked at Lizzie. "I have to take care of a few things then I'll come to the hospital." He smiled, a little uncertainly.

She gave him a small wave with her good hand. The door closed and she was staring at two back windows, through which she could see the snow swirling around.

Chapter Forty

◇◇◇

There was, she decided, only one way to find out.

STRING OF LIES—MARY ELLEN HUGHES

When Lizzie was wheeled out of the treatment room courtesy of a wheelchair and an aide, Mark rushed up to her and wrapped his arms loosely around her. He kissed her on the forehead and asked how she felt.

"Okay but sort of groggy. I missed the Christmas Eve service, though, and I so enjoy it." She smiled at him. "They have good pain meds here."

He chortled. "I talked to the doctor and it was a clean shot. More of a graze. They don't expect any complications."

"Yes, that's what he told me. I need to come back in on Thursday for a follow-up, though. What about Jensey?"

"She's in jail. Her husband came down right away with a lawyer. Doesn't look good for her, not with what I heard."

"I can't believe how this all ended. I did suspect her but not seriously. Because I knew her. I liked her."

Mark rubbed her good arm. "I know. It's hard to understand and accept."

"I can't believe you got there so quickly."

"I might as well confess. Even though I removed your visible police escort, I still had an officer tailing you. He didn't see Jensey Pollard but called in when you disappeared into the alley. That seemed a strange thing for you to do."

Lizzie took a stab at looking upset. Not very effectively, though, as it turned into a yawn.

Mark ran his fingers along her chin. "Why don't I get you home and settled. You need some rest."

She looked up at him.

He raised his eyebrows. "I can just hold you . . ."

He stopped and stared as the doors at the end of the hall flew open.

Bob and Molly came rushing toward them followed by Sally-Jo and Jacob, with Andie pushing to the front of the group.

"How are you? We're so worried! Are you okay?" they all spoke at once.

Mark held up his hand. "She's going to be just fine. She has a gunshot wound to the upper left arm but no complications."

"What are you all doing here?" Lizzie asked.

"Well, honey, we heard after church what had happened," Molly said, reaching out and stroking her cheek. "I was worried when I didn't see you in the choir. We knew there'd been a commotion in the parking lot but we went in the front door so we didn't see anything."

Andie jumped in. "And, we just got here and an ambulance came zipping in with Stephanie in it."

"Stephanie? Oh my God, is she okay? Is she having her baby?"

"She's in labor right now," Sally-Jo said, giving Lizzie a gentle hug.

Mark looked around at the book club members. "Well, I think there are plenty of friends here for Stephanie. I have to get back to the station but I'm going to get Lizzie home. She's worn out."

"No, I want to wait with everyone."

"Mark's right, honey." Molly reached out and stroked Lizzie's hair. "It could be hours. Why don't you just go on home for now and I promise to let you know." She glanced at her watch. "In a little over twelve hours we'll all be gathering at my place for Christmas dinner."

Bob shifted his gaze from Lizzie to Molly. "Well, I think you'd better go on home and rest up also. You're going to be mighty busy in a few hours, and I for one can hardly wait for that amazing turkey-and-all-the-trimmings dinner you've promised."

Molly glanced at Bob. "I truly do hate to leave her."

"Molly, go home. Now."

She smiled in defeat. "Maybe I could get a lift with you, Chief?"

"Sure thing."

A nurse in pink scrubs walked over to the group, as they were saying their good-byes. "Are you here with Stephanie Lowe?"

Molly nodded.

"She's doing just fine. That baby just didn't want to wait. Beat us to the delivery room, in fact. She's the mama of a seven-pound, two-ounce baby girl. Both mama and baby are doing just fine."

"How marvelous! Can we see her?" Molly asked.

The nurse shook her head. "It would be better if y'all waited for the morning. She's pretty tuckered out. We'll take good care of her, rest assured."

"Oh wow. Oh wow . . ." Andie said, moving from one to the other, hugging them all.

Molly hugged her back and looked around at them all. "What a blessed Christmas this is. Lizzie is safe and Stephanie is a mama."

Chapter Forty-one

◇◇◇

A guest is a jewel resting on the cushion of hospitality.

TOO MANY COOKS—REX STOUT

Lizzie sat next to Mark on one of the three silk brocade love seats in Molly's living room and looked around at her friends. Everyone was there except for Andie, who had opted to stay at her friend's house for Christmas dinner, and Stephanie, of course.

It had been quite the twenty-four hours. By the time Mark had gotten back to Lizzie's place and crawled into bed, it was going on three thirty A.M.

They'd slept in and had a leisurely espresso and some of Nathaniel's angel biscuits that had been tucked away in the freezer, while exchanging Christmas gifts. Mark had given her a silver bib necklace that she adored, and he'd seemed truly pleased with the photo of him with Patchett that she'd taken and had framed.

After a cheery lunch with Evelyn in the festive

dining room at Magnolia Manor, they'd joined in the carol singing that followed. Evelyn was all smiles when they'd finally left. Lizzie had hoped it was because she'd realized it was Christmas Day.

Their next stop was for a brief visit with Stephanie and her baby. Lizzie had been relieved to see how happy Stephanie appeared to be. Gone was the anxiety that had haunted her for so many weeks. They'd assured her of a ride home in the morning when she was to be discharged. Then, they'd made their way to Molly's for the much-anticipated Christmas feast.

Lizzie squeezed Mark's hand as Bob ushered Molly into the room.

"Just come and join us for a few minutes," he told Molly. "Let's sit and relax before we start in on the eating." He held her arm as she sat on a velvet wing chair and then handed her a glass of eggnog.

Molly laughed. "That's probably a good idea but not for long. Everything's ready to be served up. Mark, can you tell us any more about what's happening with Jensey Pollard?"

"Not too much but I can tell you that she did admit to killing Alton. She'd managed to put their affair out of her mind and get on with her life. But it was more the guilt and grief over having an abortion that took over when she saw him again. She wanted to get even."

"I think it was also fear," Lizzie added. "This had been a closely guarded secret for almost two decades and here he was back in town."

Bob nodded. "He sounds like a cocky son of a gun. I'll just bet she worried he might start telling folks about their past."

"That wouldn't do for someone with a respected role in the community. Not to mention what her husband would say if he found out," Molly added.

Sally-Jo finished her eggnog and leaned over to put her empty glass on the cherrywood coffee table. "But in the end, he did find out. Who knows what would have happened if she hadn't shot Derek."

"Maybe his ex-wife would have given it a go," Jacob said and made a face.

"This is way too sad to be discussing on Christmas Day," Molly said, standing. "Sally-Jo and I are going to get everything dished up and y'all are going to take your seats at the dining room table. And there will be no more talk about murder in this house . . . not until our next book club meeting."

"And then we'll be discussing what's written between the covers," Lizzie added.

"Damn straight," Bob grinned. "And it's my turn. Finally, a policing story."

Molly stopped at the door and turned back to them, smiling. "Merry Christmas, my dear friends."

Reading Lists

Lizzie Turner
1. Mary Jane Maffini—*The Busy Woman's Guide to Murder*
2. Avery Aames—*Lost and Fondue*
3. Julie Hyzy—*Grace Interrupted*
4. Janet Bolin—*Dire Threads*
5. Jacklyn Brady—*Cake on a Hot Tin Roof*

Sally-Jo Baker
1. Krista Davis—*The Diva Cooks a Goose*
2. Lorna Barrett—*Sentenced to Death*
3. Ellery Adams—*A Killer Plot*
4. Jenn McKinlay—*Books Can Be Deceiving*
5. Dorothy St. James—*Flowerbed of State*

Molly Mathews
1. Agatha Christie—*Hercule Poirot's Christmas*
2. Dorothy Sayers—*Busman's Honeymoon*
3. Rhys Bowen—*A Royal Pain*
4. Ann Purser—*The Hangman's Row Enquiry*
5. Louise Penny—*The Brutal Telling*

Bob Miller
1. Robert B. Parker—*Sixkill*
2. James Hall—*Dead Last*

3. James Lee Burke—*Rain Gods*
4. Ed McBain—*Hark!*
5. John Connolly—*Every Dead Thing*

Jacob Smith
1. Greg Rucka—*Keeper*
2. Lee Child—*Tripwire*
3. Paul Levine—*Flesh and Bones*
4. Phillip Margolin—*Supreme Justice*
5. Donald Westlake—*Get Real*

Andrea Mason
1. Janet Evanovich—*Visions of Sugar Plums*
2. Charlaine Harris—*Dead and Gone*
3. E. J. Copperman—*Night of the Living Deed*
4. Karen Olson—*Dead of the Day*
5. Victoria Laurie—*Abby Cooper, Psychic Eye*

Stephanie Lowe
1. Kari Lee Townsend—*Tempest in the Tea Leaves*
2. Maggie Sefton—*Unraveled*
3. Amanda Lee—*The Quick and the Thread*
4. B. B. Haywood—*Town in a Blueberry Jam*
5. Ayelet Waldman—*Death Gets a Time-Out*

Center Point Large Print
600 Brooks Road / PO Box 1
Thorndike ME 04986-0001 USA

(207) 568-3717

US & Canada:
1 800 929-9108
www.centerpointlargeprint.com